SHIFT THE TIDE

LATITUDE & LONGING
BOOK TWO

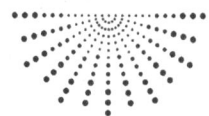

BRYCE OAKLEY

HUNGRY HEART PRESS

Copyright © 2025 by Bryce Oakley

All rights reserved. No part of this publication may be reproduced, distributed, or transmitted in any form or by any means, or stored in a database or retrieval system, without the prior written permission of the author except in the case of brief quotations embodied in critical articles and reviews. For more information, contact bryceoakleywriter@gmail.com.

This is a work of fiction. Names, characters, organizations, places, events, and incidents are the products of the author's imagination or are used for fictional purposes. Any resemblance to actual events or persons, living or dead, is coincidental.

Edited by Lemon Wells

Cover Design by Bryce Oakley

ALSO BY BRYCE OAKLEY

The Adventurers

Something Far Away and Happy

Against The Grain

Never Mine

Every Version

Latitude & Longing

One Last Run

Shift the Tide

Holiday Romances

Most Wonderful

All Aglow

Ghosted Christmas Past

The Snowy Springs Holiday Romances

Baking Spirits Bright

Rebel Without A Claus

The Kaleidoscope Album

Undone

Bewilder

Midnight

Bloom

Revel

The Kaleidoscope Album Box Set

CONTENTS

Chapter 1	1
Chapter 2	11
Chapter 3	21
Chapter 4	31
Chapter 5	39
Chapter 6	47
Chapter 7	53
Chapter 8	59
Chapter 9	69
Chapter 10	81
Chapter 11	91
Chapter 12	103
Chapter 13	113
Chapter 14	119
Chapter 15	137
Chapter 16	151
Chapter 17	161
Chapter 18	173
Chapter 19	181
Chapter 20	195
Chapter 21	205
Chapter 22	227
Chapter 23	237
Chapter 24	251
Chapter 25	265
Epilogue	275
Thank you!	281
Acknowledgments	283
About the Author	285

*For anyone who thinks it's too late.
It's not.*

CHAPTER 1

Kiera

Even asleep, Kiera couldn't stop running toward something she might never have. She was barefoot on cheap carpet, swaying to music she couldn't quite place. Izzy was in front of her, close enough to touch, with a red Solo cup in one hand, her hand resting lightly on Kiera's hip. The room was crowded, overheated. The music pulsed through the floorboards, but they were still, eyes locked.

When Izzy leaned in, Kiera didn't flinch. She kissed her back like she'd been waiting for it, like nothing else mattered. It was slow and certain and just a little messy. They smiled into it.

Then the sweetness in the air shifted. The music faded. Something too bright crept in around the edges...

Kiera opened her eyes to the scent of incense curling against her nose, sweet and leathery.

She stared at the ceiling for a long moment, still half-dreaming. Then came the singing. Off-key, far too enthusiastic. Her dad, down in the kitchen, launching into "Here

Comes the Sun" with the kind of energy usually reserved for toddlers and Broadway auditions.

The pillow muffled her groan as she pulled it over her face.

She stayed like that for a few seconds longer before forcing herself upright. The mirror caught her as she passed: loose t-shirt, yesterday's mascara, a smudge of dried toothpaste from someone's small hand on her shoulder. She rubbed at it without much conviction.

Downstairs, the day was already in full swing. Her mom stirred oatmeal on the stove with quiet focus, the incense stick anchored in a mug that said *World's Okayest Mom*. Her dad was crouched beside the fridge, balancing on the balls of his feet like he was about to leap into a yoga pose.

"Morning, Sunshine," he said cheerfully.

"Barely," Kiera muttered, heading straight for the coffee maker.

Kiera's mom, ever the devoted herbal tea drinker, gave her a look as she poured herself a generous cup of coffee. "You know, caffeine just adds to your stress levels."

"So does existing," Kiera said, taking a deep sip.

Eliza burst in a moment later, crayon drawing in hand, her cheeks pink with excitement. "Mama! I made you something."

Kiera set down her mug. The paper was an explosion of marker colors, purples and golds, with two figures in the center with dark hair and a glittery crown.

"We're fairy queens," Eliza explained proudly.

"Of course we are," Kiera said, pulling Eliza in for a quick forehead kiss. "And it's *beautiful*."

Quinn arrived just behind her, dragging a blanket and clutching a scribbled mass of green and black lines.

"I'm a monster truck," she announced.

Kiera nodded in quiet agreement, giving Quinn's hair a ruffle. "Well, naturally. I wouldn't expect anything less."

CHAPTER 1

They settled at the table. Her dad produced strawberries from the fridge like a magician pulling scarves from a sleeve. Her mom set bowls down with soft clinks and gave Kiera a familiar glance — the kind that meant, *What's your plan today?*

Before the question came, Kiera preempted it. "Same as yesterday. Apply for jobs. Wait for the universe to respond."

"You could call the co-op," her mom said, not unkindly.

"I could."

The silence that followed wasn't hostile. Just familiar.

After breakfast, the girls migrated to the living room and began rearranging couch cushions with single-minded purpose. Their voices rose and overlapped — Eliza demanding structural integrity, Quinn arguing for more aesthetic sparkle. Kiera sipped her coffee and let them build.

She opened her laptop at the dining table, the screen lighting up to the same set of open tabs she'd left the night before: district job boards, a half-filled spreadsheet of application deadlines and dead ends.

Her inbox had two new emails. One was a coupon for a local pizza place. The other was from a charter school she didn't remember applying to.

She opened it anyway.

Thank you for your interest... At this time, we have decided to move forward with other candidates.

Kiera cleared the table while her parents shifted into small talk. Her dad launched into a summary of a documentary on sustainable farming he'd watched the night before—something about vertical gardens and aquaponics. Her mom nodded along, skeptical but patient.

It was all normal. All familiar.

Still, Kiera felt miles away from herself.

In the living room, Eliza and Quinn were mid-construction, balancing throw pillows between dining chairs, the couch, and an ottoman that had already been commandeered as a throne. Kiera leaned in to help, draping a blanket higher than Eliza could reach.

They beamed at her like she'd built it single-handedly.

There were moments, like this one, where the noise in her head softened. Where their laughter filled up the room enough to drown out the rest. They were okay. That was something.

Resilient in a way only children could be, Kiera thought. They took each change in stride — new house, new school, new rules — and somehow still found ways to delight in it. She envied that ease. That capacity for bounce-back. Hers had long since eroded.

Eliza knelt beside her, folding another blanket with serious concentration. The same curve to her brow, the same clipped way she pressed her mouth when she focused — it was like looking at a younger version of herself. Quinn, on the other hand, was all chaos and stubborn joy, more like her father than Kiera liked to admit.

Kiera sat back on her heels, watching them.

The divorce hadn't been contentious. That, in its own way, had been worse. Alex had stayed in Omaha, entirely fine with Kiera taking the girls to Denver. He hadn't fought her on custody, hadn't fought her on much of anything. He'd agreed to split the house sale evenly and start over with his new life, his new girlfriend, his version of a clean slate.

Kiera had walked away with the girls and not an ounce of regret.

Sometimes she thought that should've felt like a win. Other times it just felt like abandonment.

She'd refused alimony. Aunt Jade had offered to help, of course — had paid for the legal side of it all without blinking — but Kiera hadn't let her pay for anything beyond that. She couldn't. Not even when Aunt Jade had dangled the promise of a down payment.

Without a steady job, signing a lease or taking on a mort-

CHAPTER 1

gage felt reckless. So she'd stayed. Her childhood home turned into something temporary but indefinite, her parents reminding her daily, in small ways, that she was welcome, that she had time.

In return, she cooked. Cleaned. Folded everyone's laundry while the girls were at school or when she wasn't picking up a sub shift. She made it work. Or tried to.

Her phone buzzed from the coffee table.

A message from Maggie.

> **MAGGIE**
> Hey! What time do you get in on Friday? Can't wait to see you!

Kiera picked it up slowly, thumb hovering. The trip had sounded like a good idea when it was just an idea. A beach house in San Diego. Ocean air. Her old college friends, Maggie, Danica, Pete, and Izzy. Her parents had practically forced her to go, promising they'd manage everything here. That it would be good for her.

Now it felt less like a vacation and more like a performance.

> **KIERA**
> Hey. I get in around 2 p.m. Can't wait to see you, too.

It wasn't a lie. But it also wasn't the full truth.

Another buzz.

> **DANICA**
> Hey, I wanted to check in before the trip. You're coming right?

Kiera's stomach tightened. She hadn't expected to feel nervous about hearing from Danica, but there it was, the familiar worry and shame.

They used to talk every day. Now, messages like this

carried the careful tone of people still holding one another at arm's length.

Danica had been her anchor for years, the person she called when things cracked or collapsed. But lately, their conversations felt careful, like their connection was fragile and precarious all at once.

She thought about Telluride. About how fast everything had unraveled. Back then, she hadn't known Danica had broken off her engagement. She'd only seen the way Danica and Pete moved around each other — too close, too easy — and something in her had buckled. It had reminded her of the lie she'd lived in for so long with her husband's affair, of holiday parties and polite smiles, of everyone knowing before she did.

So she'd done something she couldn't take back. She'd reached out to Danica's ex, told him maybe he should come. At the time, it had felt like the right thing — like fairness. Like truth.

She hadn't meant to hurt anyone, but intentions didn't matter much after impact.

She hadn't known it was betrayal until it was too late. And even now, the weight of it lingered. Quiet. Unresolved.

She typed out a reply, slow and measured.

KIERA

> Yeah, I'm excited to be there. It'll be a nice break from real life.

Danica responded almost immediately.

DANICA

> Seriously. Work's been crazy. Looking forward to this weekend, though. It'll be good to see everyone.

Kiera hesitated, fingers hovering over the keyboard. She started to type *Looking forward to reconnecting,* then deleted it.

CHAPTER 1

"Of course," Kiera said automatically.

Her mom didn't push, just nodded. "Tonya always says to look ahead."

Kiera blinked. "Who's Tonya?"

Her mom looked exasperated. "My new spiritual guide. I've told you about her. We meet over Zoom."

Kiera gave her a long, blank look.

Her mom sighed. "Anyway, Tonya says the future responds best to clarity. You just need to decide what you want."

"I'm trying," Kiera said. "But it's hard to look ahead when I feel like I'm failing the girls. And when it seems like I've disappointed everyone I care about."

Her mom didn't hesitate. "You're not failing them. You're doing your best. They're happy, Kiera. That's what matters. And as for disappointment? Never. Surprised, sometimes," she added with a smirk. "But never disappointed."

Kiera blinked back sudden tears.

"If those women are truly your friends," her mom continued, "you'll find your way back to each other. This weekend could be the start of that."

"I hope so," Kiera said, her voice thinner than she meant it to be. She turned back to her suitcase. The packing still wasn't done. But the tea was warm, and the silence felt a little less heavy than before.

Her mom gave her hand a gentle squeeze and stood. "And if you need your dad and me to come pick you up from the slumber party early, just say the word."

Kiera snorted softly. "Mom, that was *one* time."

CHAPTER 2

Izzy

Izzy Tierney felt weightless, her surfboard slicing through the water as though it were an extension of her body. The wave — perfect, glassy, and cresting just right — held her in a fleeting, magical balance. The salty air kissed her skin as she leaned into the turn, her toes gripping the waxed surface of her surfboard. This was what happiness felt like. Pure, uncomplicated, blissful.

She rode the wave all the way to shore, leaping off her board at the last second and landing knee-deep in the foamy surf. With a grin, she turned to watch the ocean reclaim her wave, the sea as endless and inviting as the sky above. Life wasn't perfect — she was still figuring out her place at Second Star — but here, she was content. Or at least, she was supposed to be.

The beach stretched out before her, quiet except for the rhythmic sound of the waves and the distant chatter of tourists from the small surf school set up a few hundred feet away in the direction of Carmen Beach.

Izzy dropped her board next to her beach towel and sat

down, the sand warm beneath her. Santa Teresa wasn't a typical lounging beach — there was more of a rocky stretch than the perfect beaches that existed all throughout Costa Rica — but she liked that. It was a surfing haven, and she barely had to compete for a towel spot.

She'd been in Costa Rica for two weeks now, working with Pete's nonprofit, Second Star. She'd only been with the organization for a little under a year, and she still felt like an imposter most days. The organization provided funding for children's homes to offer extracurricular activities, and Izzy's job was to ensure the partnership was working well for the organization and adjust as needed. The two children's homes in Costa Rica were in San Jose, but she always preferred to spend at least one or two days of her trip surfing on the Nicoya Peninsula, particularly at her favorite beach this time of year, Santa Teresa. The work was fulfilling, the weather flawless, and every day ended with sunsets that seemed to be painted just for her. It was the kind of life she'd dreamed about during her restless nights as a bartender back in San Francisco.

The buzz of her phone from her beach bag pulled her back to reality. Izzy leaned over to grab it, the screen lighting up with a message from Maggie.

MAGGIE

What time do you get in on Friday?

Izzy stared at the message for a long moment, the afterglow of her perfect wave fading into something more complicated. Another trip with the group meant seeing Maggie, Pete, Danica… and Kiera.

Kiera Phillips. Just the thought of her name sent a ripple of restlessness and something warmer, more bittersweet, through Izzy. They hadn't spoken since the Telluride trip, where Kiera had managed to alienate most of the group by playing referee between Pete and Danica, who hadn't yet figured out that they were meant for each other. Kiera's attempts to keep them apart had felt to everyone else as misguided and unnecessary, but Izzy had seen the strain in Kiera's eyes, the way she was trying — maybe too hard — to keep the group dynamic from changing.

Izzy sighed, tossing her phone down on the towel. She stretched out on her back, letting the sun dry the last traces of seawater on her skin. Of course, she wanted to see her friends. Maggie's chaotic humor, Pete's unshakable confidence, Danica's steady presence. But Kiera? That was... complicated. They had kissed once in college — a fleeting, impulsive moment during a party. Izzy still remembered how soft Kiera's lips were, how her laughter had turned into something quieter, more tentative, before their mouths met. It hadn't gone any further, and neither of them had brought it up again, but Izzy often wondered what might have happened if they had.

Her phone buzzed again. Another text, this time from Pete.

PETE

> mags told me she texted you! don't make me come drag you to the beach house myself because i'll do it!!!!

Izzy couldn't help but laugh. Pete's blend of tough love and relentless support was one of the reasons they'd been best friends for so long. If Pete was going, there was no way Izzy could say no. She tapped out a quick reply to Maggie.

IZZY

> Early. I'll rent a car and meet you at the beach house.

As she slipped her phone back into her bag, a flicker of nerves stirred in her chest. Seeing Kiera again would be... something. Maybe a chance to clear the air, maybe just a new way to get knocked sideways. Izzy wasn't sure. Lately, she wasn't sure about a lot of things. But she'd already spent too much time keeping people at arm's length. And whatever this turned into, she'd face it. Let it come. Let it pull her under, if it had to.

THAT EVENING, the world around Izzy softened into a slow, golden hush. The air, thick with salt and the scent of blooming jasmine, clung to her skin as she wandered back to her rented bungalow — a small, sun-bleached space with uneven wooden steps and a crooked porch light that flickered at dusk. It wasn't fancy, but it was hers for a few days, and it was quiet. Peaceful.

Izzy grabbed a cold Imperial beer from the tiny fridge, the bottle sweating instantly in the humid air. She stepped outside to the creaky hammock strung between two posts and sank into it with a sigh. The hammock rocked lazily with every movement, the worn fabric familiar against her bare legs. Before her, the sky stretched endlessly, painted with ribbons of lavender, peach, and molten orange as the sun melted into the Pacific.

She'd spent a lot of time alone lately — not because she wanted to, exactly, but because it felt simpler. Less complicated. Being around people, even people she loved, sometimes made everything feel louder inside her head. Out here, with no one expecting anything from her, she didn't have to explain the ache she couldn't quite name. She could just sit in it. Let it hum quietly under the moon and pretend it wasn't still waiting to be answered.

It should have been enough — this life she'd carved out, simple and beautiful. The kind of existence that was supposed to quiet the constant itch of restlessness inside her. But the moment she let herself relax, her thoughts found their way back to the one thing she didn't want to think about.

CHAPTER 2

To Kiera.

Izzy tried to push the thought away — tried to focus on the soft crash of the waves or the slow hum of crickets starting their nightly chorus — but her mind kept pulling her back. The memory of Kiera's hopeful, awkward smile in Telluride haunted her like a half-finished song. She hadn't expected to miss her. Hell, she hadn't expected to *think* about her.

And yet... there she was, lodged in her brain like a splinter she couldn't remove.

Her phone buzzed on the armrest. She almost ignored it. But when she glanced down and saw Pete's name flashing on the screen, she sighed and answered.

"Hey, troublemaker," Izzy said, trying to sound light, like she wasn't coming apart under the weight of her own thoughts. She ran a hand through her short hair, tugging at the blonde strands.

"You better not be ditching on me," Pete shot back, her voice carrying a familiar warmth wrapped in playful gruffness. "I will personally fly down there and drag you to San Diego if I have to."

Izzy forced a laugh, pushing her hair out of her face and adjusting herself in the hammock until the fabric cradled her more securely. "Relax. I'm coming. You know I wouldn't miss a chance to witness all of you make fools of yourselves."

The pause on the other end was slight but noticeable. "You've been quiet," Pete said, her usual teasing tone dialed down. "Not just missing calls. Like... *gone* quiet. Is this one of your disappearing acts?"

Izzy tipped her head back, resting the cold beer bottle against her forehead. "I'm here," she said, which wasn't the same as *I'm fine*, but still not the truth. "Just laying low."

Pete made a small, unimpressed sound. "Laying low or pushing everyone out before they get too close?"

Izzy's jaw tensed. "I'm not pushing anyone out. I've just

been surfing for a few days, and you know what I do for work. I'm just enjoying being on my own."

"You're always on your own," Pete said gently. "And for someone who claims to love it, you don't sound all that happy about it."

Izzy didn't respond right away. The sun had dipped below the horizon, and the sky was sliding into blue-gray. She watched the tide move in slow, steady pulses — indifferent, unbothered, sure of itself in a way she wasn't.

"How's married life?" Izzy asked, clearing her throat.

"Okay, deflection queen. I get it. And Danica and I aren't married yet. You'd know. You'll be my best person up there," Pete said.

"That's cute. I will gladly hold your bouquet for you," Izzy teased.

"I'm very excited to get you a bit drunk and play therapist about your weird deep-seeded issues this weekend." Pete said.

"Did you just say deep-seeded?" Izzy said, her smile clearly evident in her near-laugh.

"Yeah."

"Deep-seated. Like the seat is deep."

"That doesn't make sense. It's seeded, like you plant the seed really deep," Pete said, stubbornly.

"No, bud. That's…"

"Stop trying to distract me from your deeply sown issues," Pete said with a laugh.

The tightness in Izzy's chest loosened. She was excited to see Pete again, and Maggie, and Danica. Kiera would just be a part of the weekend she could avoid if necessary, she supposed. The sun had disappeared completely now, leaving the sky streaked with the soft gray of early twilight. The waves crashed on, steady and constant, unbothered by human fears and mistakes.

"I'm here for you anytime, okay?" Pete's voice was gentle

now. "You're doing a damn good job in Costa Rica, and I know you're like a bazillion miles away but you're not in this alone. In anything alone, if you don't want to be."

"Fine. Now, let me off this invisible therapist couch," Izzy groaned, but Pete's words did warm her.

They hung up a minute later, but Izzy didn't move from the hammock. She sat there for what felt like hours, watching as the sky shifted from gold to purple to deep, endless black.

And when she finally went inside and climbed into bed, Kiera's name was still tangled up in her thoughts, stubborn and quiet like the tide pulling back to shore.

Danica named the conversation, "The Gay Agenda (And Snacks)".

DANICA

Okay, listen up, everyone. We need to lock down the plan for SD tomorrow.

PETE

MAGGIE

Is the plan not just... go to the beach and vibe?

DANICA

No. We need logistics. Who's getting groceries? Who's picking up the rental car? What time does everyone land?

MAGGIE

I'm bringing sunscreen and vibes. That's all I'm committing to. I will not be opening a spreadsheet.

DANICA

We cannot survive on vibes alone.

PETE

challenge accepted

KIERA

I can coordinate the snacks.

PETE

as long as they aren't too healthy

MAGGIE

Define *healthy*.

KIERA

Fruit? Or my parents have me addicted to these gut biome bars that are actually pretty good.

CHAPTER 2

PETE

booooooring! bring chocolate-covered pretzels!

MAGGIE

Let's just Instacart things over a beer when we get there. Ta-da. Check that one off, D-sizzle.

DANICA

PEOPLE. Focus. We also need to coordinate who's driving from the airport.

PETE

uber. next problem

DANICA

No, that's expensive and—

PETE

shh the vibes have spoken

KIERA

I can drive the rental car.

DANICA

THANK YOU, Kiera. It's so nice having a responsible adult here.

MAGGIE

Wow passive-aggressive much?

DANICA

It's not passive-aggressive, it's just *aggressive aggressive* because you're all impossible.

MAGGIE

So, what's the alcohol situation? Are we planning tequila or rum vibes?

DANICA

THIS IS NOT THE PRIORITY.

PETE

tequila obvi

IZZY

Why isn't "who's picking up the booze" at the top of the list?

MAGGIE

Izzy! You DO look at your texts!

DANICA

I'm actually going to lose my mind.

MAGGIE

We love you, Dani. You're doing amazing, sweetie.

DANICA

I feel like I'm organizing a circus.

PETE

you knew who we were when you chose to love us

KIERA

You've got this, Danica. I'll help with food and logistics.

DANICA

THANK YOU, Kiera.

CHAPTER 3

Kiera

The soft hum of waves greeted them as they stepped into the beach house, late afternoon sunlight streaming through the massive floor-to-ceiling glass doors that opened onto a patio overlooking the Pacific. The home was luxurious yet warm, with terrazzo tile floors; a minimalist modern kitchen; and colorful, plush furnishings that contrasted beautifully against the soft neutral tones of the walls. But all Kiera could focus on was the awkward tension filling the air as the group settled in.

Pete clapped her hands together, surveying the open-plan layout. "This is it, folks! Home sweet home for the next few days. Let's not burn it down."

Danica laughed, nudging Pete with her elbow. "No promises." Her smile softened as Pete leaned down to press a kiss to her cheek, whispering something that made Danica laugh even harder. The ease and affection between them were palpable, a quiet reminder of how far they'd come since Telluride. They moved in sync, as though they shared an unspoken language, and Kiera couldn't help but feel a pang of envy — not in a bitter way, but in a way that reminded her of everything she'd lost.

Maggie walked toward the doors, sighing dramatically as she took in the ocean view. "I might just stay out there and become a beach hermit. Y'all can send me snacks."

Kiera smiled faintly as she set her bags in the entryway, trying to stay unobtrusive. She could feel Izzy's gaze flit toward her and then away just as quickly. The dismissal stung more than she'd expected, though she supposed she shouldn't have been surprised. Izzy hadn't said much to her during the car ride from the airport, offering only clipped responses to Kiera's attempts at conversation.

"Bedrooms are upstairs," Pete announced, already climbing the sleek wooden staircase. "Who's bunking with who?"

"Izzy, Maggie, and Kiera each get their own room," Danica said, glancing at Pete with a playful smirk. "And that leaves us sharing, obviously."

Pete grinned mischievously. "Wendell, I'm pretty sure there's bunk beds in one of these rooms."

Danica rolled her eyes, swatting Pete's arm.

Maggie, Kiera, and Izzy all groaned. Pete had been stuck with the bunk room at Aunt Jade's condo in Telluride — bunk beds that saw Danica and Pete's... reconnection. Kiera had opted to leave an extremely large Venmo tip for the cleaning company. She didn't want to know any details about what had happened on those bunk beds. And now, seeing Pete and Danica happily together made Kiera feel awkward and out of place — their happiness felt like a glaring spotlight on everything she'd almost messed up back in Telluride. Everything that everyone here was either trying to ignore or still holding a quiet grudge about.

"Guess it's all sorted," Maggie said, grabbing her bag. "Now I'm off to claim the room with the best view."

The group dispersed to claim a room and unpack. Kiera

CHAPTER 3

wandered upstairs, tossing her bag onto the bright white bedding in a random room. She stood at the window for a moment, staring out over Pacific Beach. The afternoon sun glittered on the water, where surfers carved through gentle waves with practiced ease. She could hear faint laughter and shouts carried by the breeze.

She watched as one surfer stood smoothly, riding a wave all the way to the shore before hopping off with casual confidence. Kiera's chest tightened. There was something beautiful about the effortless grace of it, about the way these strangers seemed so comfortable, so at home on the water. She'd spent so long feeling like an outsider in her own life, like she was always paddling against the current and barely keeping afloat. Here, on this beach, it seemed like everyone else had already found their rhythm.

The thought brought a lump to her throat, and she pressed her hand against the cool glass of the window, grounding herself. She could do this. She could find her own rhythm again, even if it was uncomfortable. The beach trip was supposed to be a step forward, a way to reconnect with her friends and with who she was before her marriage. She just hadn't expected it to feel so hard.

When she'd found out about Alex's affair, she hadn't even wanted to get divorced at first. It felt unbearable, like an insurmountable wall. Her marriage seemed like something she should be able to work through, like the affair was just another hurdle. After she'd returned home from Telluride, Danica's quiet voice in her head felt more like a scream — "*As a child of divorced parents, I can assure you it sucks, but it would have been worse to see my parents fight and be miserable all the time.*"

Danica was right. Her girls deserved better, and more than that, they deserved for her to be a better role model.

In the end, divorce felt mostly like running face first into that insurmountable wall, over and over, and then eventually just bursting through Kool-Aid Man-style, leaving all of the chaos and destruction in her wake.

The playful banter downstairs eventually drew her out of the room, and Kiera walked back to join the group. Pete and Izzy were passing a soccer ball inside, Danica was in the kitchen, and Maggie was sitting on a bar stool with a glass of wine in hand.

"Kiera!" Pete called, kicking the ball toward Izzy. "She emerges. Hey, I forgot to ask earlier — how's life in Hippieville?"

"It's good," Kiera said with a long exhale. "Mom's been fermenting her own kombucha. Dad's building a chicken coop in the backyard."

"Do you have chickens?"

"No, oddly enough. I fear it may be a very subtle attempt at making an ADU for me," Kiera admitted.

Maggie laughed. "Are they hoping you'll be laying eggs as rent?"

"I, for one, would like to try the kombucha," Danica said. "What's the flavor? Lavender? Elderberry? Grass clippings?"

Kiera snorted despite herself. "It's turmeric and ginger, actually. Very earthy."

"Sounds... healthy," Maggie said, holding up her glass in a mock toast. "Wine's healthier. Grapes, antioxidants, you know."

"And no fermentation explosions," Pete added with a grin.

"Let's hope," Kiera said, finally allowing herself a small smile.

"Alright, enough kombucha talk," Maggie interjected. "Danica's handling dinner, but I need someone to help with dessert. Any takers?"

"I'll do it," Kiera offered, eager to occupy herself with something other than awkward small talk.

"Perfect. Danica's in charge of the main course, so she'll

let you know what's off-limits. Just don't let Pete near the frosting. She'll eat half of it before it gets on the cake."

"No trust!" Pete protested, holding her hands up in mock offense. "When have I ever done that?"

"Last week." Danica shook her head.

Soon the group gathered in the open dining area, passing bowls of Danica's coconut curry. The massive doors were open, letting the salty ocean breeze drift inside.

Pete grabbed a spoonful of curry and took a bite. Her eyes widened as the heat hit. "Damn, Wendell. Did you put ghost peppers in this?" she asked, coughing.

Maggie passed Kiera a bowl of extra coconut cream to add to her curry. Kiera hoped that they'd added milk to the Instacart order. If the curry was that spicy, they were going to need it.

"It's just a little kick," Danica said with a grin. "Can't handle it?"

Pete's expression turned competitive. "Are you challenging me?"

"Maybe I am," Danica said, crossing her arms and raising an eyebrow. "Bet you can't eat a whole bowl without water."

Maggie leaned back, laughing. "Oh, this is going to be good."

"You're on," Pete said, digging in as the group cheered her on. Her nose began running — the first sign of trouble, sniffle by sniffle — and beads of sweat formed on her forehead. Izzy handed her a napkin while Kiera shook her head, amused.

"You know, there's no shame in bowing out," Danica teased, clearly enjoying herself.

Pete stubbornly took another bite. "Never," she said, though her voice was strained.

By the time she finished, Pete was gulping down water

while the others laughed. "Alright, you win," Pete admitted, wiping her face. "But next time, I'm cooking."

The laughter felt easy, almost natural. Kiera relaxed, letting herself enjoy the moment. Maybe this weekend wouldn't be so bad after all.

Maggie raised her glass, tilting it toward the center of the table. "Alright, now that Pete's survived Danica's inferno curry, how about a toast? To friendships that survive time, distance, and questionable spice levels."

Everyone laughed and clinked glasses, even Pete, who muttered, "My taste buds may never recover, but sure. To friendships."

"Do you guys remember our junior year winter break?" Maggie asked, leaning forward with a mischievous grin. "The road trip to New Mexico?"

Pete groaned. "The trip where Danica decided to trust her GPS over actual road signs and we ended up on that dirt road in the middle of nowhere, worried about an over-eager rancher who kidnapped us for torture?"

Danica shrugged unapologetically. "I stand by my decision. The GPS said it was faster."

"Faster to what? Ritualistic cult murder?" Pete teased, making everyone laugh.

"Hey, that detour was the highlight of the trip," Danica said, pointing her fork at Pete.

Pete winked with comic exaggeration. "I wouldn't say it was the best part of the trip. There was that shitty motel, with those super springy beds, and you and I spent all night—"

Danica flushed red, while Maggie and Izzy were openly cringing. Kiera interrupted Pete's tangential trip down memory lane with, "We found that little diner."

Maggie sighed dreamily. "The best pancakes I've ever had."

"And the worst coffee," Kiera added, smiling at the

memory. "It tasted like it had been brewed with swamp water."

"But you drank three cups of it," Danica pointed out, raising an eyebrow.

"That was self-preservation," Kiera shot back. "I was the one driving while you all slept like babies."

"Not me," Maggie said. "I stayed up to keep you company."

"By playing the same five songs on repeat," Kiera replied, rolling her eyes. "I still can't listen to Fleetwood Mac without hearing your off-key singing in my head."

Maggie feigned offense, clutching her chest. "Off-key? I'll have you know, my rendition of 'Dreams' is iconic."

"Iconic is one word for it," Izzy said dryly, earning a laugh from Pete.

Familiar memories and jokes fueled easy conversation. At one point, Maggie's phone buzzed, and she glanced down at it with a sigh. "Gwen says hi. She's wrangling the kids into bed and wanted me to remind you all that you're invited to Austin anytime."

"How are the twins?" Kiera asked, ignoring the unexpected pang she felt in her chest at the idea of having a caring spouse at home, parenting without worry.

"They're absolute tyrants," Maggie said with a laugh. "Arlo's figured out how to pick locks, so nothing is safe anymore, and Jude has decided he's the boss of the household."

"Sounds like they're taking after their mom," Pete said with a grin.

"Absolutely," Maggie said proudly, raising her glass again in acknowledgement.

"So, speaking of chaos — surfing tomorrow?" Pete asked between bites, grinning at Izzy. "We're on Pacific Beach. It'd be criminal not to."

"Obviously," Izzy replied, her tone carrying a spark of enthusiasm for the first time that evening.

Danica raised an eyebrow. "What about paddle boarding? I saw a rental place down toward Mission Beach. Less chance of Maggie breaking an arm this time around."

"Exactly!" Maggie chimed in. "I'm all for paddle boarding."

Izzy snorted, leaning back in her chair. "What's the point of coming here if you're not going to surf? Tourmaline is essentially a beginner spot."

Maggie stuck out her tongue. "Beginners like me don't want to face-plant into a wave, thank you very much."

Kiera hesitated before speaking up. "I think I'd prefer paddle boarding, too." It seemed like the safest choice, both in the way of bodily harm and trying to reconnect with Danica and Maggie.

Izzy's gaze flicked toward her, quick and unreadable. Kiera's cheeks flushed with self-consciousness as she forced herself to focus on her meal.

Danica interjected. "Why don't we just split up tomorrow? Surfers can surf, paddle boarders can paddle, and we can all meet up for lunch."

"Works for me," Pete said, raising her glass. "To whatever floats your board!"

The toast earned a round of laughter, though Kiera noticed that Izzy didn't look her way again for the rest of the meal or during dessert. As they cleaned up and the group began to scatter for the evening, Kiera lingered in the kitchen, wiping down the counters as an excuse to stay busy. She could hear Danica and Pete laughing in the living room, their voices easy and familiar. Danica perched on the arm of Pete's chair, her hand absentmindedly running through Pete's curls as they FaceTimed Gladys, their dog.

Izzy and Maggie sprawled across the couch, reading separate sapphic romance novels. Apparently Maggie had gotten

Izzy hooked on a new Australian author and they'd been voraciously reading a series together.

When she retreated to her own room to call her family, Kiera sat on the edge of the bed, staring out the window at the dark expanse of ocean. The sound of the waves was soothing, but it couldn't drown out the undercurrent of tension in the house. She'd planned to rebuild her friendships on this trip, but a mix of forced normalcy and Izzy's awkwardness made it far more complicated than anticipated. She reached for her phone and dialed home. Her mom answered on the second ring, her warm voice immediately bringing a sense of comfort. "Kiera! How's the beach house?"

"It's... nice," Kiera said, leaning back against the headboard. "How are the girls?"

"Oh, they're great. Hold on. Eliza, Quinn, come say hi to Mommy!"

There was a brief clatter on the other end, followed by Eliza's excited voice. "Hi, Mommy! We're painting rocks!"

"Painting rocks?" Kiera repeated, picturing the inevitable mess. "Where did you find rocks? And more importantly, why are you up so late?"

"Grandpa took us to the creek," Eliza explained, her words tumbling out quickly. "And now we're painting them to look like animals. Mine's a chicken! She's going to live in the new coop."

Kiera couldn't help but smile. "That sounds... fun. Are you making a mess?"

"No!" Eliza gasped in reply. "Grandma put down newspapers everywhere. Quinn got paint on her face, though."

In the background, Kiera could hear her dad laughing and Quinn giggling loudly, followed by her mom's voice saying, "It's organic and made from eggs, don't worry!"

Kiera shook her head, the image of her parents orchestrating this chaotic art project both heartwarming and mildly stressful. "Sounds like you're all having a blast."

"We are!" Eliza said. "Do you want me to save you a rock to paint when you get home?"

"Of course," Kiera said softly. "I'd love that."

Her mom came back on the line, her voice tinged with amusement. "Don't worry about us, Kiera. The girls are doing fine and we've got everything under control. You just focus on relaxing and having a good time."

Kiera hesitated, a small lump forming in her throat. "Thanks, Mom. I really appreciate it."

"Anytime, sweetheart. We love you."

"I love you too," Kiera replied, ending the call. She set the phone down on the nightstand and stared at it for a moment, her chest tight with conflicting emotions. Her parents were wonderful with the girls, and she was grateful beyond words for their help, but *needing* their help had only highlighted how much she still felt like she was barely keeping her head above water — both as a mother and as a person.

As she lay back against the pillows, Kiera closed her eyes and let the sound of the waves fill the room. She needed to figure out how to make things right — with herself, with her friends, and with everything else that had gone sideways in her life.

CHAPTER 4

Izzy

Izzy's eyes fluttered open to the faint glow of early dawn filtering through the sheer curtains of her bedroom. She stretched lazily, the sound of the waves drifting in from the beach like a soothing morning song. For a moment, she just lay there, letting the rhythm of the ocean seep into her, lulling her into a rare sense of peace. But as the minutes ticked by, the restlessness crept in. It always did.

She slipped out of bed, grabbing her wetsuit from the chair where she'd draped it the night before. The house was quiet, still steeped in sleep, as she padded barefoot through the front door and out onto the sand. The horizon stretched in every direction, still gray from dawn's light. She knew she'd be surfing later with Pete, but she wanted a moment to enjoy it alone.

Izzy loved this part of the day — when the world felt wide open and the air buzzed with the promise of something new. She didn't have to think too much about anything except catching the next wave. Pulling her wetsuit on and taking a moment to awkwardly fumble with the long zipper pull, she grabbed her board and waded into the cool water, letting it bite at her skin and wake her up completely.

The first wave was small, an easy ride to test her balance. She stood up smoothly, the familiar rush of adrenaline coursing through her as the wave propelled her forward. By the time the next one rolled in, she was ready, leaning into the movement with practiced grace. For a little while, it was perfect. The world was just her and the ocean.

But even here, where she felt most free, something felt... off. Maybe it was the weird way she felt around Kiera, still. She was so angry at Kiera for trying to ruin her best friend's happiness back in Telluride, and it was the kind of grudge that came with a long history of complications.

Now, Kiera was divorced, like Izzy. Divorce was its own kind of scar — visible to anyone who cared to look closely enough. Maybe Kiera's meddling in Telluride hadn't just been about Pete and Danica. Maybe it had been about trying to make something — anything — work, even if it wasn't hers.

The anger was there, but there was something else. An uncertainty. She couldn't name it, but it was there, a quiet hum beneath the surface of her thoughts. As she paddled back out, waiting for the next set of waves, her mind wandered. She'd spent years chasing this — freedom, movement, the kind of life that looked wide open from the outside. And she did love it, most of the time. But lately, she'd started to wonder if all the motion was just a way to outrun stillness.

Izzy sighed and lay back on her board, staring up at the lightening sky as the waves gently rocked her. She shook the thought away. This wasn't the time for an existential crisis. She was here, in San Diego, surrounded by friends she hadn't seen in over a year. That was what mattered.

WHEN SHE RETURNED to the house, damp and sandy but exhilarated from the morning session, the smell of coffee and frying bacon greeted her. The great room was bathed in sunlight now, the windows flooding the space with warmth. Pete stood at the stove, wielding a spatula with dramatic flair, while Maggie and Danica hovered around the counter, cutting fruit and pouring orange juice into glasses.

"Look who decided to grace us with her presence," Pete called out, flipping a pancake in the air. "How many waves did you conquer this morning on dawn patrol?"

"More than you, yawn patrol," Izzy shot back, grinning as she grabbed a towel from a nearby chair to pat her hair dry. "And enough to know I'm starving. Where's the coffee?"

Danica pointed toward the French press on the counter. "Help yourself. But if you want pancakes, you're going to have to be nice to Pete."

"Unlikely," Izzy said, pouring herself a mug of coffee and taking a grateful sip. She turned to the dining table, where Kiera sat nursing her own mug, her dark bobbed hair still slightly mussed from sleep, her large glasses sliding down her nose as she stared at her phone. Izzy slid into the chair across from Kiera, not making eye contact.

Kiera set down her phone, looking pleased with herself. "I just finished Wordle in two guesses."

"Hell yeah, Kier," Maggie said, settling into the seat beside Izzy. "That is all skill, no luck."

"Do people still play Wordle?" Izzy asked as she blew onto her coffee.

"I still play it, and I'm a person, so all signs point to yes," Kiera said, her tone playful.

Izzy shrugged, looking back toward Pete who was nuzzling Danica's neck. She was happy for her friends but did they have to be so fucking cute and annoying about their love? Kiera and Maggie followed Izzy's line of sight.

"Disgusting," Maggie muttered with a hint of a smile as she turned back with an exaggerated eye roll.

"Horrible," Izzy concurred.

"The worst." Kiera added, her eyes moving to Izzy's wet hair. "Did you already go surfing?"

"Yep." Izzy studied her for a moment. Kiera looked... off. There was something about the way her shoulders curved inward, the faint puffiness around her eyes. For a moment, she hated how standoffish she'd been to Kiera, how she'd dismissed every attempt at conversation since they arrived. But the chaos Kiera had caused, the unnecessary drama... It wasn't something she could easily forgive or forget, no matter how tired or vulnerable Kiera looked now.

Izzy let the silence stretch for a beat before Pete plunked down a plate of pancakes in front of her with a flourish. "For our local mermaid," Pete announced. "I made them surfboard-shaped for you."

The pancakes in question were indeed surfboard-shaped, in that they were roughly oval in appearance, but Izzy grinned at Pete's enthusiasm. "They look great," Izzy said, saluting Pete with her fork before digging in.

The morning unfolded with the easy banter of old friends. Pete's pancake-flipping show prompted teasing from Maggie, while Danica playfully rolled her eyes at their silliness. But Izzy couldn't help glancing at Kiera now and then, noticing the way she stayed quiet, only chiming in when someone asked her a direct question.

After a quick breakfast, Danica noticed the glaring omission of sunscreen. Everyone was unprepared except Maggie, who fiercely guarded her precious Korean sunscreen, muttering about its exquisite formulation and how it was far too precious to share. Danica volunteered Kiera and Izzy to make a quick run to the local market. "Pete and I already did our good deed for the day by cooking breakfast. You two can handle this one!"

Izzy shot a pleading stare at Pete, but her best friend was concentrating on cleaning a corner of the counter with fervor. Was Pete... hiding a smile?

CHAPTER 4

Izzy arched a brow at Kiera, who gave a small shrug. "Guess it's us," Kiera said, grabbing her bag.

The market was a short walk away, the kind of charming local spot that sold everything from organic produce to handmade candles. The silence between them stretched, heavy and awkward, as they walked along the sidewalk. Kiera cleared her throat and tried to start a conversation, her voice hesitant.

"So, uh, you started working at Pete's foundation?" Kiera asked.

Izzy didn't look at her, keeping her gaze fixed on the path ahead. "Yep." She kept her response brief. She'd survive this grocery trip, but that didn't mean she had to enjoy it.

Kiera nodded, fiddling with the strap of her bag. "That sounds... good. Traveled anywhere fun lately?"

"I was in Costa Rica last week, and next week we're meeting with a new organization in Denver. Pete wants to focus on more things stateside in the next few years, given we don't know how much funding is going to be cut over the next few years with this administration," Izzy replied, her voice neutral.

"Smart, given how shitty America is becoming for anyone who isn't a billionaire white guy," Kiera muttered.

"Exactly," Izzy said curtly, nodding.

Kiera answered with a small laugh, even though it sounded a bit forced. "Well, you've got the tan to prove you're doing something right out there."

Izzy's lips twitched, but she didn't smile. "Guess so."

They entered the market, the air conditioning raising goosebumps on Izzy's arms as her sandals slapped against the linoleum flooring.

"Are you a mineral sunscreen person?" Kiera asked as they paused to stare at the end cap display of various sunscreens, her voice intentionally light, hoping to ease the tension. "You know, the whole coral reef-safe debate?"

Izzy crossed her arms, her gaze skimming over the rows

of bottles. "I usually just grab whatever works," she said flatly. "I don't overthink it."

Kiera tilted her head, picking up a bright blue bottle and examining it. "Mineral's supposed to be better for sensitive skin," she offered, trying to fill the silence.

Izzy exhaled with exasperation, reaching for a bottle of chemical sunscreen. "This works fine for me."

"But isn't it bad for marine life? I mean, with all the studies—" Kiera started, her tone edging toward defensiveness.

Izzy cut her off, her voice sharper now. "Not everything has to be a debate, Kiera."

The words hung in the air, stinging. Kiera blinked, her hand faltering as she set the bottle back on the shelf. "I wasn't trying to start a debate," she said softly. "I just thought—"

"You just thought you'd lecture me about sunscreen." Izzy grabbed a bottle and tossed it into the basket she'd grabbed near the entrance.

Kiera's cheeks flushed, and Izzy instantly felt a pang of regret for the harsh words. That wasn't like her. She was a go-with-the-flow person, but Kiera brought out something more difficult to manage within her.

"I wasn't—" Kiera stopped herself, shaking her head. "Never mind."

"'Kay," Izzy said flatly. Her guilt wasn't going to make things instantly better between them. The basket swung in Izzy's hand as she headed for the self-checkout. Kiera froze for a moment before she followed, her steps hesitant.

The weight of the unspoken tension followed as they left the store, pressed down harder with every step, thick like the humid ocean air. Izzy walked ahead with deliberate, purposeful strides, her shoulders set as if bracing against something unseen. Kiera followed a half-step behind.

By the time they reached the house, sunscreen in tow, Izzy's frustration had dulled to a simmering ache in her chest.

CHAPTER 4

The walk back had been quiet, crowded with words unsaid. She didn't even know why she was so angry — no, that wasn't true. She knew exactly why.

It had been easier to be mad at Kiera. Easier to replay all the ways she'd meddled during that mess in Telluride, to keep the story simple: Kiera made things harder. Full stop. Izzy clung to that version because it let her avoid the truth — that even back in college, and again on that chaotic trip, there had been moments when she'd wanted to lean in instead of pull away. Moments that scared her more than any argument ever could.

But now? Now the silence felt safer. The distance gave her room to breathe — and to hide. Because if she let the anger go, she'd have to face what was underneath: a question she didn't know how to answer, a feeling that refused to stay buried. And Izzy wasn't ready to look at that. Not yet.

Guilt clawed at her anyway. She shouldn't have snapped at Kiera like that — over sunscreen, of all things. It wasn't fair. But every time Kiera tried to bridge the gap between them, Izzy felt the old annoyance from Telluride pulse under the surface. She wasn't ready to forgive Kiera just yet, not after how much Kiera had hurt Danica and Pete, not after the mess she'd made.

And yet, seeing Kiera's face when she shut her down — a flicker of hurt, quickly masked by polite detachment — made Izzy feel even worse.

It would be so much easier if she could just stop caring altogether.

Back inside the house, the others were already prepping for an afternoon at the beach, laughter filling the space. Izzy stayed by the door for a second longer than she needed to, staring down at the bottle of sunscreen in her hand.

It doesn't have to mean anything. That had been her mantra after that stupid kiss back in college. A mistake. A moment of weakness. But every time Kiera looked at her with that hesitant, hopeful softness, it chipped away at the carefully built mantra just a little more.

Izzy set the sunscreen on the counter with more force than necessary and slipped away before anyone could notice her lingering discomfort. She needed air. She needed space.

She stepped out onto the back deck, the ocean breeze tugging at the loose strands of her hair. She tried to remind herself of how simple things were supposed to be here — surf, sun, and friends. But the longer she stood there, staring out at the waves, the more complicated it all felt.

You're being ridiculous, she told herself. *You don't owe Kiera anything, not even after years of friendship.*

But deep down, she wasn't sure that was true.

CHAPTER 5

Kiera

The salty breeze wrapped around Kiera as she balanced on her paddleboard, the gentle waters of Mission Bay rocking her like a cradle. The sun had climbed higher in the sky, its rays warm against her skin as she adjusted her stance. Maggie paddled lazily beside her, her sunglasses glinting as she tilted her face up toward the sun, while Danica floated a little farther ahead, her paddle cutting smooth arcs through the calm water.

"This is the life," Maggie declared, stretching her arms dramatically and nearly toppling off her board. She righted herself with a laugh. "No screaming kids. Just us and these unsteady boards ready to dump us into dark, depthless water."

"Do you guys think there are sharks in here?" Danica asked, staring off to the side of her paddleboard.

"Probably," Kiera answered.

"What? Really?" Danica looked up at Kiera frantically. "Like, *shark* sharks?"

"Shark sharks? As opposed to regular sharks?" Kiera responded with a grin.

"They're actually fairly harmless," Maggie said. "More people are killed by donkeys each year than sharks."

"Even Spielberg said he regrets giving sharks such a bad reputation after making *Jaws*," Kiera added.

"When a shark eats me, can you two add both of those lovely shark propaganda talking points to my eulogy?" Danica looked between the two of them, and Maggie and Kiera burst out laughing.

"Just a eulogy? Why not the tombstone, too? Here lies Danica. That shark thought she was a seal, honest mistake," Maggie said.

Kiera smiled, adjusting her sun hat. She glanced toward Maggie. "Donkeys, really?"

Maggie nodded solemnly. "Izzy taught me that."

Kiera frowned, grateful for her sun hat and giant sunglasses to hide her reaction to Izzy's name. Izzy had been so weird at the market, like Kiera had personally attacked her.

Kiera had watched Izzy out on the waves that morning, the petite woman cutting through the water with a natural ease that made it impossible to look away. There was something mesmerizing about the way she moved, a seamless blend of precision and freedom as if she belonged out there more than anywhere else. Even from the shore, Kiera could see the grin on Izzy's face when she caught a wave, a flash of pure, unguarded joy. It wasn't just the surfing — it was Izzy herself. In the years she'd known Izzy, she'd always admired the effortless happiness Izzy seemed to exude, the kind of energy Kiera had spent years trying to cultivate but could never quite grasp. Watching her that morning, she had felt a pang of longing, not just for the life Izzy seemed to embody, but for that spark of unburdened lightness Kiera had lost somewhere along the way.

CHAPTER 5

Danica glanced back over her shoulder, her face framed by wisps of hair that had escaped her ponytail. "At least we can all agree this beats sitting on the sidelines while Izzy and Pete try to out-surf each other."

Kiera gazed toward the distant shoreline, where she could see the outline of palm trees and colorful kayaks and boats docked along the bay. "It *is* nice," she admitted.

Danica's tone was both soft-spoken and knowing. "I'm glad you're here."

"Are you?" Kiera responded more quickly than she intended, though she hoped her tone was more worried than accusatory.

Danica looked caught off-guard. "Of course I am."

Then why don't you ever return my calls? Kiera wanted to ask, but she held back the words. Instead, she forced herself to nod. "Thanks for saying that." Kiera looked down at the clear blue water, watching the sunlight ripple across the surface. She wanted to believe Danica, but a part of her couldn't accept that Danica would ever forgive her.

"You okay?" Maggie asked, her voice gentle.

Kiera shifted uncomfortably, her paddle dipping in and out of the water as she tried to articulate her thoughts. "Between our last trip and the divorce and the move... everything has just felt hard for so long, you know?"

Maggie let out a sympathetic hum. "Oh, Kiera, of course everything feels hard right now. But, Izzy is divorced, too. She might be able to give you ideas on how to get through it."

"I don't want Izzy's ideas," Kiera said automatically.

Danica and Maggie exchanged a look, and then Danica cleared her throat. "I'm sorry you're having a hard time, Kier. It sounds awful. I'm sorry we haven't spent more time together since you landed in Denver. Between work and travel and Pete and Gladys... It's been a lot of adjustment."

Kiera's throat tightened with emotion and embarrassment. Danica had once been her best friend, and now she hadn't made much of an effort to see her in the last year. "It's okay, I know you're busy."

Danica looked like she wanted to say more, but she glanced toward Maggie and then stopped, chewing on her lower lip.

Kiera's chest tightened further, but before she could ask Danica what she was about to say, Maggie pointed toward a small inlet nearby, bordered by a sandy strip and a few paddle boarders resting in the shallows. The inlet seemed quiet, a pocket of serenity tucked away from the busier parts of Mission Bay. As they drifted closer, the soft rustle of palm fronds and the chirping of unseen shorebirds created a tranquil soundtrack. "Let's head over there," Maggie suggested, her voice eager. "It looks nice and quiet and shark-free."

The trio paddled toward the inlet, the sound of the waves growing softer as they entered the sheltered area. The water was still and clear, offering a perfect view of the sandy bottom, scattered with shells and flowing seaweed. Maggie was the first to slip off her board and wade into the shallow water.

"This is amazing," Maggie said, her voice carrying over the stillness of the bay. She tilted her head back, letting the sunlight dance across her face.

"We should've brought snacks." Danica laughed, sitting cross-legged on her board as they watched Maggie explore the sandy beach. "This is the perfect picnic spot."

Kiera smiled faintly, leaning her paddle against her board and dipping her fingers into the cool water. The quiet companionship of the moment felt fragile but welcome, a brief respite from the awkwardness she'd been feeling since they arrived.

Danica's gaze lingered on Kiera for a moment before she spoke. "I love you, you know."

Kiera blinked, caught off guard by both the softness in

CHAPTER 5

Danica's voice and the directness of her statement. "I love you, too. And I'm sor—"

Danica held up a hand. "I know. It's just hard to let it all go. I'm hoping this weekend will help, you know? I miss you, but what happened..."

"Sucked," Kiera said flatly.

Danica let out a huff of a laugh. "It sucked."

Kiera sighed. "I know. It was really stupid, and believe me, I've had a lot of time to think about it."

Maggie waved toward them, shouting, "I found a little crab!" Danica and Kiera waved back like a pair of indulgent parents.

"You're doing a good job, you know. With the girls. With leaving Alex. It's not easy, but I'm proud of you," Danica said, her tone gentle but firm. "You're doing the best you can, and that's enough."

The words settled over Kiera, unexpected and comforting. She swallowed hard, her throat tight. "Thanks," she murmured, not trusting herself to say more without turning into a blubbering mess.

"You think he'll stay on my paddle board?" Maggie asked, cupping the tiny creature in her hands as she waded back into the shallows.

"No, babe," Kiera said flatly, shaking her head.

Danica sighed. "You cannot bring him back with us or Pete will name him, and we'll end up with a mascot that none of us can bring on a plane."

Maggie furrowed her brow, as she gently released him back into the water with a dramatic flourish of her hands. "A good point. So long, Sir Crabbington of Paddleboardshire."

The three of them lingered in the inlet for a while longer, relaxing and floating and taking their time. Watching Maggie and Danica's easy banter, she realized the rift between her and Danica might not be insurmountable after all. The shared memories, the quiet understanding, and the bond they once had — it all felt within reach again.

After an hour or so, the group met up again on Pacific Beach. Pete and Maggie tossed a frisbee back and forth, while Danica crouched near the water's edge, building an elaborate sandcastle, complete with a moat. Kiera sat cross-legged on the sand, watching Izzy out of the corner of her eye as she unpacked a small cooler that she and Pete had grabbed from the house.

After a long moment of silence, Kiera ventured, "This is nice."

Izzy shrugged, her expression unreadable as she busied herself with arranging bottles of water and a few snacks. "Yeah."

The awkwardness between them lingered like a low-hanging cloud, but Kiera pressed on. "With your divorce... how long did it take you to feel like a normal human being again?"

Izzy finally glanced at her, and Kiera thought she caught the faintest flicker of something softening in her eyes before the guarded wall returned. "I thought things worked with Paisley because we didn't need each other too much, but I don't think we truly ever let each other in," Izzy said quietly, surprising Kiera. "It didn't end in some big fight. It just... wore me down. Like I gave and gave, and I only got polite silence in return."

Kiera frowned. "That sounds awful."

"It was awful. I felt so distant and hollow after." Izzy chewed her lip, staring out at the horizon. Then, as if snapping out of a daze, she cleared her throat. "I don't know if I've ever felt like a normal human being, to be honest."

Kiera let out a bitter laugh. "I know that feeling well."

Izzy made a faint noise of agreement.

"So, the divorce was mutual? I don't really know anything

CHAPTER 5

about her.... about Paisley," Kiera said, hating Paisley immediately regardless of a lack of facts.

"We weren't married long, and we didn't have kids," Izzy replied, as if that negated telling her more details.

"Yeah," Kiera said. "That makes things less complicated on paper, but maybe not less complicated in reality."

Izzy took a deep breath and relaxed her shoulders as she kicked her unpainted toe in the sand. "Listen, about this morning at the market…"

Kiera hesitated, feeling the weight of everything unspoken between them. "I get that things are still weird," she said quietly. "You don't have to be nice to me just because I'm going through something right now."

Izzy's gaze lingered on her for a moment before she looked away, focusing on the waves. "Everyone screws things up, Kiera. But some things are harder to forgive than others. The question is whether you're willing to do the work to fix it and prove you're not just going to repeat the same mistakes."

The words stung, but Kiera nodded. "I am," she said simply. "But we all—"

Izzy held up a palm to stop her. "None of that. Own it."

Kiera took a deep breath, nodding. "I own it. I did the wrong thing. And because of that, everyone hates me."

"No." Izzy's short blonde hair ruffled in the ocean breeze as they watched one another for a long moment. Kiera could have sworn Izzy's gaze dropped to her mouth. Izzy's light blue eyes looked up to meet hers as she bit her lip, self-conscious. "I don't *hate* you, Kiera." Her voice was soft as she said it, a gentle, chiding reminder that it didn't help anything to be hyperbolic in her shame.

"Okay." Kiera smiled faintly, grateful for the small olive branch.

"Okay," Izzy said with finality. She turned toward Danica, who was now grimacing as one of her turrets was swept away in the current of her moat. "Need help, Danica?"

"God, yes. Please. Why are sandcastles so fucking difficult?" Danica looked up, a dejected frown on her face. Izzy sighed and pulled herself up from the sand, taking a step toward the castle.

Even Kiera couldn't help but laugh at the pained expression on her friend's face. A tiny bit of hope bloomed in her heart that she and Izzy could fix their friendship as she walked behind her. She missed that, the ease of familiarity between them. The weight on Kiera's shoulders lightened, however slightly, for the first time in ages.

CHAPTER 6

Izzy

THE LONG, GOLDEN RAYS OF THE SETTING SUN BATHED THE BEACH house in a warm glow as Izzy and Pete stood alone on the deck. Maggie and Kiera were calling their kids while Danica finished up dinner. She'd fired them as sous chefs after Pete had sliced the cherry tomatoes incorrectly. Pete leaned against the railing, her cheeks sunburnt, her fingers idly tracing the weathered wood, while Izzy swirled her glass of wine, her gaze fixed on the horizon.

"What were you and Kiera so heatedly discussing at the beach earlier?" Pete asked.

"Just the usual. She said she's trying not to screw things up again, which is just…" Izzy let out a long exhale, shifting her weight from foot to foot.

"Kiera is definitely trying," Peté said after a long pause, her voice low but deliberate. "You can see that, right?"

Izzy sighed, setting her glass down on the railing. "Trying doesn't erase what she did. She invited Eddie to Telluride after they'd already broken up. Who does that?"

Pete's jaw tightened, and she glanced toward the sliding

glass door. "I'm not saying it wasn't messed up. Believe me, I've had my own share of choice words about it. But Danica wants to move past it. So I'm... following her lead. I love that you're my tiny bodyguard but it's okay. You can calm the ferocity down."

Izzy turned, crossing her arms as she studied Pete's profile. "She didn't just hurt you and Danica. Her meddling ruined the trip."

"Meddling," Pete snorted in amusement. "You sound like Maggie."

Izzy chewed her lower lip.

Pete's voice pitched lower. "What else is going on?"

Izzy hesitated, her fingers curling around the edge of the railing. "Nothing."

Pete watched her with a bored expression. "Mmhmm. Sure. Spill it."

Izzy rolled her shoulders. "Fine. You know, back in college, when we kissed, I thought maybe... I don't know. I thought there could have been more to it. But I never let myself believe it. And then in Telluride there were a few times we were alone, skiing or on the lifts or at the house, and it seemed like... I don't know. It's stupid."

Pete turned to her, an eyebrow arching. "Isabel Tierney, have you been harboring feelings for a straight woman all this time? You saucy little minx."

"No," Izzy said quickly, shaking her head. "Not feelings. Just... She's..." She ran a hand through her short hair, tapping her Chacos against the railing. "Straight."

"And newly-divorced."

"Yep."

"And a mom."

"Pete, I get it," Izzy said with an eye roll.

"So what I'm saying is, she's definitely your type," Pete said with a small grin.

Izzy raised her eyebrows. "My type? Do you mean, complicated?"

Pete tilted her head. "I was going for: completely unavailable and thus unable to ever get close enough to see you, much less hurt you."

"Fucking ouch," Izzy scoffed, rubbing at her sternum, where she felt the invisible wound of Pete's words.

Pete's grin returned, softer this time. "Hey, at least she's single now. You know, if you wanted to test that theory."

Izzy snorted, rolling her eyes. "You're very annoying."

"I'm just saying," Pete said, holding up her hands in mock surrender. "Stranger things have happened."

Izzy's gaze drifted back to the ocean, her thoughts swirling as the waves lapped against the shore. "Did you know the ocean contains more bacteria than there are stars in the universe?"

"Well, that's terrifying," Pete commented off-handedly. "Don't think you can just tell me ocean facts to distract me away from all of your weirdness, though."

"Did you know there's an underwater waterfall between Greenland and Iceland?" Izzy tried.

Pete paused at that, her eyes narrowing in skeptical interest. "How?" she asked slowly.

Izzy stifled her grin. She'd won this time. Even as she explained the Denmark Strait cataract, which was just weird enough that she'd fallen down a very long rabbit hole researching it. Even as she was describing the temperature differences that made the waterfall possible, she knew Pete was mentally noting that they needed to return to why Kiera had gotten under Izzy's skin so badly, and worse — why she'd stayed there.

She couldn't stop herself from wondering what might have been if she'd been braver back in college, if she hadn't dismissed their kiss as a fleeting, meaningless moment. There had always been something about Kiera that tugged at her in ways she didn't fully understand, something warm and solid that Izzy found herself drawn to despite everything. She was too protective over Pete to forgive Kiera so easily. but that didn't stop the ache of wondering that threatened to unravel her resolve to ignore whatever feelings were floating to the surface.

THE GROUP SAT around the dining table, finishing up another of Danica's masterfully prepared meals. Tonight's dinner was a summer salad with grilled tofu, the bright pops of fresh veggies complementing the bohemian dinnerware Maggie had found in one of the kitchen cabinets. It wasn't as spicy as Danica normally made her food, which was a small mercy.

Pete leaned back in her chair, rubbing her stomach with exaggerated satisfaction. "Wendell, you've outdone yourself. Again."

"I'm just trying to make sure we don't all live off chips and salsa this weekend," Danica said with a smirk, lifting her glass of wine to her lips.

"What's wrong with chips and salsa?" Maggie asked, frowning.

"Nothing, unless it's the only thing you're eating for three days," Danica shot back.

Izzy half-listened, swirling the last of the wine in her glass. The conversation ebbed and flowed easily among the others. Her gaze flitted to Kiera, who was seated at the far end of the table. With rosy cheeks from the wine, Kiera laughed freely, playfully chiding Pete for her earlier wipeout.

Maybe it was the talk with Pete, or her confession about always wondering, but there was something disarming about Kiera in this moment. Something Izzy hadn't allowed herself to really *see* in a long time. Kiera's laugh was warm and genuine, and her ease with Danica and Maggie was a welcome change from how awkward she'd been before.

CHAPTER 6

Izzy had been so focused on holding onto her grudge, on keeping Kiera at arm's length, that she'd failed to notice how different Kiera seemed now after her divorce. Or maybe Kiera had always been this way, and Izzy had been too stubborn to fully realize it.

"Izzy," Pete said, breaking into her thoughts. "You're awfully quiet over there. Something on your mind?"

Izzy resisted the urge to throw Pete the middle finger and quickly schooled her expression. "Just enjoying the food. Thank you for always feeding us, Danica."

Danica smiled, clearly pleased. "Of course. I'm glad you like it! I'm just very good at following a recipe."

"You don't give yourself enough credit," Kiera said, her tone light but sincere. Danica waved off their compliments, leaning into Pete, who kissed her temple.

"I have to agree with Kiera on this one, babe. You're an amazing cook, just like how you're amazing at everything," Pete said, beaming.

Izzy's gaze shifted to Kiera, catching sadness in her expression as she looked down into her wine.

Maggie glanced toward Izzy, then followed her gaze to Kiera. "You feeling okay, Kiera?" Maggie asked.

Kiera glanced at Maggie, her brow furrowing in surprise. "Yeah, of course. Why?"

Danica put a hand on Kiera's arm. "You've been going through a lot."

Kiera's expression softened as she glanced around the table. "Oh, we don't have to do this."

"Come on, spill it. We want divorce details," Maggie prodded. "I haven't seen you since you kicked Alex to the curb and I'm dying to know what happened."

Kiera's eyes remained guarded. "It's been a process," she said carefully. "Alex didn't contest the divorce, and he's barely seen the girls since we moved to Denver. Honestly, it really fucking sucks. Divorce has really made me feel like I'm starting completely over, and I hate that."

The sentiment struck closer to home than Izzy cared to admit, reminding her of late night arguments with Paisley about priorities, about how Izzy always seemed to drift through life already halfway out the door. Kiera's quiet strength in admitting her struggles felt almost like a mirror.

"That's one way to put it," Izzy said, reaching for her water glass. "It's like being thrown into a blender and hoping you come out as a gut biome-friendly smoothie instead of a disaster."

As everyone laughed, Kiera glanced at Izzy again, her smile almost shy. "I'm just trying to get through it. One day at a time."

Izzy nodded. Unexpectedly, she felt a desire to show compassion and understanding. Kiera was hurting, and Izzy suspected that she'd been hurting for much, much longer than she'd let on. From what Izzy had heard, Kiera's ex-husband had been cheating for a while, and Kiera had already known about the affair when they were in Telluride.

Kiera's gaze lingered on Izzy for a moment.

Danica cleared her throat, breaking the silence. "Alright, who's up for dessert? I picked up some ice cream sandwiches and I am dying to dig into them."

A mischievous grin spread across Pete's face. "I've got a better idea."

CHAPTER 7

Kiera

The neon glow of the Gossip Grill sign lit up the sidewalk as the group made their way inside, laughter trailing behind them. Kiera adjusted the strap of her purse, a mix of nerves and excitement bubbling under her skin. She hadn't been to a club in years, let alone one this vibrant and unapologetically queer. The moment they walked through the doors, the pulsing bass of the music and shouted conversations enveloped them like a warm, electric blanket.

"This place is amazing," Maggie declared, turning in a slow circle to take in the atmosphere. The walls were adorned with cheeky slogans and murals of queer icons, while rainbow lights shone across the ceiling. The dance floor was packed, bodies moving in sync to the DJ's rhythm.

"Drinks first, then dancing," Pete said, steering the group toward the bar. "Priorities, people."

Kiera followed, feeling a little out of her element but buoyed by the group's energy. Pete and Maggie wasted no time ordering shots for everyone, and Kiera found herself sandwiched between Danica and Izzy at the bar.

"What do you think of this place?" Kiera asked, trying to bridge the gap.

Izzy glanced at her, then gave a tight smile. "It's no karaoke bar but it'll do."

Kiera laughed. "God, if only." She turned her attention to the others, raising her shot glass as Pete proposed a toast.

"To questionable life choices and even better stories tomorrow!"

"Cheers!" they all echoed, clinking glasses before downing the shots. The burn of tequila was sharp but welcome, and Kiera looked around the crowded room.

The thrum of bass pulsed through Kiera's chest as she stood near the edge of the crowded nightclub, half-listening to Pete order more drinks for everyone.

Colorful, dim lights played over the crowded dance floor, creating an electric, slightly intimidating atmosphere. At thirty-eight, Kiera felt conspicuously out of place. Most of the people here seemed younger, more confident, and entirely at ease in their skin. She envied them, envied their certainty, their freedom to claim their space, and their identity without hesitation. For Kiera, the whole scene was disorienting — a world she didn't quite belong to but couldn't stop herself from being drawn toward.

Her gaze caught on Izzy, who moved effortlessly among the crowd, her blonde pixie cut catching the light like a beacon. A realization bubbled up inside her chest, unbidden and confusing. Kiera couldn't deny how attracted she was to her in the moment, and how that realization hit her like a punch to the gut. Worse yet was the secondary realization of how attracted she had always been to her. But did that attraction mean anything beyond Izzy herself?

Kiera had never felt this way about another woman, not once in her twelve years of marriage. Even now, the thought of labeling herself as anything but straight felt almost presumptuous. How could she claim any part of the queer label when she didn't understand her place in it? She wasn't sure if her attraction to Izzy was enough to make her belong, and that uncertainty settled over her like a heavy, invisible weight.

Kiera shifted her drink to her other hand, her fingers damp from the condensation. A part of her felt like an impostor, standing there at the edge of something she didn't quite know how to define. But another part of her, quieter but more insistent, wondered if this was the beginning of something. Maybe it wasn't about labels or fitting neatly into a category. Maybe it was just about allowing herself to feel — fully and unapologetically. She glanced back at Izzy, her stomach twisting with an unease and interest that she could no longer ignore, realizing that maybe this was less about understanding and more about courage. For once, she wanted to stop holding herself back, even if she wasn't sure what that meant just yet.

The music was infectious, a driving beat that called to her. She followed Maggie and Danica onto the dance floor, her movements stiff, her shoulders tight with the worry that someone might be watching her, judging her. But as the beat pulsed and the crowd moved in a wave of unselfconscious joy around her, Kiera began to let go.

She closed her eyes, letting the music seep into her, its rhythm grounding her in a way she hadn't felt in years. The tightness in her shoulders melted, replaced by a cozy wine and tequila-induced warmth that spread through her chest and limbs. The noise of the crowd became part of the music, a symphony of belonging. Here, in this space filled with unapologetic energy, Kiera felt a lightness she hadn't realized she needed. Here, surrounded by a community that welcomed anyone willing to step onto the dance floor, it felt right. She felt right.

Pete and Izzy eventually joined in and passed out drinks. Maggie and Danica danced somewhere nearby, lighthearted and giggly, and Kiera grinned, her confidence growing with each beat.

Her gaze drifted to Izzy, who lingered at the edge of the group, swaying and nursing her fancy cocktail in a plastic cup. Kiera couldn't help but notice how striking she was in the club's neon glow.

The DJ switched to a slower, sultrier track, and the mood on the dance floor shifted. Kiera closed her eyes again, moving with the music, her body attuned to the rhythm. When she opened them, Izzy was closer to her, her expression unreadable but intense.

Kiera stifled a smile, glancing to see that Pete and Danica were in their own world and Maggie was getting another drink from the bar.

Izzy stepped into the space in front of her, not saying another word.

They began to dance, their movements hesitant at first but gradually falling into sync. Kiera's pulse thrummed in time with the music, a deep, steady rhythm that felt like it had taken over her entire body. She could feel the heat radiating from Izzy, her presence like a magnetic force drawing her closer.

As the world around them blurred, Kiera's thoughts began to wander. This wasn't the first time she'd danced with Izzy. One of her most replayed memories came to mind, unbidden but vivid: a college party, both of them tipsy and laughing, the music loud and the room packed with people. Dancing, their hands brushing, their bodies finding an easy rhythm. It had been the night of their first kiss — their only kiss. Kiera could still remember the way Izzy had looked at her, a mixture of heady lust and something deeper that made Kiera's chest tighten even now.

She'd thought about that kiss so many times over the years, replaying it in her mind like a favorite scene from a movie. It had been fun and sexy and intense. She'd held back then, too scared to admit what she wanted — women, or perhaps just Izzy — and by the time she'd gathered the courage, the moment had passed. She often wondered what might have happened if she'd been braver, if she'd taken the next step.

Now, as Izzy moved closer, the memory felt like a spark catching fire. Kiera's senses sharpened, every detail of Izzy coming into focus: the way her eyes glimmered in the neon light, the curve of her lips, the slight friction between them as they swayed. Her skin tingled with the excitement of being so near Izzy.

The air between them grew heavier, charged with an energy that made Kiera's head spin. She was suddenly aware of everything — the faint scent of Izzy's cherry and ginger perfume, the warmth of Izzy's body so close to hers, the way Izzy's fingers brushed hers as they moved together. It felt like the rest of the room had disappeared, leaving just the two of them in this electric bubble.

Kiera's heart pounded harder, her palms damp with nerves and exhilaration. Her gaze lingered on Izzy's lips, and she felt a pull so strong it was almost involuntary. The tension between them was unbearable, stretching taut, about to snap.

Izzy's eyes flickered down to Kiera's mouth, too, then back up, and Kiera felt something shift. A silent invitation. Her pulse roared in her ears, drowning out everything but the overwhelming urge to close the distance between them.

But just as her breath caught, Izzy's expression shifted — hardening, as if she'd remembered something. Izzy took a small step back, breaking the spell between them.

"I'm gonna go try to find Maggie and grab another drink," Izzy said, her voice quieter, almost reluctant.

Kiera nodded, swallowing hard as she forced a smile. "Yeah." Danica and Pete were talking near the edge of the dance floor, but she couldn't spot Maggie. "Probably a good idea."

Izzy nodded and turned, heading back toward the edge of the dance floor. Kiera followed a beat later, her chest heavy with longing and disappointment. Izzy wasn't ready, and maybe Kiera wasn't either. Not yet.

The dance floor receded behind them, but something felt different. Within her, between her and Izzy... She couldn't name what had shifted — only that it had, and now they'd both have to live inside the new shape of it.

CHAPTER 8

Izzy

Izzy adjusted her wetsuit under her arm as she quietly slipped on her sandals by the door. The house was still asleep, the faint hum of the refrigerator and the distant crash of waves the only sounds keeping her company. Dawn light filtered through the kitchen windows, soft and muted, casting long shadows on the terrazzo tiles.

She had hoped for solitude — her usual escape. Surfing at this hour meant no one was watching, no one was talking, it was just her and the ocean. The water was the only thing that had ever made her feel truly weightless, like she could shed the world's expectations and simply exist. Out there, floating on the tide, she could disappear into something vast and steady, something that never required anything but to be present. As she turned to leave, Kiera appeared at the bottom of the staircase, her dark waves tied loosely back and her expression soft with sleep.

"Heading out already?" Kiera asked, her voice hushed as she glanced at Izzy's wetsuit under her arm.

Izzy nodded. "Best time to catch a wave."

Kiera hovered near the counter, looking as though she was still deciding whether to go back upstairs. "It's not even light out yet."

Izzy shrugged, reaching to adjust the heel strap of her sandal. "That's kind of the point." She paused, something in Kiera's hesitant expression drawing her in. "What about you? Couldn't sleep?"

Kiera smiled faintly, her arms crossing loosely over her chest. "Something like that."

For a moment, they stood there, the silence stretching between them. Izzy's thoughts drifted back to the night before, to the charged moment on the dance floor when she'd felt the warmth of Kiera's body so close to hers. That near-kiss kept her up all night. She couldn't stop thinking about Kiera's breath on her lips. Had Kiera felt it too? Or had Izzy let herself get caught up in the moment, reading into something that wasn't really there? The charged energy between them was an undercurrent she couldn't quite shake. She surprised herself by not rushing to leave. There was something disarming about seeing Kiera like this, the strain she'd been appearing to carry on this trip seemed softened by the early hour. Izzy surprised herself by asking, "Want to come with me?"

Kiera blinked, surprised. "Surfing?"

Izzy shook her head. "A walk. It's quiet this time of day. Peaceful."

The invitation hung in the air, and for a second, Izzy almost regretted extending it, feeling antsy and unsure. She half-expected Kiera to decline, to retreat back upstairs and leave Izzy to her solitary ritual. But then Kiera nodded slowly, a small smile tugging at the corner of her lips. "Alright. Let me grab a sweatshirt."

By the time they stepped onto the sand, the sky had begun to lighten, hues of gray streaking the horizon. A thin veil of early spring fog clung to the shoreline, blurring the edges of the world around them. The ocean air was rich with the scent of salt and something cool and earthy. The water glimmered under the soft dawn light, waves rolling steadily toward shore. The beach behind them was empty, save for the occasional runner or dog walker. Izzy had left the surfboard back at the house and she fidgeted with the strings of her hoodie, while Kiera tucked her hands into the pockets of her sweatpants.

They walked in companionable silence at first, the only sound the rhythm of the waves and a few far-off sea lions hollering. Izzy stole a glance at Kiera, noticing the way her shoulders had started to relax, her gaze fixed on the ocean as if it held answers she couldn't quite articulate.

"Do your girls like Denver?" Izzy asked, breaking the silence.

Kiera nodded, her expression softening. "I think so. They've been amazing about all of the changes, especially given a new school and new house and not seeing their dad, but I can't help but wonder just how terribly I'm traumatizing them. Maybe instead of a college fund, I should just start a therapy fund."

"Sounds like something all parents should start," Izzy said with a small smile.

"I should start one for myself," Kiera admitted, kicking at the sand as they walked. "I've been so caught up in... everything. I don't remember the last time I just let myself enjoy anything."

Izzy raised an eyebrow. "Why is that?"

Kiera hesitated, then shook her head. "I don't know. Maybe I'm too busy trying to keep it all together."

Izzy glanced out at the water, her jaw tightening slightly. "Telluride didn't exactly help with that, did it?" The words were out before she could stop them, and she immediately regretted the flat directness in her tone.

Kiera stopped walking, her expression clouding. "Izzy,

I…" She trailed off, taking a deep breath. "You're right. I handled that all wrong. I thought I was helping, but I only made things worse. For everyone."

The sincerity in Kiera's voice gave Izzy pause. She had spent so much time convincing herself that Kiera's actions had been selfish, but what if it had been something else? What if, beneath the interference and misguided attempts to help, Kiera had been struggling just as much as the rest of them? She'd expected Kiera to defend her actions, to try to explain them away. She hadn't expected this.

"You did make it worse," Izzy said, though her voice lacked the edge it had carried moments ago. "You acted like you didn't trust your best friend to handle her own life and make her own choices, and you hurt my best friend in the process."

Kiera's shoulders slumped, and she nodded. "I was really going through it, and I didn't even know it at the time. Things with Alex made me feel so out of control, and watching Danica be so reckless, or so I thought at the time… I did the wrong thing, and I'm truly sorry."

Izzy studied her for a moment, the vulnerability in Kiera's expression catching her off guard. For so long, she'd held onto the frustration, the hurt. But now, standing here in the soft morning light, those emotions didn't have quite as strong a hold as they once had.

"Okay," Izzy said finally, her tone softer.

Kiera offered a small, tentative smile. "Okay? That's it?"

Izzy shrugged.

"Maybe someday when I'm feeling more… I don't know, like a person, I'll be able to unpack that more. For now, you just get to tolerate this weird broken version of me." Kiera bit her lower lip.

Izzy watched as Kiera's brow furrowed. There was clearly a lot of truth behind her words. "You know what really helped me feel normal after my divorce?"

CHAPTER 8

Kiera tilted her head, holding the loose strands of her hair back from her face in the gentle morning breeze. "What?"

"Doing something I'd never done before, only for me. I took up ceramics for a while, weirdly enough. It was just some hobby that I enjoyed that had absolutely no tie to anything that could make me think of my ex-wife," Izzy said, remembering how empty she'd felt after Paisley had left her. She'd stumbled upon a queer pottery studio and started making wonky little bowls that made her inordinately happy.

Kiera's expression softened. "That's actually a really good idea."

"You will have absolutely no one else to impress or answer to about it, either. It can be something solely for you. You don't even have to be good at it." Izzy grinned, remembering how terrible she was at throwing clay on the wheel at first and how frustrated she'd been for weeks until it finally clicked. It had been such a personal victory. Meaningless in the grand scheme of things, but such a bright spot in her own little life.

"That's a good point. You know, I've been really wanting to work out again. I used to do Pilates, but maybe I'll become like one of those people obsessed with CrossFit and... throwing around tires, or whatever they do." Kiera smirked.

"Hell yeah. You should try it." Izzy nodded, picturing Kiera with massive muscles, talking about WODs. She grinned.

They continued walking, the tension between them easing slightly. After a while, Izzy nudged Kiera with her elbow, a glint in her eyes. "Want to see something cool?"

FIFTEEN MINUTES LATER, Izzy had driven her rental car to the rocky coastline of Point Loma to show Kiera the Cabrillo tide pools. They climbed down the cliffs, the rocky ledge of pools stretching out before them. An early morning marine layer rolled in, cloaking the cliffs in mist and giving the area an otherworldly feel. Waves crashed against the rocks, sending sprays of seawater into the breeze. Kiera crouched down, peering into one of the pools where tiny hermit crabs scuttled along the rocks.

"My parents met in San Diego when my dad was in the Navy, so I grew up visiting here," Izzy said, watching as Kiera trailed her fingers through the water. "It's one of my favorite spots."

Kiera looked up, a soft smile on her lips. "I didn't know your dad was in the Navy."

"He was. He's dead," Izzy said with the same detached air she always reserved for that statement.

Kiera's eyes widened. "I'm so sorry."

Izzy nodded. "It's been like nearly twenty years. It's okay."

Kiera watched her for a second, like she was really seeing her, and Izzy's stomach clenched with nervous energy.

"This place is beautiful," Kiera said finally, reaching into the tide pool to lift a rock and examine it.

Izzy shrugged, stuffing her hands into her pockets. "Figured you might appreciate it. Something about watching these little creatures just living their lives, oblivious to everything else going on… it's kind of nice, isn't it?"

Kiera nodded, her gaze lingering on the water. "Yeah. It really is. Lucky dummies."

They stood there for a long moment, side by side, the wind tugging at their clothes, the ocean stretching endlessly before them.

Izzy loved how otherworldly this place was. The red and beige rocks all around, the tiny sea life hiding out in the tide pools… no where else ever felt like this place, which was both reassuring and made her heart ache with nostalgia. As she watched Kiera crouch and smile, looking at a starfish, she was surprised with herself for even bringing Kiera here. She was

CHAPTER 8 65

surprised mostly because she'd *wanted* to share this with Kiera, a place she hadn't even brought Pete before.

Kiera glanced up, her eyes gleaming with excitement as she pushed her large glasses back up her nose, looking at Izzy. Izzy's stomach did a giddy flip in response. *Oh no. What was that?* Her heart pounded uncomfortably in her chest, and she suddenly felt too warm despite the cool sea spray misting over them. It was one thing to acknowledge that Kiera was attractive — that was an objective fact — but this was something else. This was wanting to reach out and tuck that loose strand of hair behind Kiera's ear, wanting to see if her skin was as soft as it looked under the morning light.

This was dangerously close to the pattern she'd never tried to break — it was easier to chase someone who could never love her than to face someone who might, risking that they might not stay.

Izzy forced herself to look away, to focus on the shifting tide instead of this attraction, this pull toward Kiera. It was ridiculous. She barely tolerated Kiera most of the time — so why did she suddenly want to know what it felt like to have Kiera's fingertips graze hers as they both reached for a seashell at the same time? Why did she have to notice the way Kiera's hoodie slipped off her shoulder slightly, exposing a sliver of skin that Izzy couldn't seem to ignore?

She inhaled sharply, stuffing her hands in her pockets as if that could keep her emotions in check. This was Kiera — straight, recently divorced, a mom, and not someone Izzy should be entertaining thoughts about. And yet, she felt herself drawn in, her chest tight with something that felt too much like longing.

This was what she always did. Pete had been right. Kiera was unavailable, and that was why she was attracted to her now. Izzy had better be careful, or Pete was going to crow for days about this revelation.

"You okay?" Kiera's voice was soft and gentle.

Izzy startled, glancing away quickly as if she could physically shake off the thoughts flooding her mind. "Yeah, fine," she said, clearing her throat.

Kiera tilted her head, studying her. "You're quiet all of a sudden."

Izzy forced a small laugh, rubbing at the back of her neck. "Just thinking."

Kiera didn't push, but her gaze lingered, searching. Izzy resisted the urge to fidget under the scrutiny, her heartbeat a steady thrum in her ears. She needed to get out of here — away from the pull of Kiera's presence, away from her own traitorous thoughts. "We should head back," she said abruptly.

Just before Izzy turned to walk away, Kiera straightened from where she'd been crouched beside the tide pool, brushing a lock of hair from her face.

Kiera's eyes sparkled behind her glasses. "You make that face when you're flustered."

Izzy blinked. "What face?"

Kiera stepped closer, just enough to make Izzy's breath catch. "The one where you stare really hard at the ocean so you don't have to look at me."

Heat rushed to Izzy's cheeks. "I do *not* make that face."

Kiera laughed softly, turning back toward the parking lot. "It's cute, don't worry."

Izzy gaped, but something very annoying and very tender clenched in her chest as she hurried after Kiera.

***

As they walked into the beach house, Izzy could feel her chest tightening with every step closer to reality. The tide pools had been quiet and secluded, where she wouldn't have to worry about everyone else noticing what she was so desperate to hide. But now, back in the orbit of their friends, with the house looming ahead and the wide stretch of sand

CHAPTER 8

inviting them down to the shoreline, Izzy's panic set in full force.

She needed space. Needed air. Needed Kiera to stop looking at her with that soft, open expression that made something inside her unravel.

"I think I'm going to head down to the water and try to surf a bit," Izzy said abruptly as they stepped inside, already toeing off her sandals by the patio doors. The house smelled like coffee and sunscreen, the others clearly awake and already moving about. Pete's voice carried from the kitchen, something about eggs being overrated, while Maggie and Danica laughed in response.

Kiera hesitated, brushing a strand of dark hair behind her ear. "Oh. Do you... do you want company?"

Izzy swallowed hard, something about Kiera's casual question making her feel cornered. "Nah," she said, a little too quickly. "I just need to move." She forced a smile. "You should, uh, grab some breakfast. Danica's probably already made something."

Kiera's expression flickered, unreadable, but she nodded. "Alright. Maybe I'll see you down there."

Izzy didn't answer. She just turned, grabbed her board, and strode down the path toward the beach like she had somewhere urgent to be.

By the time she hit the sand, the weight in her chest hadn't eased. If anything, it pressed heavier. She walked straight toward the water's edge, the morning tide licking at her ankles as she tossed her towel and board onto the sand and stood there, hands on her hips, watching the horizon.

This was ridiculous. She was being ridiculous.

Kiera was still trying to piece together her life after everything crumbled, and Izzy was feeling this intense draw over a woman who didn't even see her that way.

And yet.

No.

She squeezed her eyes shut, but it didn't stop the image from flooding her mind — Kiera's wind-tousled hair at Point Loma, her dark eyes glinting with amusement as she'd teased Izzy, the way her lips had parted slightly when they'd stood too close on the rocks, like maybe she'd been thinking about this attraction, too.

Izzy groaned, pressing her palms against her face. No. No, she was not doing this.

She needed to push these feelings down, bury them deep where they belonged.

With an exhausted exhale, she picked up her board and headed out toward the waves, toward the only place where her mind felt clear.

CHAPTER 9

Kiera

The sun beat down on the sand, warm and relentless, though their cluster of umbrellas provided some much-needed shade. Kiera stretched out on a lounge chair, her wide-brimmed straw hat tilted low over her face as she sipped from a can of sparkling water. Around her, Maggie and Danica had settled into the same lazy rhythm, chatting or half-dozing as the waves rolled in a steady, hypnotic rhythm.

Pete and Izzy, predictably, couldn't sit still. A few yards away, they tossed a frisbee back and forth with a couple of guys who had wandered over, eager to join in. The men were the typical San Diego beach type — sun-kissed skin, tousled hair, an effortless cool to their movements. Kiera barely paid them any mind, more focused on applying sunscreen to her legs, making sure to get every inch.

Maggie, stretched out beside her under the umbrella, let out an amused sigh. "Do you think Izzy and Pete realize they're being flirted with?"

Kiera glanced over at them, watching as one of the guys laughed a little too enthusiastically at something Izzy said, brushing his hand through his hair in a way that was painfully obvious. Oblivious to her admirer's attempts, Pete remained engrossed in her world, showcasing her expert frisbee skills with sniper-like precision.

"Nope," Kiera replied, smirking. "Not even a little."

Danica, lying on a towel beside them, adjusted her sunglasses. "It's honestly painful to watch. That guy is literally flexing every time he throws the frisbee."

"I respect the dedication," Maggie murmured, taking a sip from her bottle of water. "Even if it's wildly ineffective."

Kiera chuckled, leaning back against her chair. It was nice, the easy camaraderie of the moment. No silent grudges, no awkwardness. Just a group of friends enjoying the kind of afternoon that felt endless and golden, the kind of day that was meant to be tucked away for safekeeping.

Danica propped herself up on her elbows, nodding toward the group still playing. "I swear, if Pete catches that frisbee mid-air one more time, that guy's going to propose on the spot."

Maggie snorted. "I give it ten minutes before he starts asking her if she surfs."

"Oh, absolutely," Danica agreed. "The other one's going to turn to Izzy and say, *'You ever try paddle boarding at sunset? Changed my life.'*" She dipped her voice lower into a silly imitation of a frat bro.

Kiera laughed, adjusting her hat. "Please. Izzy will be the one who ends up lecturing him about ocean pollution and the carbon footprint of beach tourism."

Maggie grinned. "You've gotten that lecture, too? I don't know, some people could be wooed by that sort of talk."

Kiera hesitated just a beat too long before replying, "I mean... it's not *not* attractive."

Danica raised an eyebrow behind her sunglasses. "Oh?"

Kiera groaned, tossing her empty soda bottle toward the cooler. "Don't start."

"Too late," Maggie sing-songed. "I saw you at the bar last night. Kiera's got a cru-ush."

"I do not." Kiera grabbed her book and opened it dramatically. "I just appreciate passionate environmental rants. Like any sane person."

"Sure," Danica said. "And I only watch *Outlander* for the gorgeous period-appropriate costumes."

Maggie laughed. "It's okay, Kier. You could have worse hypothetical taste in women. Izzy's cute."

Kiera peeked over her book, eyes on Izzy again — the way her short blonde hair bounced when she ran for the frisbee, the way her smile was wide and easy as if carried on the sea breeze. "Yeah," she said softly, mostly to herself. "She kind of is."

Danica made a humming sound of interest, and Kiera knew that she'd never live this down. Her friends were like vultures, circling their next meal.

Out of the corner of her eye, Kiera saw a frisbee soaring through the air, an errant throw. One of the guys, of course, had miscalculated his angle. Kiera barely had time to register its trajectory before it smacked directly into Maggie's face with a sickening *thwack*.

There was a stunned moment of silence, interrupted only by a loud, "Fuck!" Maggie clutched her nose, doubling over, her voice muffled through her hands.

Danica moved to kneel in front of Maggie, her face going full professional-in-crisis mode. "Shit, Maggie! Let me see."

Pete and Izzy abandoned the frisbee game, rushing over, the guys trailing behind them, looking appropriately horrified.

"Oh my god, I am so sorry," the guy who threw it stammered, his tan face turning pale.

Maggie pulled her hands away, revealing a trickle of blood running down toward her lips. Her nose was already swelling, an alarming shade of red.

"Does it look broken?" Maggie asked, her voice nasally, which was probably not a great sign.

Danica leaned in, examining her with a clinical focus. "Yeah, I'm pretty sure it's broken."

Maggie groaned, grabbing a towel Pete was handing her. "Of course it is. Because what's a trip with you guys if I don't sustain at least one major injury?"

Kiera exchanged a look with Izzy, who was biting her lip with an unreadable expression, unsure whether she was concerned or about to laugh, or both.

"Should we take her to the ER?" Pete asked, glancing at Danica.

Danica sighed, rubbing a hand over her forehead. "Yeah, she should get it checked out. They might need to set it."

Maggie groaned louder. "I hate this. I *hate* this trip. I hate frisbees. I hate men."

The guilty frisbee guy took a step back, looking like he wanted to melt into the sand.

Izzy finally lost it, letting out a snort of laughter. "Okay, yeah, but to be fair, you've always hated men."

Maggie pointed at her with a bloody hand. "That's not the *point*, Izzy."

Kiera sighed, already standing up. "Alright, let's get you to a doctor before you start cursing *all* recreational sports."

Maggie muttered something under her breath about *burning every frisbee in existence*, but let Danica and Kiera help her to her feet, wobbling slightly.

The two men were still lingering, looking like they wanted to help but not sure if they should. The one who threw the frisbee shuffled forward, clearing his throat. "Uh, can I — can I do anything?"

Maggie, deadpan, stared at him over her blood-streaked hands. "You can *leave*."

Kiera bit back a smile as the guy mumbled another apology and stumbled in the sand to flee.

CHAPTER 9

"Well," Pete mused as they started gathering their things, "at least we'll always have this beautiful memory of Pacific Beach."

"Make sure you get a photo. You can put it in the scrapbook," Maggie grumbled.

Kiera patted her shoulder. "Oh, don't worry. We will."

Danica helped Maggie shuffle toward the house, still holding a bloodied towel to her nose and muttering about her hatred for frisbees and men. Kiera, Izzy, and Pete carried their beach bags and chairs, while Danica lectured Maggie on not tilting her head back, her doctor-mode fully activated.

"We'll text when we know something," Danica called over her shoulder before sliding into the driver's seat of the rental car parked in the driveway.

And just like that, they were gone, leaving Kiera and Izzy alone, the sound of the waves and distant chatter of other beachgoers settling between them.

"Well, should we go try to relax until they come back?" Izzy suggested.

Kiera glanced back toward the beach, where their own umbrellas and chairs still sat. "Might as well." They walked back down into the sand, an awkward silence stretching between them that hadn't been there that morning on their walk.

Izzy didn't sit back down. Instead, she busied herself with brushing sand off her chair, adjusting her sunglasses, and brushing nonexistent flecks off her Patagonia shorts. Kiera noticed how Izzy kept her body angled away, almost like she was trying to physically avoid looking at her.

Ever since the tide pools, Izzy had been acting... off. Not just distant, but weirdly avoidant. Normally, Izzy was blunt — if she had a problem, she'd say it, not dance around it. But now, it felt like there was an invisible ocean between them.

Kiera sighed, settling back into her chair. "You're being weird."

Izzy, still standing, tensed slightly. "What? No, I'm not."

Kiera tilted her head, squinting at her through her prescription sunglasses. "Yeah, you are."

Izzy huffed out a small laugh, but it sounded forced. "I'm literally acting normal."

"You've barely looked at me since we got back from the tide pools this morning."

Izzy paused, her fingers fidgeting with the edge of her towel. "I don't know what you're talking about," she said.

Kiera arched a brow. "So you're saying you *didn't* full-body flinch when I asked you a question at lunch?"

Izzy rolled her shoulders in a shrug, finally dropping back into her chair with a sigh. She pulled on a baseball cap, obscuring part of her face. "I don't know. I guess I'm just tired."

Kiera studied her for a long moment, debating whether to push or let it go. She didn't want to let it go, though. Not when the morning had been so easy between them.

She leaned forward in her low beach chair, resting her arms on her knees. "Is this about me? Did I do something? Did you get offended when I said you were cute?"

Izzy stiffened just slightly. "No," she muttered.

Kiera narrowed her eyes. "You *are* lying."

Izzy exhaled sharply through her nose, tilting her face up toward the sky like she was praying to the Sun God for patience. "Kiera. You didn't do anything. I don't know what you want me to say."

Kiera searched Izzy's expression, the set of her jaw, the way she kept picking at the hem of her shorts. It was like Izzy was holding something back. Kiera swallowed hard and leaned back again, feigning casualness in her tone, even as something tight curled in her chest. "Fine. Whatever."

Izzy didn't respond. She just lay back on her towel, crossing her arms behind her head like she was completely

CHAPTER 9

unbothered, even though Kiera could *feel* the awkwardness radiating off her.

And that was it. The conversation ended, the silence stretching between them, filled only by the sounds of others on the beach shouting, laughing, playing, and rhythmic crash of the ocean waves.

Kiera crossed her arms and forced herself to look *anywhere* but at Izzy. The ocean, the sky, the joggers passing by on the packed sand — literally anything to keep her from noticing the way Izzy's legs stretched out, sighing as she finally seemed to settle.

Izzy pulled a book from her bag, some fantasy novel with a dragon and a sword on the cover. Kiera should've known better than to look up at Izzy's face. But she did.

Izzy, with her sun-kissed skin and tousled blonde hair, turned her baseball cap backward on her head, pushing her sunglasses up her nose before flipping the paperback open. She held it casually in one hand, her fingers resting lightly against the pages as she shifted onto her side, propping herself up on an elbow. Izzy's barely perceptible frown, the minimal movement of her lips while reading, and the absent-minded scratching of her shoulder captivated Kiera.

She'd always thought Izzy was attractive. Objectively, Izzy was the kind of effortlessly cool that Kiera had never been. But this? There was something unbearably *hot* about the way Izzy read. Something about the ease of it, the casual confidence of a person completely absorbed in her book, oblivious to the world around her. She licked the tip of her finger to turn the page, brow twitching slightly as she concentrated, and Kiera had to drag her eyes away, biting the inside of her cheek.

Kiera cleared her throat and turned toward the water, willing herself to think about anything other than Izzy's fingers against the soft, worn pages. Or the way the sunlight traced over the line of her jaw.

Kiera forced her gaze out toward the horizon, pretending she was deeply fascinated by the waves rolling in. *Act normal, Kiera. Get it together.,*

"What?" Izzy asked, her tone light. Her voice held a hint of hesitation, like she wasn't sure she wanted to know the answer. Izzy shifted, glancing at her over the top of her sunglasses, her lips quirking into something almost — *shy?* No, that wasn't right. Izzy didn't do shy. Stoic, at her most quiet, but never shy.

Kiera's stomach flipped. Great. Izzy caught her staring. Now she looked like a creep.

"Nothing," Kiera responded quickly, but the way her voice squeaked with surprise probably gave her away.

Izzy raised an eyebrow, looking as if she was holding back a laugh. "Right..." she said slowly.

Kiera scrambled for a reasonable excuse. "I — I was just thinking about, um, sunscreen."

Izzy blinked. "Sunscreen."

"Yeah," Kiera rushed out, nodding way too fast. "Like, if I should reapply. You know, UV rays and all that. I don't want to pull a Pete and get sunburnt."

Izzy just stared at her for a beat. Then, with a small shake of her head, she turned back to her book, clearly deciding not to question the nonsense that had just come out of Kiera's mouth.

Kiera exhaled, dragging a hand down her face, feeling even more ridiculous.

Izzy flipped another page, shifting slightly. "You should probably reapply," she murmured absently, eyes still on the text.

Kiera swallowed hard, suddenly feeling too warm, and reached blindly for her bag. Anything to give her hands something to do. She fumbled with the sunscreen bottle, nearly dropping it into the sand as she twisted the cap off.

She squeezed a dollop onto her palm and started rubbing

it into her arms with way too much concentration. She could feel Izzy beside her, still reading, still entirely herself, completely unaware of the ridiculous state Kiera had worked herself into.

Izzy let out a small sigh and set her book down, tilting her head to look at Kiera. "Do you want me to get your back?"

Kiera's brain stalled. She turned toward Izzy too quickly. Izzy looked at her with a perfectly neutral expression, like she'd just asked her if she wanted water. Like this wasn't a *thing*.

And maybe it wasn't. Maybe it was only a thing in Kiera's head.

"Oh," Kiera said, voice coming out a little too high. "You don't have to..."

Izzy rolled her eyes, already reaching for the sunscreen. "You'll burn if you miss a spot. Just turn around."

Kiera hesitated for a second before obeying, shifting so her back was to Izzy, her pulse suddenly too loud in her ears.

Izzy's hands were warm when they touched her shoulders, spreading the cool sunscreen in slow, careful movements. Her fingertips pressed firmly but gently, gliding over Kiera's shoulder blades, down the line of her spine, then sweeping outward again.

Kiera clenched her jaw, staring at the ocean like her life depended on it.

It was just a friend helping a friend avoid melanoma. Nothing more. Kiera shouldn't want to read into the way Izzy's hands felt on her bare skin, how they dipped under the shoulder strap of her bikini top, then lower. She wasn't aware a shoulder blade could even be an erogenous zone until Izzy's thumb traced the soft curve.

Izzy's hands smoothed lower, following her ribcage out toward the sides of her waist. Kiera squeezed her eyes shut, her skin tingling in a way that had absolutely nothing to do with sun exposure.

"There," Izzy said after what felt like an eternity, giving her shoulder a quick pat before pulling away. "You're good."

Kiera let out a breath she didn't realize she'd been holding, turning back around with what she hoped was a casual nod. "Thanks," she said, her voice only slightly strained.

Izzy was already reaching for her book again, like the whole thing had been an average day-at-the-beach experience. Like it wasn't currently short-circuiting Kiera's entire nervous system.

Kiera picked up her water bottle and took a long, desperate sip, willing herself to get a goddamn grip.

Kiera twisted the cap back onto the sunscreen bottle, still feeling the lingering heat where Izzy's hands had been. She needed to say something — anything — to shake off the weird energy building between them.

She cleared her throat. "Do you think Maggie will be okay?"

Izzy didn't look up from her book. "Yeah. Probably."

Kiera paused at the noncommittal response. "I mean, she seemed in good spirits when she left, but you know how she is. Always brushing things off like they're no big deal."

Izzy exhaled, still not looking at her. "I'm glad Danica is with her. And at least Pete can help entertain them while they wait."

Kiera hesitated, trying to figure out if she'd done something wrong. "Are you sure you're good? You seem kind of... on edge."

Izzy turned a page with just a little too much force. "Kiera, you're distracting me."

Kiera blinked at the bluntness in her tone. "Right. Sorry." She shifted awkwardly, pressing her lips together. Okay. That was... something. Izzy had been weird all day, but this? This was new.

She pulled her knees up to her chest, staring out at the ocean again, determined not to let the sting settle too deep.

CHAPTER 9

Izzy sighed heavily and shut her book with a decisive *thump*, scrubbing a hand over her face. "Okay, that was rude. Sorry," she let out a long sigh. "What I mean is, you're... very distracting." Her tone was soft and quiet, like the admission humbled her greatly.

Kiera studied her. Izzy wasn't just annoyed — she was uncomfortable. She now sat stiffly, tension woven through every line of her body, like she was forcing herself to stay put when all she wanted to do was bolt.

Kiera hesitated for half a second before pressing, keeping her voice gentle. "I'm sorry to... distract you."

Izzy's tongue darted over her lower lip, and Kiera found herself leaning forward. "For what it's worth, you are also extremely, extremely distracting."

Izzy's gaze flicked down toward Kiera's mouth, and Kiera could feel the moment building. She was sure that Izzy felt the same way, felt the same inevitability of whatever was drawing them together.

The buzz in her pocket jolted her back to reality. Kiera winced, cursing under her breath, but instinct made her reach for it. Danica's name flashed across the screen.

Kiera exhaled, still breathless from the moment that had shattered between them. She answered the call with fumbling fingers. "Danica?" She put the phone on speaker.

"Hey," Danica said, voice calm but a little tired. "Just wanted to let you know Maggie's nose is definitely broken, but she'll be fine. They gave her some pain meds. Pete's getting her checked out now, so we'll be back soon."

Izzy nodded, then stood, packing up her chair and shuffling around her things.

Kiera watched Izzy while trying to stay focused on the call with Danica. "Oh, thank goodness. I'm glad she's okay." Danica promised to send a text when they were on their way back.

"I'm going to go take a shower and start dinner. You can stay here if you want, though," Izzy said.

"Okay. I'll be in soon to do the same," Kiera said, and Izzy nodded again, then picked up the small lounge chair and headed back up the beach.

For a second, Kiera just sat there, her pulse still racing, her body caught in the space between what almost happened and what *didn't*.

CHAPTER 10

Izzy

The sun had long since set, leaving the beach house wrapped in the warm glow of the dining room lights. The sliding doors were open, welcoming in the cool night air, and the ocean sounds were a steady backdrop to the hum of conversation. The long wooden table was cluttered with half-empty wine glasses, serving bowls, and the remnants of dinner, but most of the attention was fixed on Maggie's swollen and bruised nose, now covered in a comically large bandage.

"I swear to god," Maggie muttered, her voice thick and nasally, "if I end up with a permanent bump, that guy's paying for my rhinoplasty."

Pete smirked, taking a sip of beer. "I'm just saying, you should've ducked."

Maggie's head snapped up. "Excuse me? *Should've ducked*? That thing came at me like a heat-seeking missile!"

"It really did," Danica said sympathetically, hiding her smile behind her glass of wine. "Honestly, it was kind of impressive."

Kiera, seated diagonally across from Izzy, reached for the salad bowl and almost met her gaze. Izzy had been all-to-aware of her all evening, but every time they got too close to making eye contact, she looked away, feigning interest in her food.

"I think you should lean into it," Kiera said. "Tell people it was a heroic act, like you saved a child from an oncoming frisbee. Or took a hit to win the championship point in an ultimate frisbee match."

Maggie rolled her eyes, but a grin tugged at the edge of her mouth. "Yes, my valor will be remembered forever. At least it's on the last full day of the trip, and I can go convalesce in peace tomorrow."

Pete pointed her fork at Maggie. "Honestly? I think it makes you look *very* cool."

Maggie looked helpless for a moment. "What if it like, heals weird? Or scars?"

Danica elbowed Pete, a knowing smile tugging at her lips. "Women *love* scars."

"Why do you have to call me out like that?" Pete shot back playfully.

Danica held her hands up. "I wasn't naming names."

Maggie's smirk deepened, shimmying her shoulders suggestively.

Pete blushed, burying her face in her hands as laughter rippled around the table.

Izzy chanced another glance at Kiera, only to find her already looking. It lasted less than a second — just long enough to send a jolt through Izzy's chest — before Kiera looked away, pretending to focus on her plate. Izzy took a long sip of her drink, willing herself to shake off the feeling.

After dinner, Pete and Danica excused themselves for a "walk on the beach," which everyone at the table understood to mean they were sneaking off to make out in the dunes.

CHAPTER 10

Maggie, still groggy from her pain meds, mumbled something about watching TV before shuffling off to her room.

Izzy lingered in the kitchen, rinsing her glass, aware of Kiera moving nearby, stacking dishes. The silence between them was palpable, tangible in its intensity.

Kiera leaned her hip against the counter. "Sorry, was I being too distracting?"

Izzy rolled her eyes. "You're really never going to let me forget I said that."

"Of course I won't."

Izzy smirked. "I stand by it."

Kiera shut a cupboard door, hooking her drying towel over her shoulder. "You're being so weird. And every time I feel like we're getting close, you leave." She shook her head. "Am I reading something wrong? I just — if I did something, if I made you uncomfortable, just tell me."

Izzy swallowed hard. "You're not reading it wrong."

Kiera turned to face her, arms crossed, her expression skeptical. "Then what's with all the walking away? What do you want?"

Izzy knew she had two choices: lie and save face or tell the truth and risk her dignity and her friendship.

Her pulse thundered in her ears. And then, before she could second-guess herself, before she could talk herself out of it, she stepped forward, grabbed Kiera's face between her hands, and kissed her.

It wasn't soft. It wasn't tentative. It was all the frustration, confusion, and unspoken longing crashing together in one reckless act.

For half a second, Kiera froze.

Then she melted.

Her hands found Izzy's waist, pulling her closer. Izzy could feel the warmth of her, the way they fit together. The world outside the kitchen — the waves, the murmurs of wind through the open doors, the distant sound of Maggie's TV — faded into nothing.

Then, Kiera pulled back, breathless, searching Izzy's face like she was trying to make sense of what had just happened.

"Izzy," she whispered.

Izzy's chest heaved. Kiera's lilac perfume was fresh and intoxicating, and Izzy wanted to bury her face in Kiera's neck. "Yeah?"

Kiera's gaze flickered down to her lips, then back up. "Is this a good idea?"

Izzy had no idea, but she wanted to find out. Instead of answering, she kissed Kiera again. Thankfully, this time, Kiera didn't hesitate.

Her hands slid up Izzy's arms, tentative at first, then firmer, fingers curling into the fabric of Izzy's hoodie like she was anchoring herself there. Izzy sighed into the kiss, hands trailing down to grip Kiera's hips, tugging her closer.

Kiera tasted like wine, and Izzy couldn't think straight. Didn't want to think straight.

She sure hoped Kiera wasn't thinking straight, either.

Kiera's fingers skated under the hem of Izzy's hoodie, brushing against her skin. The touch sent a shiver down Izzy's spine, and she deepened the kiss, pressing Kiera back against the counter, her hands splayed against her ribs.

Kiera made a quiet sound in the back of her throat, her fingers tightening against Izzy's hips, and suddenly this felt real. Like something inevitable. Something that had been waiting for them both to stop running from it.

And then, just as Izzy was starting to lose herself completely, Kiera hesitated.

Not a full stop, not pulling away completely — but enough.

Izzy felt it like a cold rush of air between them. She stepped back, breath unsteady, suddenly aware of just how quiet the house was.

CHAPTER 10

Kiera blinked, lips still parted, looking as dazed as Izzy felt. Her gaze flickered to the hallway, toward Maggie's room and where Pete and Danica would eventually return.

Kiera's expression shifted — not regret, but uncertainty. Izzy felt it settle around them like a weight. Izzy took another step back. The kitchen, which had felt so charged just seconds ago, now felt too small and too quiet.

Kiera opened her mouth like she was going to say something, but then closed it again, pressing her lips together. "Wow. Um. I—" Kiera started.

"Yeah," Izzy cut in, forcing a lightness she didn't feel.

They stood there, staring at each other, both waiting for the other to say something, to make the next move. Neither of them did. Because there wasn't a simple answer.

Now that everything was out in the open, Izzy was absolutely terrified.

Izzy was forced to do what she did best, which was act cool and unbothered. She needed to avoid getting any more wrapped up in someone who wasn't available. Again. Always. Kiera was straight, newly divorced, finding herself — she was unavailable whether she knew it or not. It was like the more someone couldn't possibly give Izzy what she needed, the more she wanted it.

Izzy grabbed her bottle of water from the counter, and walked away before she could do something really stupid, like kiss Kiera again.

Izzy LAY IN BED, staring at the ceiling, the sound of the waves rolling in through the open window. It should have been soothing. Normally, it was. The ocean had always been her place, the thing that calmed her when nothing else could. But tonight, the waves did nothing to quiet the electricity still running under her skin.

The taste of their kiss still lingered. The feeling of Kiera's hands gripping her waist, the way she had leaned in so hesitantly and then kissed her with such passion, only to look so utterly confused after — it played over and over in Izzy's mind like a song stuck on repeat. She should have expected it. Of course, Kiera would have doubts. Of course, she would second-guess. She was still figuring out who she was outside of being a wife and a mother. She didn't even think Kiera was interested in women that way. The last thing Kiera needed was more uncertainty. Izzy didn't want to complicate her life further.

And yet, Izzy hadn't been able to stop herself. Not when Kiera had been looking at her like that, not when they had been standing so close in the dim kitchen, heat pooling between them.

Izzy turned onto her side, exhaling sharply, rubbing a hand over her face. She shouldn't have done it. She knew better than this. Kiera wasn't ready, and Izzy wasn't trying to fall back into her habit of only chasing unavailable women. When she'd met Paisley, she seemed emotionally grounded and independent. Her coolness felt mature, sometimes even alluring. But it wasn't long until she realized that Paisley was unreachable in the ways that mattered. They avoided conflict, didn't talk about hard things, and wanted everything to stay on the surface. In the end, her marriage had turned distant and hollow. She'd told herself that it wasn't Paisley's fault, that she was just hard to love.

Maybe it was better to make that call now, with Kiera. Even if Kiera *was* available, which she wasn't, she didn't need anything difficult added in her life right now.

She reached for her phone on instinct, her thumb hovering over her flight itinerary. She hadn't planned to leave until the late afternoon the next day, around the same time as everyone else, but the thought of staying, of pretending like nothing had happened, made her stomach twist. It would be easier to go early, to rip the bandage off before this got messier than it already was. She pulled up the airline app, searched for an earlier flight, and found one leaving first thing in the morning. Without hesitating, she changed her ticket, locking her phone and tossing it onto the nightstand before she could second-guess herself.

She closed her eyes, willing herself to sleep, but it didn't come easily.

THE HOUSE WAS STILL DARK when Izzy crept down the stairs, her duffel bag slung over her shoulder, her sandals tucked under her arm to keep from making noise. She walked as quietly as she had while sneaking out for an early surfing session, slipping into the kitchen for a granola bar before heading for the door. It was better this way. No drawn-out goodbyes, no awkward conversations. Just a clean break.

She had almost made it when a voice stopped her. "*Seriously?*"

Izzy cursed under her breath and turned to find Pete standing in the doorway, arms crossed, looking very unimpressed for someone who had clearly just rolled out of bed. Her dark curls were sticking up in all directions, her oversized sleep shirt hanging loosely over her frame, but her eyes were sharp, taking in the duffel bag. "Sneaking out? Really?"

Izzy sighed, adjusting the strap on her shoulder. "It's an early flight."

"That's not an answer," Pete said, brow raised.

Izzy exhaled through her nose, already tired of the conversation. "Change of plans."

"Bullshit."

Izzy pinched the bridge of her nose. "Look, I don't have the energy for this right now, Pete."

Pete leaned against the doorframe, studying her. "Does this have anything to do with a certain someone with short brown hair and glasses?"

"Nope." Izzy rolled her eyes, turning back toward the door.

Pete snorted. "Right. Because it seems to me like you're avoiding something big here by leaving without saying goodbye to anyone."

Izzy sighed, running a hand through her hair.

"Why are you so afraid of things working out for you?" Pete asked, crossing her arms.

"I'm not," Izzy said.

"You're a terrible liar." Pete didn't move, still watching her, like she was waiting for Izzy to crack. The scrutiny of it made Izzy's skin itch. Pete knew her too well. She knew when Izzy was running, when she was making excuses. And Izzy could tell she was about two seconds away from calling her on it.

"I don't know how to do this," Izzy said finally.

"Do what?"

"Kiera. I don't know what to do there, and I just can't... face it. Wanting is familiar, but being wanted? That's terrifying."

"You're leaving because Kiera told you she wanted you?" Pete asked, her voice dipping lower to a whisper. "Isn't that like best case scenario?"

"No," Izzy said, her voice also dropping to a harsh whisper. "It's the worst case."

Pete shook her head. "I'll tell Danica you had an emergency, I guess," Pete said finally, her voice dripping with sarcasm. "She'll be so sad to miss giving *you* the lecture about bailing this time around."

Izzy hesitated, gripping the strap of her bag tighter. "I'll text you when I land."

Pete sighed, blowing her dark curls out of her face. "Fine. But promise me you'll talk to a therapist about this, because you're being irrational."

Izzy forced a smirk that didn't quite reach her eyes. "I

promise I'll Google a therapist at least one time and consider it."

She turned before Pete could say anything else, stepping outside into the cool morning air. The sun hadn't even started rising yet, the world still half-asleep, the beach house quiet behind her.

Her Uber was already waiting at the curb, its headlights casting long beams through the pre-dawn darkness. She pulled the car door open, sliding into the backseat without a word.

The driver glanced at her through the rearview mirror. "Airport?"

Izzy nodded. "Yeah. Airport."

As the car pulled away, she kept her eyes forward, willing herself not to look back.

She wasn't running. She was just leaving before it got worse.

Before she let herself hope for something that was never going to happen.

CHAPTER 11

Kiera

Mid-afternoon sun cast the cabin in dim light as Pete, Danica, and Kiera shared snacks, the plane's hum a steady background to their makeshift inflight feast. Kiera and Danica were sharing a selection of trail mix, dried mango, and dark chocolate covered pretzels. Pete, on the other hand, was working her way through an entire bag of Sour Patch Kids with the reckless abandon of someone who had never once worried about a sugar crash.

Kiera, needing a distraction more than food, picked the pepitas from her trail mix. The conversation around them had dulled to an indistinct murmur, with most passengers either dozing or mindlessly scrolling through their phones. Across the aisle, a man snored softly against the window, his head bobbing with each minor bump of turbulence. The hush of the plane, coupled with the dim glow from the overhead reading lights, gave the moment a surreal feeling of being paused in time.

Kiera could still see Izzy's back as she'd walked away, disappearing into her bedroom. Then, this morning, disappearing completely without saying goodbye. Kiera had expected awkwardness, had anticipated tension, perhaps even a little giddiness, but she hadn't expected Izzy to flee like she was escaping a crime scene. She'd awoken with the intention of having a long talk with Izzy about what that kiss meant, but Pete had broken the news gently over a cup of coffee. Danica and Maggie were surprised that Izzy had to leave early, and Pete had given her a long, knowing look. How the tables had turned since Telluride, when Kiera had been the one giving knowing looks and leaving early.

The mood had shifted into something slightly awkward and reserved, but the last day of a trip was always difficult for various reasons, with Danica trying to convince everyone to be at the airport four hours early and Maggie attempting to put makeup on around her bandage. They'd gone to brunch, then carpooled to the airport in the rental car. The terminal was small enough that they could all sit together before their flights, though none of them were very energized after the three day trip. After Danica had made sure Maggie took a decongestant and ibuprofen to help with her nose swelling, they'd parted ways to board their own flight.

Now, Danica stretched her legs as best she could in the cramped row, sighing as she shifted against the headrest. "I wish this plane had First Class."

"Okay, bougie girl. I let you fly First Class three times and now you're too good for Comfort Plus?" Pete sighed dramatically and shook her head.

"You only have yourself to blame," Danica joked, before glancing sideways at Kiera.

Kiera said nothing, too distracted and disconnected to pay attention, and reached for her water bottle to take a slow sip.

"You doing okay? This weekend was weird, right?" Danica asked. "What was with Izzy leaving so suddenly?"

"I'm fine." Kiera hadn't told anyone about the kiss, and

she wasn't sure if Izzy had told Pete. She shifted uncomfortably in her seat and pushed her glasses up her nose, fidgeting.

Danica let out a quiet snort, shaking her head as she turned toward Pete. "You know, it's pretty rich, because Izzy called me a coward for running away in Telluride."

Pete, who had been mid-chew, stilled. Her usual lazy grin flickered, her eyes narrowed just a fraction. "Come on," she said, her voice quieter, gentle. "She's just protective."

Kiera glanced between them, catching the way Danica's expression softened. "She is very protective over *you*, and vice versa. Clearly. That doesn't mean she's not being slightly hypocritical," Danica said, her eyebrows raised.

Pete shook her head, popping another sour gummy into her mouth.

Danica exhaled, running a hand through her hair before offering a small, reluctant nod. "In Izzy's defense, she was right at the time," she said, backtracking with an apologetic smile.

Pete silently snagged a piece of dried mango from Danica then nodded, like that was all she needed to say.

Kiera watched the quiet exchange, the way Pete's fingers brushed against Danica's wrist as she leaned back into her seat, the way Danica's smile turned softer, her body relaxing just a little. Years of mess and uncertainty couldn't break them. They found their way back to each other, a simple, unshakable bond.

She busied herself with rifling through the trail mix to pick out more pepitas, looking away as Pete leaned in to whisper something into Danica's ear. Whatever it was, Danica laughed, tilting her head toward Pete like magnetism alone drew her in.

Kiera had never had that. Definitely not with Alex.

She thought about the night she left him, the way she had stood in their too-large kitchen, staring at the backsplash she had picked out herself, and said, *I'm leaving. I know you're having an affair, and I'm done.* She had expected a fight, some kind of protest, but Alex had only sighed, tired and resigned, and said, *Alright.*

That was it. *Alright.* As if anything would ever be right ever again. There were no grand declarations, no last-minute attempts to salvage their life together. Just the continued quiet unraveling of something that had already frayed beyond repair.

Then had come the custody talk, or rather, the lack of custody talk. Alex had agreed to Kiera taking full custody of the girls, with a few visits during school breaks. He'd come to see the girls around Christmas, and he planned to take them back to Omaha for a week or two in the summer, but that was it. That disconnection hurt more than any other part of the divorce, but it was no longer her job to make him into a father.

The overhead speaker crackled, and the pilot announced their descent into Denver. Pete and Danica exchanged a glance before Pete reached over and squeezed Danica's knee, grinning as Danica rolled her eyes but didn't move away.

Kiera exhaled, adjusting in her seat as she stared out the window at the city lights blinking below. The lingering pain of the heartbreak of divorce felt familiar as her chest ached now, thinking of Izzy landing early in San Francisco, pretending none of this ever happened.

And Kiera had no idea what to do about that.

When Kiera finally pulled up to her parents' house, she immediately spotted the sleek silver car parked in the driveway.

Frowning, she climbed out of the Uber, exhaustion pressing down on her as she grabbed her bag and made her way inside.

The smell of her mom's burnt sage hit her first, but it was

CHAPTER 11

the familiar scent of rose perfume that made her pause in the doorway.

"Aunt Jade," Kiera realized aloud, as she stepped into the living room.

And there she was, poised effortlessly on the couch, a half-empty glass of red wine balanced between two perfectly manicured fingers. Aunt Jade was opposite to her sister in every way — modern, chic, refined, practically glowing with self-assurance. Her tailored linen pants were a stark contrast to the loose, patterned dresses Kiera's mom favored, and the delicate gold jewelry she wore looked like it belonged in a magazine spread.

"Well, well," Jade said, setting her glass down on the coffee table with a warm smile. "Look who finally decided to return to civilization."

Kiera sighed, dropping her bag at her feet and giving her aunt a gentle hug, afraid she might wrinkle her carefully pressed clothing. "Hi, Aunt Jade."

She barely had time to steady herself before a blur of strawberry-stained cheeks and tangled dark hair came barreling toward her.

"Mama!" Eliza shrieked, launching herself at Kiera with all the force of a child who had spent the past few days running free and untamed. Quinn was only a second behind, her little arms wrapping around Kiera's waist as she squeezed in between them.

"You're back!" Eliza beamed up at her. "Grandma and Grandpa let us name the new chickens!"

Kiera blinked, her travel-weary brain struggling to catch up. "Wait, what new chickens?"

"The new chickens, Mama!" Quinn echoed, bouncing on her heels. "Grandpa built them a house and everything!"

Kiera shot her parents a look over her daughters' heads, but her dad just grinned, unrepentant as ever, as he casually sipped his tea.

"Of course he did," she muttered, before turning her attention back to her girls. "Alright, hit me with the names. What'd you pick?"

Eliza, held her head high to share the news. "Mine is named Chiquitita," she declared proudly. "Like the ABBA song!"

Kiera pressed a hand to her heart, overwhelmed with pride. "That is an excellent name."

Quinn wiggled in excitement, already impatient for her turn. "And mine is Chicken Nugget Rocketship!"

Kiera let out a bark of laughter, scooping Quinn into her arms as she kissed the top of her head. "Wow, that's... that's also a name, alright."

"I was gonna name her just Chicken Nugget, but then I thought, what if she wants to fly?" Quinn explained, entirely serious.

"Very wise." Kiera smiled, glancing at her dad. "And you let them do this?"

Her dad spread his hands wide, his sun hat hanging by a string around his neck. He smiled and attempted to look bashful. "They made compelling arguments."

Her mom, clearly trying to suppress a laugh, placed a warm hand on Kiera's shoulder. "They've been in the garden all afternoon. Thankfully, they don't have Jade's fear of mud."

"You should see the state of their nails," Aunt Jade said, and Kiera could have sworn her eye was twitching.

Kiera finally took in the full picture — both girls were caked in dirt, their fingernails practically black, their socks grass-stained. She sighed but smiled all the same. "Alright, my little garden fairies, go upstairs and shower before dinner, please."

Eliza and Quinn groaned in unison, but Kiera was already ushering them toward the stairs. "No arguments. If you want to play with Chiquitita and Chicken Nugget Rocketship after school tomorrow, you need to at least *pretend* to be clean humans."

As they dragged their feet toward the hall, Kiera turned back to Aunt Jade, who was watching the whole scene with an amused expression, twirling her glass of rosé between two fingers.

"You, my dear niece, could use a summer somewhere with fewer farm animals and more cocktails," Jade said with a tip of her glass.

Kiera sighed, rubbing her temple. "Give me a minute. I'm still processing the fact that Mom and Dad have chickens."

Her mom appeared from the kitchen, wiping her hands on a towel. "We *rescued* them."

Kiera narrowed her eyes in skepticism. "Where did you rescue the chickens from?"

"Just a neighbor down the street. They were going to *eat* them," her mom said with a concerned expression.

"Tell me you didn't steal our neighbor's chickens, Mom."

"No, your father went up to the door and paid for them, of course. We're not criminals."

Aunt Jade closed her eyes as she sighed. "Ask John what he paid for them."

"Two Costco rotisserie chickens," her dad said proudly.

"And that worked?" Kiera blinked, looking back and forth between her parents, feeling a combination of worry, amusement, and general confusion.

"No," her dad laughed. "They wanted $50 each for them."

"You paid $100 for chickens?"

"No," her mom said with a laugh. "Jade did, though."

Aunt Jade dissented loudly, but all three were still laughing as Kiera's mom and dad headed upstairs to check on the girls.

"You're just as bad as they are," Kiera said, looking back to her aunt with a laugh of disbelief.

"I did bring wine, if that helps," Aunt Jade said, shrugging and daintily crossing her legs.

Kiera collapsed onto the couch beside her, exhaustion pulling at her limbs. "It does. So, what's the occasion?"

Aunt Jade arched an eyebrow. "Can't I just visit my favorite niece?"

Kiera raised a skeptical brow.

Aunt Jade sighed dramatically, pouring Kiera a glass from the bottle on the coffee table. "Alright, I came to talk about your next steps. Why are you still chasing a teaching job like it's your dream?"

Kiera groaned, rubbing her hands over her face. "Aunt Jade…"

"Just hear me out," Aunt Jade interrupted smoothly, reaching for her wine again. "I know you decided against alimony, and even with Alex paying you for your half of the house… How can I help? If it's a down payment for a house you need, I'm here for you, my love."

Kiera sighed. "You've already helped plenty. And it's not just money."

Aunt Jade blinked slowly, watching her. "Then what is it?"

Kiera hesitated, swirling her wine glass slowly, watching the deep red liquid catch the dim light of the living room. It wasn't just one thing — it was everything. Signing a lease would make it real in a way it hadn't been before. And then there was Alex, who had worked and traveled so much that the girls barely asked about him now. Alex, who had barely blinked when she walked out, who had treated their marriage like a worn-out sweater — comfortable but ultimately disposable. She wasn't sure what she was waiting for. Closure? A sign? A version of herself prepared to leave it all behind without looking back? She exhaled sharply, shaking her head. "It's complicated," she finally admitted. "And I've applied to so many jobs. I'm just waiting to hear back."

Aunt Jade sighed and sipped her wine. "What districts are

you applying in? Maybe I know someone who can pull a string. Or, perhaps there's an extra certification I can help you pay for to make your application stand out. Have you thought about branching out to other grades?"

Kiera groaned, rubbing her hands over her face. "Aunt Jade, I do appreciate the worry. Really. I'm fine, though. I'll figure it out."

"I know it's far, but if you'd like to stay at the condo—"

"To be honest, the idea of letting my children into your perfect condo in Telluride is enough to make me want to set myself on fire," Kiera admitted. "It was bad enough trying to convince my friends not to break things."

Before Aunt Jade could respond, the sound of feet stomping down the stairs interrupted them. Eliza and Quinn appeared, their hair still damp from their showers, looking up at Kiera expectantly.

"Pizza party?" Eliza asked, eyes wide with hope.

Quinn nodded furiously. "Grandma said we could!"

"Pizza sounds perfect," Kiera said with a nod. The girls cheered, and Kiera stood, knowing full-well that her parents were going to try making some strange dough recipe with an alarming amount of nutritional yeast.

Jade gave her a knowing look. "Consider it, darling."

Kiera rolled her eyes but clinked her glass against Jade's anyway. "I'll think about it."

KIERA HAD SET out for a Pilates class, taking Izzy's advice to heart. She adjusted her gym bag over her shoulder and slowed as she passed a sleek studio with floor-to-ceiling windows. The gold lettering on the glass read *Luna Pole & Aerial*. Just as she glanced inside, two effortlessly cool women — one sporting bright pink hair and the other filling out a pair of booty shorts that screamed confidence — opened the door to the sounds of laughter and Chappell

Roan. The way they entered, strong and self-assured, made Kiera slow.

She paused at the window, her sneakers scuffing against the sidewalk as she stopped, taking in the way the polished chrome poles gleamed. She had never considered pole fitness before, but the space, the women of all shapes and sizes walking in without a second thought, intrigued her.

The door swung open, and a woman with a high ponytail and an easy smile paused, holding it open for her. "Are you here for the 6 p.m. class?"

Kiera's mouth opened, but no sound came out at first. She had mentally, physically, and emotionally prepared herself for Pilates. She knew what to expect there, knew the routine. Pole fitness? That was an entirely different world. She'd heard pole fitness was a hard workout, and Kiera wasn't sure she possessed the right amount of sex appeal she'd need.

"Oh, no. I mean, no, I'm just—" With a vague gesture, she attempted to justify her presence outside, peering through the window like a voyeur. "Sorry, no, I'm not."

The woman gave her a knowing smile but just nodded. "Maybe next time."

Kiera forced a small smile and hurried away, heading for the Pilates studio down the block. Inside, the scent of eucalyptus and the low drone of meditative music surrounded her with familiarity, but she still felt out of place. She glanced at the women on each reformer beside her and instantly felt self-conscious — about not only her body, but also her tax bracket. She kept thinking about the pole fitness studio, about the way those women had walked in without hesitation. She contemplated the terrifying yet intriguing prospect of trying something that frightened her.

Chapter 11

The Group Chat™

MAGGIE

Made it home in one piece. Nose and all.

PETE

are you SURE it's in one piece though? pretty sure it's two now

MAGGIE

Bold talk for someone who thought sunscreen was optional on Day 1. How's the peeling going, lobster?

PETE

that was a tactical error

my body is molting

i'm becoming stronger

DANICA

Or just crispier.

Pete named the conversation, "Nose Job Security".

MAGGIE

This group chat is harassment, actually. I'll be billing you all for emotional damages AND rhinoplasty.

KIERA

We'll pay you back in friendship. And maybe a lifetime supply of sunscreen for Pete.

PETE

this sunburn is a personal growth opportunity

IZZY

Yeah, personally growing new skin.

DANICA

Someone please stop them before the dad jokes get worse.

MAGGIE

Too late. This group chat is officially one giant cringe-fest.

DANICA

Miss you guys already.

KIERA

Same! Miss you guys!

PETE

okay, emotions? nope

group hug later

for now, who's down for a video call next week?

DANICA

Only if we can toast Maggie's "Broken Nose Era."

MAGGIE

You're all the worst. But yeah... I'm in.

CHAPTER 12

Izzy

Izzy pulled up in front of Pete and Danica's new home, whistling under her breath. It was a beautiful old house in West Highland — pastel siding, a porch swing, and an understated yet colorful xeriscaped yard. It suited them, she thought. The chaotic, cramped apartments of their twenties had been fun. Even Danica's condo had been nice when she'd visited before, but this place looked like a home. Settled. Permanent. She loved that for Pete.

She killed the engine and lingered for a moment, staring at the house. The last time she had visited, they'd still been in that small condo, talking about home ownership like it was a distant dream. Now, they had something real. Something lasting. The thought made Izzy's stomach twist, though she wasn't sure why.

Grabbing her bag from the passenger seat, she headed up the driveway, barely making it to the front steps before Pete yanked the door open with a grin. "You made it!" she exclaimed. It had only been about a month since they'd seen each other in San Diego, but she loved how Pete was a classic golden retriever human, always excited to see her again.

Izzy barely had time to set her bag down before Pete wrapped her in a bear hug, lifting her slightly off the ground. "Damn, okay," Izzy laughed, patting Pete's back. "I get it. You're freakishly strong."

"Don't forget it," Pete said, setting her down and stepping aside so Izzy could enter. "Come on in. I've got cold beer or that weird prebiotic soda Danica likes."

Danica appeared in the kitchen doorway, holding a brightly colored can of said weird prebiotic soda. "Hey, you." They hugged, then Danica forced Izzy to take a glass of water, saying something about dehydration and altitude.

Izzy scanned the space as she walked through. High ceilings, warm lighting, the scent of citrus in the air. It was undeniably Pete and Danica — laid-back but carefully curated, a mix of Pete's casual style and Danica's quiet elegance. It made Izzy's chest tighten, but she ignored it.

Before she could say anything, a blur of fawn-colored fur came barreling toward her. Gladys, Pete and Danica's pittie mix, wiggled excitedly as she shoved her big, blocky head against Izzy's legs. "Well, hello, gorgeous," Izzy said, laughing as she crouched down to scratch behind the dog's ears. Gladys grinned up at her, eyes squeezed shut in bliss, a well-loved Lamb Chop toy clamped in her mouth.

"She's been dying to see you again," Danica said, crouching to rub the dog's back.

"She's obviously a fan of the finer things in life," Pete added. "Like good company and extremely overpriced organic dog treats."

Izzy grinned, pressing a kiss to the top of Gladys' head before standing. "She has good taste."

"So," Pete said, waving an arm dramatically. "What do you think of the house?"

Izzy smirked. "I think you finally have a place where you can't get away with leaving piles of laundry on the couch."

"That is *not* true," Pete said immediately, at the same time Danica said, "Thank you."

Izzy chuckled, following them into the living room. She sank onto the couch, stretching out her legs as Pete flopped down beside her. Danica, somewhat more graceful, took the armchair across from them, tucking her legs beneath her. Gladys climbed onto Pete's lap like she was a ten-pound lap dog instead of a fifty-pound hippo.

"So," Pete said, nudging Izzy's knee. "Let's talk business."

Izzy sighed dramatically. "I just got here."

"You're on the clock," Pete said, though Izzy knew she was teasing.

Izzy rolled her eyes. "I'm salaried. Can't we bask in the glow of your homeowner status first?"

"Nope," Pete said, popping the *p* with a grin. "We've got shit to do."

Danica's phone buzzed, and she held up a finger. "One sec, it's Annie." She stood, already heading down the hallway as she answered the call of her coworker, leaving Izzy and Pete alone. Gladys' nails tapped on the hardwood as she followed Danica with a wagging tail.

Pete leaned forward, resting her elbows on her knees. "Alright, what's the latest on Second Star's Denver expansion?"

Izzy took a sip of wine before setting the glass down on the coffee table. "Well, it's entirely up to you where to go from here."

"No, give it to me straight."

"Like you had mentioned before—"

"Iz, you don't have to preface everything with this being *my* company. I know it is. And now it's yours, too."

Izzy sipped her water. "Okay, well, we're making progress. The funding is solid, and the community outreach has been better than expected. I think people are really responding to the idea of extracurricular grants for the kids."

Pete nodded. "Good. Any issues?"

Izzy hesitated, then sighed. "Some of the local orgs are hesitant about partnering with an outside nonprofit."

Pete frowned, considering. "They want assurances that we're not just another group parachuting in, making promises we won't follow through with, and then leaving. Makes sense. So, we double down on the partnerships and the mentor program. Show them we're here for the long haul."

"That's a great approach." Izzy sipped her water quietly.

The fear of overstepping was always there, a persistent worry in the back of her mind. Izzy had joined the foundation after Pete had already built it from the ground up. It was her baby, her passion project, fueled by years of dedication and hustle. Izzy didn't want to be the person who came in and disrupted that delicate balance. She never wanted Pete to question whether hiring her had been the right move, or worse, to regret bringing her into something so personal and meaningful. That worry kept Izzy constantly on edge, making sure she stayed in her lane, never pushed too hard, never took up more space than she felt she deserved — regardless of the dozens of reassurances from Pete, the imposter syndrome was still too palpable. Even as her role grew, even as she began leading her own projects and seeing successes pile up, that nagging voice always whispered: *Be careful. Don't screw this up.*

Danica reappeared then, phone in hand, looking amused. "Kiera just sent me a picture of the girls with their chickens."

Pete laughed, already reaching for Danica's phone. "Are the chickens finally growing on her?"

Izzy raised a brow. "Chickens?"

Danica handed it over. "Apparently, her parents got them while we were in San Diego."

Pete squinted at the screen, then snorted.

Danica grinned. "Eliza named hers Chiquitita. Quinn named hers... and I quote... 'Chicken Nugget Rocketship.'"

Pete let out a delighted cackle. "That kid is going places."

Izzy grinned, looking over the photo. Kiera, standing in the sun, her daughters beaming beside her, dirt smudged on her cheek, smiling like she belonged in the garden — it was a vision Izzy hadn't expected to hit her so hard.

The near-kiss at the bar had been intense, leaving her heartbeat rattling in her chest like a loose drawer every time she thought about Kiera's face so close to hers. She was so surprised by that split second where it had felt like inevitability had them both in its grip. Then there was the next morning, the quiet, disarming softness of sharing space together, just the two of them in that shy silence. The vulnerability of it all, the way Kiera had looked at her like maybe, just maybe, she didn't want the distance between them anymore — it was too much. And then, finally, the kiss in the kitchen — desperate, intense, charged with every bit of pent-up tension they'd been dragging around since college. It had left Izzy spiraling.

It had all felt so wrong when Kiera had pulled back, and offered her a nervous, hesitant smile that didn't quite reach her eyes. Every millisecond after that felt like walking barefoot across glass, and Izzy had bolted in embarrassment. Kiera's openness over the weekend made Izzy realize she hadn't been fair to Kiera. And Izzy, as much as she hated herself for it, kept second guessing every word, every look, every touch. Now, she didn't know how to be around Kiera without feeling like she was waiting for the floor to drop out from under her again.

So she left. It was easier to throw herself into work, to stay busy in the endless tasks and responsibilities that came with Second Star, than to give herself even a moment to consider what might have happened if Kiera hadn't given her that look of regret. Seeing Kiera like that — close enough to taste but still somehow oceans away — was too much. And Izzy wasn't sure she was strong enough to keep pretending that it didn't hurt. It was easier to put space between them, easier to convince herself that it didn't mean anything.

She'd been so doing well at that until Danica announced, "I invited Kiera over for dinner."

Despite a perfectly set table with wine and food, an odd heaviness filled the room. Izzy felt it with every stolen glance, with every moment that her eyes almost met Kiera's before darting away. Pete and Danica noticed it, too. Pete kept raising an eyebrow at Izzy, as if waiting for an explanation. Danica — always the peacemaker — kept trying to smooth the conversation over, filling awkward silences with pleasant small talk that nobody actually responded to.

Kiera looked effortless as always — perfectly fitting jeans, an oversized button-down shirt. But Izzy couldn't shake the feeling that something seemed just slightly different about her. Maybe it was the way she kept adjusting the cuff of her rolled sleeve or how she tucked her hair behind her ear one too many times. She looked like herself, but there was an undercurrent of discomfort beneath it all.

"So, Kiera, how are the girls adjusting to the chicken life?" Danica asked.

Kiera smiled, but it looked a little strained. "They're obsessed. They check on them first thing in the morning and last thing at night."

Pete chuckled. "Better being obsessed with chickens than some other terrible thing, like drag racing."

Kiera laughed. "I mean... when you put it like that..."

Danica laughed, too, but Izzy could feel her own shoulders tensing. The small talk felt forced, the energy between her and Kiera humming like a frayed wire. She barely tasted the food. Every time Kiera shifted in her chair, Izzy felt exceptionally aware of her presence.

After dinner, they ended up in the kitchen together after Kiera offered to clean up and Izzy was volunteered to load the dishwasher. They moved around each other in a quiet, careful dance. The clatter of dishes, the rush of running water, the excuse to keep their hands busy — it all felt like a buffer against the truth hanging between them. Izzy rinsed a plate, her fingers scrubbing at a stubborn bit of sauce as if the task required her full concentration. Kiera moved behind her, reaching for the fridge to put away leftovers, her arm nearly brushing against Izzy's back. Izzy felt the shift of air, the warmth of Kiera so close.

When their arms finally did brush, the touch was fleeting, but Izzy's entire body felt electric. The last time they were alone in a kitchen together... The entire room felt suddenly too small.

Finally, Kiera cleared her throat. "Izzy... can we talk?"

Izzy inhaled, nodding once. "Yeah." The word barely came out, her throat tight. She hadn't stopped thinking about the kiss since it happened. And now, with Kiera standing there, waiting, looking at her with hesitation in her eyes, Izzy felt like she was seconds away from combusting into a thousand pieces of nervous energy.

They stepped out onto the porch and sat on the swing, a slight breeze cool against Izzy's skin. The air carried the faint scent of salt and fresh-cut grass, the distant sound of music drifting from a neighbor's open window. A dog barked somewhere down the street, followed by the muffled sounds of people lingering outside in the late spring warmth.

With her fingers curled around the wooden swing arm, Izzy fought to relax her stiff shoulders but felt utterly tense. Her pulse thrummed unevenly, and for a second, she let herself look at Kiera, taking in the way the porch light cast a glow over her features, the way her lips pressed together like she was waiting for something.

The silence stretched unbearably, her heartbeat hammering against her ribs. Then, before she could stop herself, Izzy blurted, "The kiss meant nothing." It came out with more force and decisiveness than she'd intended. "Just like our first one in college."

Kiera's expression faltered. "Right. Of course."

Izzy told herself she was doing the right thing. She had convinced herself that keeping things simple, brushing it off, was the best way forward for their friendship, for Kiera, for her own heart. But as she watched the expression on Kiera's face shift, she felt like she'd just slammed a door she wasn't sure she wanted closed.

Izzy cleared her throat. "What I mean to say is, it doesn't have to mean anything." She stared out into the dark street beyond the front yard, her heart beating wildly in her chest in anticipation. She could feel Kiera's eyes on her.

"And if I do?" Kiera's voice was a whisper, her entire body stiff beside Izzy's. "Want it to mean something?"

Biting her lip, Izzy allowed herself to look at Kiera. The dim porch light obscured Kiera's expression, yet Izzy felt they shared the same uncertainty. The feeling was exhilarating and unnerving, a chaotic mix of excitement and powerlessness.

The first few lines of Sam Cooke's "You Send Me" began playing softly from inside. Kiera glanced over her shoulder through the window. "Are they... dancing?"

Izzy leaned to look, finding Danica and Pete slow dancing in the kitchen. Danica's head rested against Pete's shoulder, and both had their eyes closed as they swayed together.

"Dear god, I've never felt more single in my life," Kiera said with a furrowed brow.

"Big time," Izzy affirmed. As usual, Danica and Pete existed in their own little world. A part of her felt annoyed and bitter, but mostly she just felt happy for her best friend.

Still, she didn't want to sit there and watch two people in love in a way she wasn't sure existed for her. She turned to Kiera. "Do you wanna get out of here?"

"And go where?" Kiera whispered, as if she was being careful not to ruin the moment for Danica and Pete, even from outside.

"Literally anywhere else," Izzy said. "My hotel has a bar."

Kiera was already standing from the porch swing. "Sounds perfect."

CHAPTER 13

Kiera

Kiera stepped into the bar, the rich scent of aged whiskey and citrus curling around her as she took in the space. Polished mahogany and floor-to-ceiling windows showcasing Denver's glittering lights created an intimate, sleek atmosphere. A curved bar stretched across one side of the room, its glass shelves glowing with the reflection of hundreds of bottles, while clusters of low leather booths lined the opposite wall. Soft jazz murmured from hidden speakers, the kind of background music designed to make everything feel luxurious.

It was the kind of place that encouraged whispered conversations, knowing glances over the rim of a cocktail glass, hands brushing on smooth tabletops. Anticipation coiled in Kiera's stomach as she searched for Izzy.

They had each driven their own cars, a choice that had seemed sensible when she proposed it. She paused just inside, sensing an underlying intensity. Being there alone, looking for Izzy among so many strangers, felt electrifying. It made this feel like something else. Not just two old friends meeting for a drink.

Something about that both thrilled and unnerved her.

Her eyes landed on Izzy at the far end of the bar, already perched on a stool, her fingers wrapped loosely around the stem of a martini glass. With her legs crossed, posture relaxed, and hair tousled with studied casualness, she looked devastatingly attractive. The dim lighting softened her small features, casting golden shadows along the line of her jaw, the slope of her nose. She wasn't dressed up, not exactly — just a fitted olive-green T-shirt and perfectly broken-in dark jeans — but she looked unfairly good, like she always did.

Kiera took a breath, straightened her shoulders, and made her way toward Izzy. Arriving at the bar, she perched beside Izzy, offering a slow, teasing smile instead of a greeting.

The bartender approached. "I'll have whatever she's having," Kiera said, tilting her head. "And bring her another, too."

Izzy turned toward her, arching an eyebrow as if taking her in for the first time. She leaned back slightly, letting her gaze sweep over Kiera with exaggerated interest, her expression one of deliberate intrigue. "Careful," she said, swirling the clear liquid in her glass. "Mine's got jalapeño in it."

Kiera bit back a grin. "I like a little heat."

Izzy smirked. "I do enjoy a woman confident enough to order mystery cocktails and flirt with strangers."

Kiera tasted her drink, some kind of jalapeño Dark and Stormy, rum and ginger and warmth.

Izzy made a show of considering her, then stated, "So, mystery cocktail girl," she leaned in slightly, voice lower, playful. "What's your name?"

Kiera smirked. "Why don't you guess?"

Intrigued, she tilted her head, as if Kiera were a captivating mystery. "Hmm. You don't strike me as a Stephanie or Lauren... Maybe a Jessica?"

CHAPTER 13

"Wow. You really think I look like a Jessica?" Kiera balked.

"Okay, you're right. I take it back. You're more of a..." Izzy bit her lip, and Kiera could barely drag her eyes away. "Kiera."

Kiera feigned surprise. "How'd you guess?"

Izzy's mouth twitched. "Lucky guess. Or, I've got a sixth sense for interesting women."

Kiera ran a finger along the edge of the cocktail napkin in front of her, feigning contemplation. "Hmm, interesting? What's your sixth sense telling you now?"

"That I should probably ask for your number."

Kiera let herself lean in just a fraction as she sipped her drink, feeling emboldened by the game, by the subtle push and pull between them. "You're pretty confident that I'll give it to you..." Kiera let her eyes drag over Izzy's face, then lower.

"Izzy." Izzy took a slow sip of her drink, her gaze steady. When she set the glass down, her mouth curved just slightly. "I'm not really the forgettable type."

The words sent electricity through Kiera's veins, but she couldn't help but grin and roll her eyes. "Such a line."

Kiera *felt* Izzy's stare everywhere. The slow, creeping warmth that curled through her stomach, pooling low, making her pulse flutter against her throat. She had been playing, flirting, pushing at the edges of something undefined, but now that Izzy was looking at her like that — like she was worth the chase — the game felt real. Who could she be if she had any choice in the world? What could she do? That realization sent a delicious shiver down her spine.

"What can I say? You're really bringing out my A material tonight." Izzy's gaze flickered over her, assessing, lingering just long enough that Kiera had to suppress the urge to shift in her seat. Her body was betraying her — heart hammering, skin prickling with awareness, her fingers cool against her glass. She felt seen, and not in the casual way old friends saw each other, but in a way that made her wonder what else Izzy might see in her.

"Are you always this forward with strangers in bars?" Kiera said with a shy laugh.

"Only when I meet someone I don't want to forget," Izzy murmured back, and her voice was lower now, smoother, slipping through Kiera's ribs like warm honey.

She had thought — well, she wasn't sure what she had thought, only that she had walked in here knowing she wanted to see Izzy. She hadn't planned for Izzy to play along. She hadn't planned for the way her skin would flush hot, for the way her breath would catch just from the look in Izzy's eyes. She reached for her drink again, more for the distraction than anything else. When she took a sip, she barely tasted the alcohol. "You're lucky I'm a sucker for bold women."

Izzy drummed her fingers against the wooden bar top, her smirk lingering at the corner of her lips.

Kiera's smile was slow. "And here I was *just* about to swear off strangers in bars."

"Lucky for me, I'm hoping to be something else entirely." The confidence in Izzy's voice wasn't just playful — it edged toward cocky, and somehow, it worked. Kiera found herself leaning in, drawn to it.

Kiera lifted an eyebrow. "Oh? And what exactly would that be?"

"That depends." Izzy's voice dropped, the words like silk against Kiera's skin. "Would you want to see me again?"

For a long moment, neither of them spoke. Kiera could feel as Izzy shifted, then the steady press of Izzy's knee against her thigh. Izzy's focused attention was intensely distracting. Suddenly self-conscious, she felt her pulse pounding, her breath quickening, and a flush of heat spreading through her, settling between her thighs.

Kiera barely resisted the urge to shiver. She had spent so much time thinking about what she shouldn't be doing —

shouldn't be imagining Izzy's hands on her waist, or the way she had looked at her on the beach, or how their kiss had felt — that she hadn't given much thought to what she wanted.

And right now, she wanted... Well, she wanted to keep playing.

Kiera lifted her drink to her lips, hoping her cheeks weren't as red as they felt, tilting her head slightly. "You're bold."

Izzy let out a soft chuckle, shaking her head. "And you're curious. I can tell. You want to know if I talk like this in private, too."

A small, reckless thrill curled through her chest. She could do this. Just for tonight, she wasn't going to think too hard about what it meant. "Do you?"

"Well," she said, nudging Kiera's thigh again with her own under the bar. "Only one way to find out."

Kiera watched as Izzy slid the napkin across the polished wood of the bar, her movement slow, deliberate. The numbers scrawled in dark ink were unmistakable. Room 1012.

Izzy didn't say a word. She just lifted her glass, draining the last of her drink, and then stood. Her expression gave nothing away — no teasing smirk, no challenge, just quiet intensity. Kiera's stomach flipped.

She should say something. Should laugh, make a joke, break the tension before it consumed her. But before she could even find her voice, Izzy was walking away, weaving through the low-lit bar, her stride confident, measured.

Kiera's fingers curled around the edge of the napkin.

She could leave. She could crumple the napkin, finish her drink, pretend like nothing had happened, like the heat still coursing through her veins was just leftover adrenaline from their little game.

She knew if she followed, nothing would ever be the same.

She exhaled slowly, taking one last sip. Then, before she

could think about it too hard, she stood, smoothed her shirt, and turned toward the door.

The hallway outside the bar was dim, lined with sleek modern sconces casting a soft glow. Her heels barely made a sound against the carpet as she walked toward the elevators, heart pounding in her throat. She pressed the call button. The doors slid open immediately.

And there, standing inside the elevator with a wicked grin, was Izzy.

The entire world seemed to narrow, the air between them thick with possibility.

Izzy stepped back, motioning for her to enter. "Going up?"

Trembling, Kiera stepped inside. "Floor 10, please." Izzy reached out to press the button for the tenth floor. As the doors slid shut, Kiera turned, half-ready to say something, but Izzy didn't give her the chance.

She grabbed Kiera, bodies colliding, and kissed her.

Izzy's hands were warm against Kiera's waist, her lips insistent. Kiera barely had time to think before she was kissing Izzy back, gripping Izzy's jacket like she needed something to hold onto, like she needed to steady herself.

Lost in the kiss, their desperate hands and mouths roamed. Kiera was caught up in the intoxicating heat of Izzy's tongue on her throat, the warmth of that damn cherry and ginger perfume, that she barely registered the elevator's gentle hum and the soft chimes of passing floors. This was nothing like the kiss in the beach house kitchen.

That kiss had been a question.

This was an answer.

CHAPTER 14

Izzy

Izzy had expected nerves. She hadn't expected to feel like she'd been struck by lightning.

She stood in the elevator, heart pounding in her throat, low in her belly, everywhere. Kiera was close — so close — her breath slightly uneven. The way she looked at Izzy, wide-eyed and flushed, sent a shiver straight down Izzy's spine.

She'd written her room number on the napkin as a dare, both to Kiera and to herself. She hadn't let herself believe Kiera would follow.

Izzy stepped back as the elevator door opened to her floor, her hands still tingling from where they'd gripped Kiera's waist and motioned toward the open doors. "This is us."

Kiera hesitated. Frozen.

It was slight, barely noticeable, but Izzy caught it instantly. She paused, blinking at Kiera, whose lips were still parted, her breath still uneven, but her eyes — her eyes had changed. A moment ago they'd been darkened with heady lust, and now they just looked wide in panic.

She stepped back toward Kiera, her hands slipping from

her waist. "Hey," she murmured, keeping her voice careful, controlled. "You okay?"

Kiera opened her mouth, then closed it again. She swallowed hard, shaking her head just slightly, and Izzy felt something crack inside her chest. The elevators doors shut, but they stayed put, neither daring to move.

"I... I don't know," Kiera admitted finally, her voice quieter now, like she hated having to say it out loud.

Izzy nodded, exhaling through her nose, willing herself to be okay with this, to not let the sharp pang of rejection sting more than it should. She shifted back further to give Kiera space.

Kiera pressed her hands over her face for a second, taking a deep breath, before letting them fall away. She looked... conflicted. "I want to," Kiera admitted, and *fuck*, why did that make Izzy feel worse?

Izzy rubbed the back of her neck, forcing a small, crooked smile. "Wanting to and being ready are two different things," she said, keeping her tone light, gentle. "Trust me, I'm familiar with the concept."

Kiera let out a small, breathy laugh, but her eyes were still concerned. "I—" She shook her head again. "I'm sorry."

"Don't be," Izzy said immediately. She meant it. She did. But she couldn't act like she wasn't feeling disappointed and nervous for what this meant in the grand scheme of her and Kiera.

Kiera ran a hand through her hair, exhaling slowly.

"This... this is a lot," Kiera said finally, looking down at her hands like she wasn't sure what to do with them. "I don't even know what I'm doing. I'm not usually even interested in sex like this. I'm not the kind of person who makes out in elevators or makes out at all. Like, I'm a mom. And I've never been with a woman."

Izzy shook her head. "You being a mom only adds to how incredibly hot I think you are. And who you've been attracted to in the past has nothing to do with us. We have something, Kiera. I know you don't want to deny it anymore, either."

The elevator began moving down, and both of them fell into a tense silence.

She could push more. She wanted to push. But she wouldn't. Not with Kiera. Not with this.

"Maybe I should go, and we could give this some space to get our heads on right," Kiera murmured, reaching out to press the button for the lobby.

Izzy opened her mouth to say something — anything — but Kiera spoke first.

"But," Kiera said tentatively, "I do think this is worth figuring out."

Izzy blinked. The shift in her chest was immediate, warm and hopeful.

"Figuring out?" she repeated, eyebrows lifting.

Kiera gave a small, nervous laugh. "Yeah. I care about you."

"As... friends?" Izzy asked.

Kiera shook her head. "Well, yeah, and... as more. I'm done pretending there isn't something more here. I just also can't deny we've got a lot to lose, and I'm a mess—"

Izzy tilted her head, lips curving into a slow smile. "I don't mind that you're a mess."

Kiera pursed her lips. "At least no one is denying *that*."

Izzy grinned. "Don't you think honesty is going to get us a bit further?"

Kiera exhaled, the sound almost a laugh, almost relief. "Yeah, I guess you're right."

As the elevator doors slid open to the lobby, Kiera reached to give Izzy's hand a squeeze before stepping out.

It wasn't the ending she'd imagined, but it wasn't an ending at all. It was a pause. A breath. A door left cracked open.

. . .

Izzy slid into a booth at Sunny Side Up, a cozy brunch spot with mismatched mugs, checkered tablecloths, and the distinct smell of butter and coffee in the air. It was the kind of place Pete loved — no-nonsense, greasy, and perpetually packed with hungover twenty-somethings inhaling pancakes like their lives depended on it.

Pete had arrived before her and was nursing a cup of coffee, her arm draped over the back of the booth like she owned the place. She smirked as Izzy sat down. "Well, well, well. If it isn't our very own heartbreaker. Should I be congratulating you or offering condolences?"

Izzy sighed, rubbing a hand over her face. "Jesus, Pete. Can we start with coffee before you start prying into my personal life?"

Pete snorted, waving down a server. "Coffee for my very grumpy friend, please."

Izzy murmured a thanks, fidgeting with the sugar packet container. She could feel Pete watching her, studying her for some type of clue.

"So," Pete started, stretching out the word. "Are you going to tell me what happened with Kiera last night, or do I have to guess? Because I *love* guessing, but I'd hate to embarrass you in public."

Izzy leveled her with a look as the server brought coffees and cream. "You're going to embarrass me in public no matter what, so let's not pretend that would stop you."

Pete grinned, unrepentant. "Valid." She leaned forward, resting her chin on her hand. "Come on, though. Spill. You two had some *serious* tension happening at dinner. I figured something was bound to happen when you left at the same time."

Izzy stared at her coffee, debating how much to say. She and Pete had been through so much together — college, bad relationships, even worse decisions — but this? This felt too tender and new and unknown.

Pete's smirk faded slightly. "Okay, now I'm actually a little concerned. Did something bad happen?"

Izzy let out a slow breath. "I kissed her."

Pete didn't react right away, just nodded like she was waiting for the rest.

Izzy took a long sip from her mug. "And it was good. *Really* good." She hesitated, then added, "But then it wasn't."

Pete tilted her head, her expression shifting from amused to concerned in an instant. "What do you mean?"

"I don't know. It was like... she wanted it. I *felt* that she wanted it. And then, all of a sudden, she didn't. She seemed to panic, and I..." Izzy exhaled through her nose, shaking her head. "I worry that I wasn't thinking clearly, and I was too into it to realize that she wasn't ready for that yet."

Pete frowned, her brows drawing together. "Did she *say* that?"

"Kind of," Izzy admitted. "But she looked... god, I don't know. Torn? Upset? Like she wasn't sure what she was doing?"

Pete let out a breath, tapping her fingers against the table. "Did she ask you to stop?"

"No, it wasn't like that," Izzy said, shaking her head. "It was before we even got to my room."

Pete sat back, considering her. "I don't think you would have crossed a line if you were aware of that boundary. You're not that kind of person."

Izzy huffed an awkward laugh. "I just feel weird about it. I knew she wasn't ready, and I shouldn't have kissed her, but we were in the bar and... I think I just read into her flirting too much, maybe?"

Pete's eyes softened. "Izzy." She reached across the table, tapping her knuckles against Izzy's wrist. "If Kiera wasn't ready, that's on *her* to communicate with you. If she's figuring things out, she needs to be the one to say that. You can't be a mind reader."

Izzy swallowed, nodding, but the heaviness of the night before still sat on her shoulders. "I just..." She exhaled. "We talked about honesty, and I'm already reading into what she's *not* saying, and I'm worried if I'm truly honest with her, I'm going to scare her off."

Pete raised an eyebrow. "Look at me. I never told Danica explicitly how I felt, and we wasted so much time not being together just because we were both stubborn idiots. Don't make my same mistakes."

Izzy groaned, rubbing her temples. "I hate when you're right."

Pete grinned. "I know. It's one of my many gifts." She paused, tilting her head. "Look, I don't know where Kiera's head is at, but I do know she's a grown-ass woman who needs to use her words. You're not responsible to figure out for her what she is feeling."

Izzy took a deep breath, letting Pete's words sink in. She wasn't sure if she believed them yet but hearing them out loud made her feel just a little bit lighter.

The server arrived with their food, and Pete immediately stole a bite of Izzy's hash browns, grinning as she did it. "So. Are we done with the self-loathing? Because I'd like to enjoy my eggs without you brooding at me like a sad Victorian widow."

Izzy rolled her eyes, but she couldn't stifle her smile as she reached for a bite of Pete's pancake. "You're insufferable."

Pete grinned. "And yet, you love me."

Izzy shook her head. Maybe Pete was right, but that didn't make the next step clearer. She worried about reaching out first, or responding too quickly, or acting too eager. "Hey, can you not tell Maggie yet? I know there's no chance of Danica not knowing, but I want to tell Meddling Maggie myself."

Pete nodded, silently chewing.

They ate in companionable quiet until Izzy stabbed at the remains of her Eggs Benedict. Across from her, Pete stretched back in the booth, fingers drumming idly on the table, her coffee cup pushed to the side.

"You ready to talk about work?" Pete finally asked, tipping her head as she studied Izzy.

"Yeah, of course." Izzy set her fork down and leaned back, crossing her arms. "You mentioned partnerships yesterday. Tell me what to do, and I'll do it."

"What do you think?"

Izzy paused, taking a long sip of her coffee. "I think you're the brains and I'm the boots on the ground. So, you tell me what direction to go in and I'll go."

"I want to hear what direction you think we need to go in." Pete watched her with skepticism.

"I have no idea." She exhaled, staring at the salt shaker like it had answers.

"Come on, I know that's not true."

"You probably have better ideas, Pete," Izzy confessed, shifting in the booth.

Pete's brow furrowed, and for once, she didn't jump in with a joke. "Do you think I hired you out of pity or something?"

Izzy winced. "Not pity. But… I don't know. Maybe because we're friends?"

Pete snorted. "Bullshit. You think I'd let anyone into my business just because we're friends? If that was the case, Maggie would be our head of PR, and Danica would be performing impromptu physicals in the break room."

Izzy let out a laugh, despite herself. "That's horrifying."

"Exactly." Pete shook her head. "Listen, you have a good eye for people. You're great at figuring out what people need. You know how to connect. That's not something you can fake." She tapped the table with her index finger. "And you're fucking good at it, Iz."

Izzy stared at her for a moment, unsure what to say.

Pete took another sip of her now-cold coffee, then set the

cup down with a thud. "You've been pretty passive, though. You're a part of Second Star, but you're still acting like an outsider looking in. You wait for me to tell you what to do instead of taking the initiative. That's gotta change."

Izzy frowned. "I don't want to step on your toes. It's *your* vision."

Pete leaned forward, leveling her with a look. "It *was* my vision, but you're part of it now, so start acting like it." She took a beat before adding, "So, what do *you* think? About Denver, about expansion, about where we should go next?"

Izzy blinked, caught off guard by Pete's directness. Pete wasn't giving her an out.

She hesitated, but then she thought about the last few months — the meetings, the outreach, all the times she'd had ideas and stifled them, too nervous to voice her opinion.

"I think…" She exhaled, choosing her words carefully. "I think to succeed in the states and especially in Denver, we need to focus more on long-term engagement. We're great at funding, at getting kids into programs, but we don't track what happens after that. Are they sticking with it? Are they growing? Are we actually making an impact, or just throwing money at things? That's the kind of data that will help grow our partnerships here. That is the kind of data that builds trust."

Pete's lips curved into a slow smile. "Now *that* is what I want to hear."

Izzy sat a little straighter.

Pete leaned back, looking satisfied. "So. How do we do that?"

Izzy took a sip of her coffee, rolling her shoulders back. "I have a few ideas. We need a mentorship program," she said, the words forming as she spoke. "We're good at funding activities, but if we want these programs to succeed beyond just funding, we need a way to connect the kids to people who can guide them. Not just teachers and coaches — actual mentors who've been through it."

Pete nodded slowly, her expression thoughtful. "You mean like former participants?"

"Yeah, that could work in places where similar programs already exist," Izzy said, warming to the idea. "In Denver that could mean people in the industries we're supporting — artists, musicians, athletes. We always talk about access being the biggest barrier, but what about *belonging*? These kids need to see themselves in the spaces we're opening up for them."

Pete leaned back in her chair, nodding. "That's gonna take work. But you're right — we can't just be a revolving door. We've gotta be a foundation."

Izzy felt a small thrill of validation, her nerves settling. "Exactly. And I'd include training the mentors and giving them check-ins to ensure it's going in the right direction. We don't want mentors who meet these kids once and fall off the face of the earth, you know? We have to make sure we're starting with a solid foundation, or we're never going to differentiate ourselves from something like Boys & Girls Club, who are already doing exceptional work."

Pete bit her lip, considering. "That all makes total sense…" She drummed her fingers against the table, thoughtful. "Alright. Let's start with the mentorship thing. We can run a pilot in Denver. If it works, we expand it."

Izzy nodded eagerly.

"Oh, by the way," Pete said, waving down their server for the check. "We should talk about a longer term hotel or rental, because you're leading this."

Izzy blinked. "Wait, what?"

"You heard me," Pete said breezily, handing her card to the server. "You're the one who came up with it, you're the one who's gonna make it happen."

Izzy blinked in shock. "I… Pete, I don't even know where to start."

Pete shrugged. "You'll figure it out." She moved to put on her light jacket.

Izzy sat there for a moment, still processing, as Pete stood up and clapped her on the back. "Come on, boss babe. We've got work to do."

THE CITY outside her hotel room window was quiet in that late-night way that always made Izzy feel a little untethered, like everyone else had found their place to land, and she was still hovering just above the ground.

The day had been long, full of discussions and planning, emails piling up faster than she could answer them, but it wasn't work that kept her awake now. It was Kiera.

It was Kiera, in her head. Again.

In the soft, pale blue glow of her phone screen, Izzy sat cross-legged on her bed. Kiera's name was at the top of their most recent text message thread. The last message hung there between them, unanswered for the last few moments.

> **KIERA**
> Can I call you?

Izzy stared at it. Her heart beat faster, like every second she hesitated, she was more likely to miss her moment.

She didn't respond. Instead, she hit *call*.

It rang once. Twice.

"Hey." Kiera's voice was soft. A little breathless, like she'd been waiting.

"Hey," Izzy replied, her voice low, steady. She swallowed hard. "Everything okay? You're up late."

"I couldn't sleep." There was a pause, long enough that Izzy almost said something. But then Kiera's voice came back, quieter this time. "I keep thinking about you."

Izzy leaned back against her headboard, phone pressed tighter to her ear. "Yeah?"

She was rewarded with a breathy laugh and "yes" from Kiera, then, "I... I keep thinking about that kiss."

Relief flooded over Izzy. She hadn't misread the situation the night before — not entirely, not in the way she'd feared. All day she'd been stuck in her own head, replaying the night before on a loop, second-guessing every playful flirtation. She'd convinced herself she'd pushed too far, moved too fast, that maybe Kiera had only kissed her because it had been late and emotional and impulsive after their game in the bar. "I can't stop thinking about you, either," Izzy admitted, voice quiet. "I just want you to know that I don't ever want to pressure you. And that I just think you're so... Is it too much to say sexy? Is that okay?"

The sound of Kiera's breath caught on the other end of the line. "I can't think of the last time anyone thought I was sexy."

Izzy swallowed. She wanted to strangle Kiera's ex-husband for ever letting Kiera think she wasn't an absolute goddess. "Well, I happen to think you're *very* sexy."

A soft laugh. "Well, the feeling is *very* mutual."

"*Very* glad to hear it," Izzy teased.

Another soft laugh. "I'm sorry, I just... I can't stop thinking about yesterday. I'm... this is all new to me. I spend most days feeling entirely invisible," Kiera said.

Izzy smiled to herself. "Stop apologizing, first of all. You're not invisible to me. I see you."

There was silence. A beat too long. And then Kiera whispered, "I wanted you, too. Want. Present tense."

A nervous flutter in Izzy's stomach turned into a full-blown somersault. "I want you, too."

Kiera was quiet for a moment, though Izzy could still hear her quiet movements and breaths on the line.

"Tell me what you're thinking about that's keeping you awake," Izzy said, her voice softening. If Kiera was so worried she wasn't able to sleep, Izzy wanted to reassure her.

Kiera's breath hitched again. "You. Your hands on me. How it felt when you pulled me close in the elevator. Izzy..." She broke off with a quiet moan.

Oh.

Oh.

She just thought Kiera was letting herself be vulnerable again, letting the walls fall for a second. Izzy would've taken that. Happily. It wasn't until Kiera's breath caught, sharp and uneven, that Izzy felt the shift. Something in her tone, her rhythm, the way she exhaled Izzy's name like it *meant* something — that's when it hit her. This wasn't just closeness. This was want. This was Kiera reaching for her in a way Izzy had barely let herself hope for.

Izzy exhaled slowly. She was ready. "Tell me what you want, Kiera."

There was nothing but the sound of their breathing on the line for a moment.

"I want to feel you again," Kiera whispered, breathless and open. "I want to feel you dig your fingers into my hips again. I want... I want to remember what it felt like when you kissed me. Like I was the only thing you wanted."

"You are."

"Izzy."

And just like that, the tension between them snapped into something sharp and undeniable, something sparking, electric and real.

The way Kiera whispered her name, Izzy wanted every second of it. "Close your eyes," Izzy said, her voice low and sure.

The line was quiet for a heartbeat, and then Kiera's voice came through, barely a whisper, but steady. "Okay."

Izzy steadied her own breath as she settled deeper into the bed, letting the quiet stretch between them — not uncomfortable, but charged with something far more intimate. Every ounce of hesitation from earlier had slipped away, leaving behind a palpable connection.

"Tell me where your hand is," Izzy murmured.

There was a pause on the other end of the line. She could hear the sound of Kiera's breath, a soft rustle like she was shifting in bed.

"I'm sliding it under the band of my underwear," Kiera whispered.

"Just let your hand drift down... feel how warm you are. Find that little spot that makes you gasp and touch it like you'd want me to. Slow. Gentle," Izzy said softly, her voice warm and encouraging.

An unsteady breath from the other end of the line. Izzy could practically picture her: lying in bed, cheeks flushed, hands trembling slightly against her smooth, fair skin. Vulnerable. Trusting.

"Izzy," Kiera whispered, but her tone had shifted into something more ragged.

Izzy's breath caught, her own skin hot and electric. "Good," Izzy murmured, letting her own hand trail lightly over her thigh, her body buzzing with anticipation. "What are you thinking about?"

The sharp inhale on the other end of the line was like a spark, like a fuse catching flame.

"I'm thinking about you," Kiera whispered, her words spilling out like a confession. "About the way your hands felt on my breasts. And your mouth on my skin. The way you were so desperate for me in the kitchen at the beach house... in the elevator..."

Izzy squeezed her eyes shut, the memory hitting her like a wave — Kiera's body pressed against hers, the heat of her breath, the softness of her mouth yielding beneath her own. She let out a low, quivering exhale.

"God, Kiera," Izzy rasped. "You have no idea how badly I

wanted to keep going. I wanted to feel every inch of you under me, hear you fall apart for me."

Another breath from Kiera, wavering and uneven. "I wanted that too. I still want it."

Izzy swallowed hard. "Tell me how it feels right now. I want to imagine you."

Kiera didn't answer right away, but then her voice came back, soft but certain. "Warm. I'm so wet. My heart is pounding. I keep thinking about the way you bite my lower lip when you kiss me, how solid you feel against me."

"I wish I was there," Izzy admitted, her fingers sliding through her own wetness, her forearm tensing as she began slow circles. "I'd show you just how much I want you. I want to take my time with you."

Kiera made a soft, involuntary sound — somewhere between a gasp and a whimper — and Izzy's stomach tightened in response.

"Izzy," Kiera breathed, voice strained with need. "God, I wish you were here, too."

"I am," Izzy breathed. "And I want this to feel good for *you*. However that looks. Just be in it."

There was a long pause, just the sound of breathing — Kiera's unsteady and quick, Izzy's low and tight in her chest. The honesty of Kiera's voice and the way she let herself ask for more hit Izzy harder than anything else could have. It was quiet, but it undid her completely.

"Kiera..." Izzy's voice came out rougher than she meant it to. "You don't have to be perfect. You don't have to prove anything. Just let yourself feel good. That's all I want."

A soft sound followed, almost a whimper, and then Kiera said, barely audible, "Tell me what you'd be doing if you were here."

Izzy exhaled slowly, her body already humming. She let the image fill her mind, let herself *want* without restraint, let herself imagine Kiera — flushed, open, and close enough to touch.

"I'd run my fingers along your thighs," Izzy said, voice quiet and certain. "Not too fast. Just enough to tease, to let you know I'm not in any rush."

She heard the way Kiera's breath caught, a slight hitch that only made Izzy sink deeper into the feeling.

"I'd kiss your stomach," she said, her tone thick with warmth, "soft and slow, until I felt you trembling. I'd glide my tongue along the inside of your thighs, feel you arch into me."

Another pause, sharper this time — like Kiera was trying not to make a sound but couldn't hold it back.

"I'd look up at you," Izzy went on, quieter now. "Just to see your face when I finally touched you. I'd make you wait for it, just a little longer, until you asked for more."

A sharp inhale on the other end of the line, followed by a breathless whisper: "Izzy..."

Izzy closed her eyes. "I've got you," she said softly. "Just feel it."

Kiera let out a sharp, stuttering breath.

"Izzy..." Kiera's voice cracked, rough with need. "You're driving me fucking crazy."

Izzy's breath hitched. "Good," she said, low and warm. "That's the idea."

There was a pause. A breath. Then Kiera spoke again, quieter now. "I wish it was your hand. Your fingers. I keep pretending it is."

The admission hit Izzy hard, heat blooming under her skin. "Me too," she said, voice softer now. "If I were there, I'd take my time. I'd learn exactly what you like and give it to you until you can't think straight."

A shaky exhale came through the phone. Izzy could hear how close Kiera was, how much she was holding onto every word.

"You're doing so well," Izzy murmured. "Just keep going. Let it build."

She could hear it in Kiera's breathing now, faster, uneven. It made something deep in Izzy tighten.

"You sound amazing right now," she said, her voice dipping lower. "I wish I could see your face, see how good it feels. I want you to keep going. Don't stop." Another soft, broken sound. Izzy's fingers curled tighter around the phone. "Kiera," she said, her voice steady, coaxing. "Are you close?"

A gasp. Breathless. "Yeah."

Izzy closed her eyes. "Then come for me," she said. "Let yourself take it. I'm right here."

Kiera's breath stuttered — shallow, uneven — then a hitched gasp slipped through the line. Izzy felt it in her gut. It wasn't just release. It was more like something Kiera had been holding in for too long, finally breaking loose.

Izzy closed her eyes as her own orgasm swept over her, quiet and consuming, like everything outside her body had dropped away.

The line went still, just the sound of Kiera breathing — each inhale a little deeper than the last. When she finally spoke, her voice was wrecked, but calm. "Oh my god, that was so hot."

Izzy let out a soft laugh, breath catching on the tail end of it. "Yeah. It really was."

Kiera's voice came again, quiet, more certain this time. "Iz?"

"Yeah?"

"Will you stay on the phone? Just until I fall asleep?"

Izzy's throat tightened with emotion. She turned onto her side, holding the phone a little closer. "Yeah. I'm here."

And that was it. No big declaration. No need to fill the space. Just two steady heartbeats on either end of the line, settling into quiet together.

CHAPTER 14

For once, silence didn't feel like absence. It felt like enough. It felt like a shift — like they'd stepped over an invisible line together and neither of them wanted to go back.

CHAPTER 15

Kiera

Kiera sat at the kitchen table, filling out the spreadsheet that Danica had forced her to create to keep track of every job application she'd put out. As she filled in the mundane details, all she could think about was Izzy and their phone call the night before — the way their voices were low like they were keeping a secret. Her body still hummed with distraction and unmet need.

Across the kitchen, her parents moved around each other in their usual chaotic dance of domesticity. Her dad was chopping an excessive amount of ginger, while her mom poured hot water over loose-leaf tea.

"You've been at that for two hours," her mom observed, setting the kettle down. "Honey, I'm sure color-coding the spreadsheet isn't *that* big of a deal."

Kiera sighed, dragging a hand through her hair. "You're probably right, but it makes me feel like I'm doing *something* at least." She paused, exhaling hard as she rubbed her temples. "I feel like I'm floundering."

Her dad, still focused on butchering a hunk of ginger, let

out a hum. "Floundering is just another word for figuring it out."

Kiera shot him a flat look. "That's not even remotely true."

Her mom slid a cup of tea in front of her. "You're going to be fine, sweetheart. The right teaching job will come once this part is behind you."

Kiera couldn't help but groan. "Trust the process, right? Well, in case you have your rose-colored parent glasses still on, I am extremely bad at that. I'm divorced, I live with my parents, and I need help raising my daughters."

Her parents exchanged a glance, the kind of silent parental communication that usually meant they were about to approach a subject *carefully*.

Her dad cleared his throat. "You're worried about the girls."

Kiera pressed her fingers into her temples. "Of course I'm worried about the girls. I'm worried I won't get a job in the fall, and that I moved them here without any kind of plan beyond 'start over and hope for the best'."

Her mom frowned. "You've always landed on your feet. This won't be any different."

"That's the thing," Kiera said, voice tight. "I don't feel like I'm landing anywhere. I feel like I'm just free-falling, hoping the application is going to magically fix everything."

Her dad finally abandoned the ginger and leaned against the counter, arms crossed. "Or maybe you're just adjusting. Starting over is hard — doesn't mean you're doing it wrong."

Kiera scoffed, shaking her head. "You don't get it. I used to *know* who I was. I was good at my job. I thought I was a good wife. A good mom. I had a system. Now I'm pretending I'm not terrified that I've made a huge mistake."

Now that the words were out there, they felt disingenuous. She knew she'd done the right thing by leaving, by bringing the girls to Denver, by ensuring that they'd see their mom being strong and standing up for herself.

CHAPTER 15

A silence settled over the kitchen, warm but weighty. Kiera stared into her tea, her pulse a little too quick, her nerves too raw.

Her mom was the first to speak again, voice softer. "Sweetheart... is this really about applications or a spreadsheet?"

Kiera swallowed. "What?"

Her dad gave her a knowing look. "You've been organizing that same column for damn near an hour. So... what else is going on?"

Kiera opened her mouth, then closed it. The words were there, but they caught in her throat. The intensity of the last few days — Izzy's kiss, the way it felt like something inside her had been knocked loose — sat like a stone in her chest.

She took a breath. "I kissed a woman." She pointedly did *not* add that they'd had epically good phone sex the night before.

There was a beat of silence before her mom let out a dramatic sigh of relief. *"Finally."*

Her dad, however, simply broke into a slow, satisfied grin. He turned to her mom with an outstretched hand, palm open. "Pay up," he said with a grin like he'd just won the lottery.

Kiera blinked. "Wait. *You bet on me kissing a woman?* On... coming out, I suppose?"

"Not *if* you'd come out — *when*," her dad corrected with a grin. "Your mom said last year. I said you'd figure it out before forty. Clearly, I had faith."

Kiera let out a strangled noise, somewhere between disbelief and sheer mortification. "Are you serious? You knew... what?"

Her dad shrugged, unbothered. "Kid, we knew you were queer long before you did."

Kiera stared at them, her heart still racing. "Okay, so you're both *shockingly* calm about this. But I'm still kind of..."

She waved a hand, struggling for the right words. "Processing."

She hadn't expected it to feel like this — like her ribs had loosened a notch, like she could finally exhale after holding her breath for years without realizing it. And still, part of her couldn't help scanning their faces for any flicker of hesitation, any shift in tone that might mean she'd read it wrong. But there was nothing. Just quiet warmth and the easy rhythm of her parents acting like they were talking about the weather.

It should've felt anticlimactic. Instead, it felt huge. Not loud or dramatic — just quietly, terrifyingly real.

She hadn't even said the words out loud until recently. And now, here she was, standing in her childhood kitchen, saying them without apology and being met with love.

Her throat tightened. Processing didn't even begin to cover it.

Her mom reached over and squeezed her hand. "And that's okay, sweetheart. But just so you know — you don't have to have it all figured out right this second. And you don't have to be scared to tell us things like this."

Kiera exhaled, shoulders relaxing slightly. "Yeah. Okay."

Her dad gave her a grin. "So... was it a *good* kiss?"

Kiera groaned and dropped her head onto the table. "Oh my god."

Her dad leaned forward, his smile widening. "I mean, we need details. Was it a *movie-worthy* kiss? A 'slow-motion, dramatic music swelling in the background' kind of thing?"

Her mom chimed in, eyes twinkling. "Or was it more of a 'whoops, didn't see that coming' situation?"

Kiera groaned again, covering her face with her hands. "Why did I tell you this?"

"Because we're your loving and supportive parents," her mom said sweetly, taking another sip of tea.

"And because you knew deep down that we'd eventually drag it out of you anyway," her dad added, stretching his arms behind his head like he had all the time in the world. "So, was this just a casual kiss? Or are we talking Big Feelings?"

Kiera peeked at them between her fingers, equal parts mortified and exasperated. "Please stop."

Her mom gasped dramatically. "Big feelings, then. Got it."

Her dad pointed at her, eyebrows raised. "You didn't deny it."

Kiera groaned, slumping forward onto the table. "I take it back. You two are *not* supportive. You're busybodies."

Her mom patted her back soothingly. "Sweetheart, we're just happy for you. And also, frankly, relieved. I knew you'd come to your senses."

"Come to my senses?" Kiera lifted her head just enough to glare at them.

Her dad nodded sagely. "Well, yeah. The way you used to talk about your totally platonic girl crushes growing up? It was painfully obvious. And in college, there was that girl you never stopped talking about. I'm just shocked it took this long."

Kiera threw up her hands. "I hate this. I hate this entire conversation."

Her mom just laughed, shaking her head. "Oh, honey. You don't hate it. You're just flustered."

"I am *not* flustered."

Her dad raised an eyebrow. "Then why is your face turning the exact color of a tomato?"

"Wait, what girl did I talk about in college all the time? Danica?"

Her mom rolled her eyes. "Yes, but not like that. I believe it was Missy, if I remember correctly."

"Missy?" Kiera repeated.

"Pixie?" Her dad added rather unhelpfully.

"Izzy?" Kiera clarified.

Her mom's eyes widened. "Yep, that was it. Izzy."

Kiera groaned again and pushed back from the table. "I'm leaving."

Her mom clutched her arm. "But sweetheart, where will you go? We know where you live."

She could see the laughter bubbling up inside her dad.

Kiera crossed her arms, grumbling, "I was *trying* to make a spreadsheet before you both turned this into a full-fledged intervention. Now I'm going to go to Pilates and forget this conversation ever happened."

Her mom leaned in conspiratorially. "Kiera, darling. What we really mean to say is that we *hoped* you would come out, but we did begrudgingly accept you as our straight daughter, as well."

Kiera turned to leave, shaking her head. "Unbelievable."

Her dad called after her, his voice still teasing, "We're just saying, if you need advice on handling complicated romantic feelings, you should just ask us. Between your mother and me, we've got so many complicated romantic feelings about each other, it isn't even funny!"

Kiera stopped in the doorway, turning back just enough to give them a dry look. "I'm not sure that a straight couple that has been married for decades can help me in this new queer adventure."

Her mom winked. "At least you admit it's an adventure."

Shaking her head, Kiera disappeared down the hall, still feeling the heat in her cheeks. But as much as she wanted to be embarrassed by the conversation, she couldn't ignore the slight weight that had lifted from her chest.

An hour later, Kiera found herself standing outside *Luna Pole & Aerial*, the studio windows reflected against the late afternoon sun. She hadn't planned on being here. She had planned to go to Pilates. She wasn't sure she enjoyed Pilates, necessarily, but it was now familiar, which meant predictable and safe.

She wasn't sure why she hesitated when she passed the pole fitness studio again. Through the glass doors, she could see two women chatting as they changed into heels, looking at ease in a way Kiera could barely comprehend.

She told herself she was just going to grab a brochure. That was all. Just information. She stepped inside before she could change her mind.

The front desk attendant, a woman with a blunt bob and a septum piercing, greeted her with a warm smile. "Hey there! Here for a class?"

Kiera opened her mouth, ready to explain that *no, she was just looking*, but then the attendant glanced at the clock.

"There's a beginner's class starting in ten minutes. If you want to join, I can get you set up."

Kiera hesitated, her stomach clenching like a fist.

She could think of a dozen reasons to say no. She had planned on Pilates, she wasn't dressed for this, she didn't know what she was doing. But then she thought about the kiss with Izzy and initiating that very hot phone sex; how she had let herself be bold for once, and *brave*; how her parents had been so unbothered when she'd told them. The relief of it. The realization that maybe, just maybe, she didn't always have to be the careful, predictable version of herself.

Maybe she could just *try*.

She squared her shoulders. "You know what? Yeah. Why not."

The woman grinned. "Love that energy. Let's get you signed in."

Ten minutes later, Kiera stood in a bright, mirrored room, barefoot, surrounded by sleek metal poles spaced evenly throughout the studio. A handful of other beginners — some looking just as nervous as she felt — stood or stretched nearby.

The instructor, a bubbly redhead named Sam, clapped their hands together. "Alright, welcome to beginner pole! Who here is brand new?"

Kiera raised her hand, nerves spiking the moment she did. She glanced around and saw she wasn't the only one, but that didn't make her feel any less exposed.

Sam beamed. "Awesome. First thing you need to know is that pole is for *everyone*. No matter your strength level, no matter your background, this is a safe space to learn, have fun, and maybe discover you're stronger than you thought."

That was... oddly reassuring.

They started with basic warm-ups — shoulder rolls, hip circles, core activation exercises — and then moved into simple grips. Kiera had assumed it would be all spins and climbing, but the first ten minutes were just learning how to *hold* the pole properly.

When they finally moved on to a beginner spin, the fireman spin, Kiera was sure she was doing it wrong. She watched Sam demonstrate, the move looking effortless, before she tentatively copied the motion. She stepped, hooked her leg, and... immediately clunked against the pole, sliding down in the least graceful way possible.

"Holy shit," she muttered under her breath, laughing as she caught herself.

Sam chuckled. "That was a perfect *attempt*. Try again but trust your momentum more."

Kiera tried again. And again. And by the fourth or fifth time, she managed a wobbly, slightly stilted spin.

Her arms ached. Her legs were already burning. She was *terrible* at this.

But she was having *fun*.

For the first time in a long time, she wasn't worrying about what came next. She wasn't thinking about Alex or the divorce or teaching or what the hell she was doing with her life or even Izzy. She was just *here*, in her body, trying something new.

And damn, it felt good.

AFTER PICKING the girls up from school, Kiera went through the well-worn motions of their afternoon routine. Shoes scattered in the entryway, backpacks unzipped and emptied onto the kitchen table, snack requests flying at her from both sides. Eliza, ever the chatterbox, launched into a story about how she and her best friend had started a "detective agency" at recess, while Quinn sat on the counter, munching on an apple, solemnly nodding along.

"Mommy, can we have a tea party after dinner?" Eliza asked, swinging her legs under her chair.

Kiera pressed a kiss to the top of her head. "Of course. You want the real tea set or the plastic one?"

"The real one," Eliza said, grinning. "But *not* the Sleepytime tea. That one is yucky."

Kiera laughed. "Noted."

Eliza paused swinging her legs and looked up at her with wide eyes. "Mama, are we gonna live with Grandma and Grandpa forever?"

Kiera's heart clenched. She glanced at Quinn, who was also watching her with interest, then back to Eliza. "No, baby. Just for a little while. We'll have our own place again soon. I promise."

Eliza asked softly, "Why don't we see Daddy anymore?"

Kiera swallowed hard. "Daddy works a lot, so you get to live with Mama and visit Daddy. Like a vacation. Isn't that fun?"

Eliza seemed to think about that response, nodding after a beat. "Okay. As long as Daddy still loves me too."

"He does," Kiera assured her. "So, so much."

Quinn, still silently eating her apple, reached over and

grabbed Kiera's hand with her tiny fingers. Kiera squeezed back, trying to anchor herself in that simple, pure connection. "I don't mind living with Grandma and Grandpa and the chickens and you, Mama."

"Me too, Mama. But you first, then the chickens," Eliza said.

Kiera smiled, her heart still tight in her chest. The fear of the unknown was still there — pressing in from all sides — but for now, she had her daughters. And perhaps she was finally piecing herself back together.

CHAPTER 15

5 Oppossums in a Trench Coat

MAGGIE

Okay, here's a good one. Would you rather never be able to eat cheese ever again or never be able to receive oral sex ever again?

DANICA

I'd give up cheese.

PETE

definitely cheese

IZZY

You guys answered that way too fast.

KIERA

...Is it weird that I need to think about this?

Danica named the conversation, "The Grate Debate".

MAGGIE

Kiera, I think you're telling on yourself.

DANICA

Yeah, Kiera, are you about to choose cheese over THAT?

KIERA:

I just really love cheese, okay??

PETE:

love cheese more than orgasms?!

bold

MAGGIE

I'm just saying, have you ever had brie on a fresh baguette? Life-changing.

DANICA

I've had something else that's life-changing, and trust me, it's not dairy.

PETE

can you cross-stitch that on a pillow, baby?

Maggie named the conversation, "Brie-yond Boundaries".

IZZY

I think we all learned something very personal about you today, Kiera.

MAGGIE

Yeah, like how you're dangerously close to starting a committed relationship with a cheese wheel.

Pete named the conversation, "Wheel-y Complicated".

KIERA

Honestly? I think I'd take cheese. Even below average cheese is better than most oral I've received.

MAGGIE

The straights are not okay.

IZZY

That sounds like a partner problem.

KIERA

I'm open to being proven otherwise.

DANICA

👀

PETE

ewwwwwwwwwwwww, we are RIGHT here

CHAPTER 15

MAGGIE

Wait, WHAT is happening right now?

CHAPTER 16

Izzy

Izzy lay sprawled across the hotel bed, one arm draped over her stomach, phone balanced loosely in her other hand. The room was dim, lit only by the bedside lamp and the faint neon glow from the city skyline outside. The sheets were cool against her skin, but she felt warm, buzzing with restless energy. She had spent the last twenty minutes flipping between apps, pretending she wasn't waiting for a reason to text Kiera. She didn't want to pressure Kiera into anything after their phone call the night before.

That conversation had played in her head all day, distracting her as she prepared for talks with potential partners in Denver, replaying on a loop in every free moment.

The excuse she landed on was nothing special, just a simple check in after reading the latest group chat.

IZZY

Hey, how was your day?

It took a few minutes for Kiera to respond, and Izzy was

trying not to analyze what that meant when her phone buzzed.

> **KIERA**
> You'll never guess what I did.

Izzy smiled, sitting up against the headboard. She sent back a silly reply, hoping to keep the mood light.

> **IZZY**
> Ate some very good cheese.

> **KIERA**
> I wish. Try again.

> **IZZY**
> Trained a chicken to do the bunny hop.

> **KIERA**
> Alas, untrue. They're just completely uncoordinated when it comes to rhythm. Terrible students.

> **IZZY**
> Noted. Okay, sorry to bring the chickens into this. What'd you do today?

> **KIERA**
> A pole fitness class.

Izzy stared at the screen, grinning. The mental image of Kiera pole dancing hit her hard.

> **IZZY**
> I am very much in favor of this.

> **KIERA**
> Oh?

> **IZZY**
> For your personal growth, of course.

KIERA

Of course.

IZZY

So, should I start calling you Magic Mike?

KIERA

More like Tragic Mike. I was terrible.

Somehow Izzy highly doubted that. Kiera's curves and confidence and just the way she kissed and moved beneath Izzy's hands... No, there was no way that Kiera could be bad at that.

IZZY

But did you have fun?

KIERA

I did, actually. Which is weird. But I think I'm done being so scared of trying new things.

IZZY

Hell yeah, look at you. Next thing you know, you'll be performing in Vegas.

KIERA

Give me six months. Maybe a year.

IZZY

I'll start making flyers now. "Introducing Kiera, the Pole Dancing Queen."

KIERA

Oh god.

Izzy's smile softened as she pondered the idea. Kiera was venturing into new territory. Stepping out of her comfort zone. A warmth bloomed in Izzy's chest, a feeling of unexpected pride for her.

IZZY

New things are good. Sometimes terrifying, but good.

Kiera's response came quicker this time.

KIERA

What do you know about terrifying things?

IZZY

Well, Pete asked me to head up the new Denver project, which is absolutely terrifying, if you ask me.

KIERA

That's exciting! You're going to kill it.

IZZY

I don't know. I'm just a bartender from San Francisco, you know? I don't... help run foundations.

KIERA

It would seem everyone knows you're definitely wrong and underestimating yourself. Including me. But I'm always here if you need an unemployed middle school science teacher's opinion.

IZZY

I thought this was your cheerleading session for trying a new thing.

KIERA

I think we've established that mutual appreciation can be a very fun thing.

Izzy's pulse picked up, and before she could talk herself out of it, she typed:

CHAPTER 16

IZZY

> So... about last night... Any thoughts?

The typing bubble appeared, then vanished. Izzy held her breath, cursing those three little typing dots. Then her screen lit up with an incoming call.

Kiera.

Butterflies cartwheeled in her stomach. She hesitated for half a breath before swiping to answer. "Hey."

Kiera exhaled a quiet laugh. "Hi."

They sat in silence for a long beat, filled with unspoken things, like they were both picking at the edges of something delicate and unspoken.

"So," Izzy started, fingers toying with the hem of her shirt, "you called."

"I did," Kiera said, a smile in her voice. "Seemed easier than texting."

Izzy huffed a laugh. "Debatable."

A pause. Then Kiera sighed. "I don't know what to say about last night. Or the night before."

Izzy swallowed. "Me either."

Another stretch of silence, but it wasn't as suffocating as she'd feared. Finally, Kiera spoke again, her voice quieter. "I don't regret it."

Izzy closed her eyes, relief blooming in her chest. "Me either."

Kiera hesitated. "But I don't know what it means."

Izzy's grip tightened on the phone. "We don't have to know what it means right now."

Kiera was quiet for a beat, then exhaled. "Okay."

Izzy could picture her then — probably pacing, or maybe sitting on the edge of her bed, her brows drawn together. Izzy felt a pang of such deep affection that her chest tightened, a painful but lovely sensation.

Izzy let out a breath, settling back against the pillows. "So, what was harder? The pole class or talking about feelings?"

Kiera let out a startled laugh. "They're both brutal."

Izzy smiled, letting the warmth of Kiera's laugh settle into her bones. "Maybe we just take it slow. Figure it out as we go."

Kiera was quiet for a moment, then said, "Yeah. I think I'd like that."

Izzy was in uncharted territory. She knew how to burn fast and pull away quicker. She knew the rhythm of want without being wanted in return. But this? Slow could mean messier. It asked more of her. Kiera wasn't rushing toward her or away from her — she was just *there*. Steady. Waiting. And it was both the kindest and most disarming thing Izzy had ever experienced. She didn't know how to hold still in love, but maybe she wanted to try.

They weren't solving anything tonight, but they weren't running from it either. That was enough.

The conversation drifted after that, shifting into lighter territory — Kiera recounting a chaotic bedtime routine with her daughters, Izzy talking about a new smoothie place Pete had dragged her to that afternoon. The easy rhythm between them returned, familiar and comfortable, like the best parts of their friendship had never wavered. But underneath the jokes and tangents, something had shifted — a quiet current neither of them named, but both of them felt.

When they finally said goodnight, Izzy lay in bed staring at the ceiling, her pulse still a little too quick. She tried to pretend she wasn't already thinking about seeing Kiera again. But she was. And for once, that didn't feel like something she had to talk herself out of.

A FEW DAYS PASSED, and Izzy threw herself into work with a level of focus she hadn't tapped into in months. Pete had been right to push her — she needed to start acting like she belonged at Second Star, prove just how invested she was. So, she did. She sat in on every meeting, spoke up when she had ideas, and didn't let Pete make all the decisions. It felt good. Like she was carving out a place for herself in something that mattered.

She barely had time to dwell on Kiera. Except, of course, when she did.

Every night, after the work emails had been sent and the spreadsheets reviewed, Izzy found herself staring at her phone. They texted every day, but that last phone conversation played over in her head, the ease of it, the warmth tucked between their words. They had left things open-ended, undefined, which should have made her feel unsettled, given how she was used to chasing unrequited affection. Now, instead of feeling unsettled, it had given her room to breathe.

Still, she kept waiting. For what, she wasn't sure. Maybe for Kiera to talk about it first, to set the terms of whatever this was going to be. Izzy was so nervous about pushing Kiera too far, too fast, but her excitement made her want to take a chance. Like Pete had said, only Kiera could make that call for herself.

Izzy picked up her phone, pulled up her last text with Kiera, and typed.

IZZY

Hey. I have a serious question for you.

KIERA

Oh god. What?

Izzy grinned, tapping her fingers against the edge of her desk before responding.

IZZY

> If I were to ask you on a date, like a real, actual date... what are the chances you'd say yes?

There. It was out in the world. No going back.

The response didn't come right away. The typing bubble blinked in and out a few times, and Izzy could practically *see* Kiera hesitating, debating, overthinking — the exact same way Izzy had done for days. Had she asked too soon? Should she have let things sit a little longer?

Then, finally, Kiera's reply came through.

KIERA

> Are you asking me on a date? Or are you just gauging my reaction for research purposes?

Izzy huffed out a laugh, relief flooding through her.

IZZY

> Hypothetically.

KIERA

> I'd say... hypothetically, I'd need to know what the date entails.

IZZY

> Oh, you know. Something classic. Candlelit dinner, wine, long walks on the beach where I try very hard not to be weird.

KIERA

> So you're planning on being weird. On the famous beaches of Denver.

IZZY

> Can't change who I am, Kiera.

There was another pause, then:

KIERA

Then yeah. I think I'd say yes.

Izzy didn't realize she'd been holding her breath until she let it out in a slow, measured exhale.

IZZY

Good. Because I wasn't just asking hypothetically.

She set her phone down on her desk, waiting, heart in her throat. The response came quickly this time.

KIERA

Then I guess I have a date with you.

Izzy stared at the words for a long moment, a slow smile pulling at her mouth before she even realized it. Warmth spread through her, low and steady, like something waking up. She didn't know what this was going to turn into, but for once, she couldn't wait to find out.

CHAPTER 17

Kiera

Kiera sat at the dining table in Danica and Pete's house, her hands wrapped around a steaming mug of coffee. The room was warm and inviting, filled with signs of their life together — cozy mismatched mugs, a half-finished crossword on the counter, Pete's leather jacket slung over a dining chair. The faint scent of cinnamon lingered, a memory of a recent breakfast.

Across from her, Danica leaned against the counter, sipping her own coffee, looking impossibly well-rested in an oversized CSU sweatshirt and joggers. The morning light filtered through the large kitchen windows, making her light brown hair glow golden, and she felt at ease around Danica for the first time in a long time.

Gladys lay sprawled on the floor beside them, her massive head resting on Kiera's foot. She let out a deep, contented sigh, her stubby tail wagging slightly even in sleep.

"So," Danica said, drawing out the word as she arched a brow. "Are we actually going to close the book on Telluride?"

Kiera took a long sip of her coffee, buying herself a few seconds. "Thought we already did."

"We talked," Danica said. "But I don't think we finished."

Kiera sighed and set her mug down. "Yeah. You're right."

She looked at Danica, her expression open for once — no edge, no evasion.

"I was wrong," Kiera said quietly. "About all of it. I pushed too hard, I overstepped, and I didn't listen when you told me what you needed. I wanted to fix things, but I wasn't actually showing up for you in the way that mattered."

Danica didn't interrupt. She just waited.

Kiera's voice dropped. "I hurt you. And I hate that I did."

The silence between them stretched, but this time it didn't feel uncomfortable. It felt honest.

"I appreciate you saying that," Danica said finally. "I think I needed to hear it in plain language. No 'I thought I was helping,' no justifications. Just... that."

"You deserved that the first time," Kiera said, her voice tight. "I'm sorry, Dani."

Danica reached across the counter and gave Kiera's hand a squeeze. "Thank you."

A beat. Then she smirked. "But if you try to fix my love life again, I'm calling in backup."

Kiera raised an eyebrow. "Let me guess. Gladys."

"She has very sharp elbows," Danica said, rubbing at a part of her ribs as if remembering that very fact.

Kiera laughed, a little breathless with relief. "Noted."

Danica tilted her head, eyes narrowing slightly. "Speaking of people you shouldn't be trying to fix... what's going on with *you*?"

Kiera blinked. "What?"

"You're glowing," Danica said, grinning. "Either you've joined a cult or you're into someone."

"I am not glowing."

CHAPTER 17

Danica just sipped her coffee, eyes twinkling. "That's exactly what someone who's glowing would say."

Kiera hesitated, but the words were out before she could stop them. "Izzy asked me on a date."

There was a sharp clatter as Pete, who had clearly been lurking in the hallway, dropped whatever she was holding. A second later, she burst into the kitchen holding a broken picture frame. "What?!"

Kiera startled. "Jesus, Pete."

Danica just blinked, watching Pete set the broken frame down on the kitchen counter.

Pete crossed her arms, eyes wide with glee. "Izzy asked you out?"

Kiera sighed, rubbing her temples. "Yes, and now I regret saying anything."

Danica, to her credit, looked pleased. "I knew it."

Pete spun on Danica. "Did you know? Did you know and not tell me?"

"I only suspected," Danica said, wiggling her eyebrows. "How do you feeeel? Do you like her? I mean, I know there's always been something there, but..."

Pete turned back to Kiera. "You said yes, right?"

"I said yes," Kiera mumbled. "I feel... I don't know. I'm nervous, but I'm excited, and I'm trying not to freak out about what it all *means*. Maybe it won't even turn into anything, and we'll just decide we're better as friends, you know? And then I've freaked out about my identity for nothing."

Danica nodded, but Pete tilted her head in confusion. "If it doesn't work out with Izzy, it's not like you're just out of luck. If you're into the idea of tiny tomboys, the queer community has plenty," Pete said.

Kiera flushed and Danica laughed, smacking Pete's arm. "That's not the point, babe," Danica chided.

"I'm trying not to overanalyze and freak out, okay?" Kiera took a deep breath.

Danica grinned. "Look at you, dating."

"It's one date," Kiera said, rolling her eyes. "Can we not make a thing out of this?"

"No, we absolutely *will* be making a thing out of this," Pete said. "You have been pining after Izzy for literal *years*."

"I have *not*—"

"College, Kiera," Danica echoed, pointing her coffee stirring spoon at her. "*College.* You didn't even tell me you kissed her, but then when I learned it, it all makes sense now."

"It was *one* kiss," Kiera muttered.

Pete raised an eyebrow. "The story changed like four times. First it was, 'We were drunk, it didn't mean anything.' Then it was, 'It was a dare.' Then suddenly it was, 'We were just experimenting.' And then... radio silence for, like, a decade."

"You think we didn't clock what was actually going on?" Danica asked, grinning. "You'd light up like a sparkler anytime she texted you. Even when it was just some dumb meme."

"And she always asked about you," Pete added casually. "Even years after graduation. Not constantly, but enough that it stuck."

Kiera blinked. "She did?"

"Oh yeah," Pete said. "Any time we caught up. 'How's Kiera?' 'Is Kiera still teaching?' Super chill, very casual, obviously loaded."

Danica leaned forward, resting her chin on her hand. "You two have been orbiting each other forever. It all makes so much sense now."

Kiera groaned, slumping back in her chair. "You're both deeply annoying."

Pete leaned over and stole a sip of Danica's coffee. "Also, you're totally glowing."

"I am *not* glowing."

Danica grinned. "See, I told you."

Kiera shook her head, but she couldn't stop the smile that tugged at the corner of her mouth.

Gladys let out a heavy sigh and dropped her head onto Kiera's lap like she was bored of all the drama.

Kiera scratched behind the dog's ears. "Even the dog thinks you're being ridiculous."

Danica set her mug down and clapped her hands together. "Alright. First date. That means we're dressing you."

Kiera groaned. "Oh, I don't—"

"Oh, *yes*," Danica said, already standing. "Upstairs. Now."

Pete grinned. "I'll get the accessories."

Kiera buried her face in her hands. "This was a mistake."

Danica dragged her off the stool, already leading her toward the stairs. "No take-backs, sweetheart."

Kiera huffed, but when she caught Pete's delighted grin and Danica's excited energy, she felt something settle in her chest — something light, something good.

Kiera fastened her earrings, smoothing a hand over her dress as she took one last glance in the mirror.

She stared at her reflection. *It's just dinner. With Izzy. Who you kissed. Twice. And who talked you through a very satisfying orgasm over the phone. As friends do.*

She was being cringey. She had been on dates before. She had been in serious relationships. She had gotten married, had kids, gotten divorced. And yet, somehow, meeting Izzy at a small Italian restaurant lit Sloan's Lake felt more intimidating than any of those things.

Tonight was supposed to be a step forward — to explore her connection with Izzy, and to do something out of her comfort zone. But before she could grab her purse, a small sniffle from the hallway stopped her.

"Mama?" Quinn's voice was thick with tears as she shuffled toward her, clutching at her ear. "It hurts."

Kiera's heart sank. She knelt down, brushing damp curls from Quinn's flushed face. "Your ear, baby?"

Quinn nodded miserably, her lower lip trembling. She'd always been prone to ear infections, just like Eliza, so at least Kiera was in familiar territory. Any thought of going out vanished instantly. Kiera scooped her daughter up, holding her close as she grabbed her phone from the dresser.

"Hey," Kiera said when Izzy picked up. "I have to reschedule. Quinn's not feeling great."

There was no hesitation in Izzy's voice. "Do you need anything? Medicine, soup..."

"No, no, we're okay. I just don't want to leave her. I'm sorry."

"Don't you dare apologize. Would it be okay if I brought dinner to you?"

Kiera's voice caught and she cleared her throat. "Izzy, you don't have to do that."

Kiera could hear Izzy's smile as she talked. "I know I don't. But I want to. I want to see you and I want to help. I could grab some pizzas and keep you all fed and happy while the little one convalesces, if that's okay with you?"

"Pizza?" Kiera hesitated, glancing down at Quinn, who sniffled but perked up slightly at the mention of pizza. There was a part of her that did want Izzy here, in her space, with her girls. "Okay," she said softly. "Yeah. That actually sounds really nice."

She texted her parents, insisting they go out to a nice dinner instead of staying home on babysitting duty, and by the time Izzy arrived, arms full with pizza boxes and a bag of snacks, Kiera started to feel more at ease

Izzy hovered in the doorway of the living room as Kiera shut the door and put the bags of snacks in the kitchen. Izzy paused, balanced the boxes and Kiera took in the scene — Quinn curled up under a blanket on the couch, Eliza sitting cross-legged on the floor, eyeing her suspiciously.

CHAPTER 17

"What kind of pizza?" Eliza demanded, arms crossed.

"Whoa now, let's use our kind words," Kiera said from behind Izzy, "Especially when we're meeting Mom's friends. Eliza, this is Izzy."

"And I'm Quinn," croaked the moving blanket on the couch.

"Thank you for bringing pizza and it's nice to meet you, but what kind of pizza is it?" Eliza said, still stone-cold.

Kiera tried to shoot a desperate look of apology toward Izzy.

Izzy glanced down, suddenly looking unsure. "Uh, cheese, pepperoni, and some fancy one with mushrooms and goat cheese."

Eliza wrinkled her nose. "That's Mom's."

Izzy pulled a disgusted face instantly. "Yeah, I figured. She's got interesting taste."

Quinn, still sniffling, peeked out from her blanket. "Did you bring dessert?"

Izzy hesitated, then lifted the extra bag she'd brought. "I didn't know what you guys liked, so I got some options. Chocolate chip cookies, brownies, and, uh... gummy bears?"

Eliza studied her for a long moment, then nodded approvingly. "You can stay."

Kiera stifled a laugh as Izzy exaggeratedly wiped her brow and let out a breath, like she'd passed some kind of secret test.

Izzy was dressed up — not anything extravagant, just a simple button-down and dark jeans, but the *effort* was there, and it caught Kiera off guard. Izzy was always more Patagonia fleece and cutoff shorts than crisp button-downs. The sleeves of the shirt were slightly too long, cuffed once at the wrists, the fabric just a little too big on her frame.

Kiera laughed. "I was going to ask if Pete dressed you, but I already know the answer."

Izzy rolled her eyes but grinned. "She picked out, like, five options. This was the least tragic."

Kiera let her eyes skim over Izzy again, the way Izzy had neatly tucked the front of the shirt into her jeans like she was trying, but not *too hard*. "I like it."

Izzy's grin softened, and Kiera's felt giddy at the sight.

The evening unfolded with a surprising ease. They sat on the couch, plates balanced in their laps, debating which Disney movie to put on. Quinn, despite her earache, kept sneaking bites of Eliza's pizza, and Eliza retaliated by stealing sips of Quinn's juice box. Izzy took it all in stride, tossing in playful commentary and glancing sideways at Kiera whenever their hands brushed.

Eventually, Eliza, turned to Izzy. "Are you one of Mom's friends who she goes on trips with?" she asked, curiosity in her voice.

Izzy froze for half a second before looking at Kiera, unsure what to say.

"Yeah, she's one of my friends from college," Kiera supplied easily.

Eliza squinted. "You look younger than my mom."

Kiera scoffed. "That's an inside thought, honey."

"Thank you. Our other friend Maggie has me on a strict tretinoin regimen," Izzy said, deadpan. "When you're older, I can share my secrets with you."

Eliza nodded sagely. "You know, you can call me Lizzie, if you want. Aunt Danica does."

Izzy smiled. "Izzy and Lizzie. What a good pair of names, huh?"

Eliza beamed. "You can sit beside me on the couch, if you want."

"Okay," Izzy said, positively beaming. "I'd love that. Can I sit beside your mom, too?"

Eliza shrugged. "If you want to."

CHAPTER 17

Kiera snorted in amusement as Izzy settled on the couch beside her, Eliza climbing to sit on Izzy's side.

As the night stretched on and Muppet Treasure Island hit its stride, Quinn, half-asleep, burrowed deeper against where she was koala-ed into Kiera's side. "Mom?" she murmured sleepily.

Kiera smoothed a hand over her daughter's hair. "Yeah, baby?"

"Can Izzy stay for a sleepover?"

Kiera glanced at Izzy, who was already looking at her, amusement twinkling in her eyes.

"I'm honored," Izzy said. "But I have to get back and feed the spider living in my hotel room or she gets mad and eats all of my left shoes."

Quinn and Eliza giggled in amusement.

Kiera shook her head, laughing softly. "Nice try, Quinn."

Quinn made a small sound of disappointment but didn't argue. Within minutes, her breathing evened out, her small body finally giving in to sleep. Eliza wasn't far behind, her head resting against Izzy's shoulder.

Kiera let out a slow breath, taking in the scene before her. The dim lighting, the comfort of a movie she'd seen dozens of times quiet in the background, the warmth of her daughter curled against her. Izzy — here, familiar, fitting into Kiera's life, cozied up with Eliza like it was the most natural thing in the world... She was surprised by how right it felt.

She had never let herself think too hard about what could be between them. About what it would mean to let Izzy all the way in. Tonight, sitting here like this, still feeling the fizzing giddiness in her stomach even with a sick kid and a kids' movie on the screen, she couldn't help but wonder.

ONCE THE GIRLS were tucked in and the house had gone calm with quiet, Kiera tiptoed back downstairs. She found Izzy in the living room, collecting plates and folding up the stray blankets that had ended up in a heap during movie night.

"You really didn't have to clean up," Kiera said, lingering in the doorway.

Izzy glanced back over her shoulder, smiling. "I know. But I wanted to."

Kiera walked over, brushing her fingers against Izzy's as she took one of the plates from her hands. That tiny contact was enough to spark something — not just electricity, but something steadier beneath it. Something that had been waiting all night for space to bloom.

"Thanks for a really nice date," Izzy said.

Kiera raised a skeptical brow. "You had to watch Muppet Treasure Island with a koala kid clinging to you. You're sure it was okay?"

"I loved it. Underrated movie, in my opinion. The cuddles were a bonus."

Kiera blushed, tenderness filling her chest.

They moved toward the door together, slow and quiet, the air between them thick with possibility. Kiera reached for the handle, but Izzy's hand got there first. Their fingers brushed again, this time staying there, neither of them pulling away.

Izzy looked up, eyes searching hers. "What?"

Kiera didn't answer. She just leaned in, let herself close the last few inches, and kissed her — slow, certain, wanting. Izzy kissed her back immediately, like they'd both been waiting for permission.

Her hands came to rest at Kiera's waist, and Kiera tilted forward into her like she couldn't help it. One kiss turned into another, deeper now, more urgent. Kiera let out the softest sigh against Izzy's mouth, her fingers curling in the fabric of Izzy's shirt.

And that's when the front door opened.

Keys jingled, the doorknob turned, and Kiera barely had

time to break the kiss and jump back — breathless, lips tingling, heart absolutely slamming in her chest.

"Oh!" her mom said brightly, stepping inside with her tote bag slung over one arm. "We're home!"

Her dad followed a second later, stopping short just behind her. "Evening."

Kiera froze, her hand still half-raised, like she could pretend she'd just been… gesturing.

Izzy straightened, cheeks flushed, but to her credit, she didn't bolt. She smiled — smiled, like this wasn't mortifying — and gave a small wave. "Hi. Sorry. I was just heading out."

Kiera wanted to crawl under the couch and die. "We were just… uh…"

"Kissing, yes, we noticed," her mom said, not unkindly. "Izzy, it's so nice to see you again after so long. We've heard so much about you lately."

"You have?" Izzy asked, voice a little too high.

Kiera groaned internally.

Her mom smiled. "Only good things, I promise."

Her dad gave a nod that somehow managed to be both chill and conspiratorial. "She lights up when she talks about you."

"Dad."

"What? It's true." Her dad raised a shoulder in a shrug, tossing his keys onto the entryway table behind Kiera.

Kiera wanted to melt into the floor. She could feel Izzy trying very, very hard not to laugh beside her.

"Well," Izzy said, eyes dancing, "I should probably go before I get you in more trouble."

"You're not in trouble," her mom said cheerfully. "Unless you count making us feel ancient for interrupting."

Izzy bit her lip, grinning now. She turned to Kiera, her voice softer. "Text me later?"

Kiera nodded, still pink with embarrassment but also strangely, absurdly happy. "Yeah. Definitely."

She walked Izzy to the door, this time without touching her, and watched her go with a flutter still working its way through her chest.

Her parents disappeared down the hall, already talking about leftovers, like nothing had happened at all.

Kiera stood there a moment longer, hand on the doorknob, trying not to grin like a fool.

She felt fifteen. And seen. And maybe just a little bit adored.

CHAPTER 18

Izzy

THE AIR WAS WARM WITH THE LINGERING HEAT OF THE DAY AS Izzy and Kiera walked side by side along the path encircling Sloan's Lake. The sky stretched out in front of them — deep oranges melting into dusky pinks, fading into the quiet glow of twilight. They walked slowly, their arms occasionally brushing, each touch easy, unspoken.

Izzy glanced over at Kiera, who was staring out at the horizon with a small, thoughtful smile on her face. The last bit of sunlight caught in the loose waves of her hair, and Izzy had the absurd thought that she wished she could take a picture, just to remember the moment

"This is nice," Kiera said, looking over at her, voice quiet but certain. "I'm glad this is our re-do and not something weird like staring at each other across a tablecloth."

Izzy smiled. "Yeah," she admitted. "I like our goo phase."

Kiera laughed. "What the hell is a goo phase?"

Izzy shook her head, but she didn't stop smiling. "Okay, so when caterpillars go into their little chrysalis to turn into a butterfly, they don't just sprout wings. They literally turn into a liquidy, soupy substance, and that metamorphoses into the butterfly. This is *our* goo phase. You know. As us."

"Goo," Kiera said, nodding. "The goo phase of metamorphosis. I like that. You know, you're adorably nerdy when you're spouting off random animal facts." She teased, bumping her shoulder against Izzy's. "It's very cute."

They walked on in silence, stepping out of the way for joggers, kids on bikes, and people speedwalking their dogs. Izzy kept glancing over toward Kiera, trying to find the right opening.

"I've been thinking about the mentorship program at Second Star," she said finally, voice more casual than she felt. "It's grown fast. I kind of built the framework on instinct and vibes — and a few too many Google Docs — but now it's real. There are expectations. Actual structure. And I want it to be more than just... throwing cool adults at overwhelmed teens."

Kiera smiled. "Cool adults are a good start."

"Sure," Izzy said. "But I need someone who knows how to turn all this potential into something sustainable. You know education — how kids learn, how to meet them where they are. You know how to scaffold things, and evaluate progress, and—" She broke off, realizing she was rambling. "Basically, I trust you to help make this more than a pretty idea."

Kiera was quiet for a beat, processing. "You already have the heart of it, Izzy. You know what these kids need. I just speak fluent 'lesson plan.'"

"Exactly." Izzy looked at her fully now. "That's why I'm asking. I don't want a consultant. I want *you*. I want your opinion. Your ideas. Your voice on this."

Another pause — longer this time — then Kiera nodded, that small, thoughtful frown she always made when she was weighing something she cared about.

"Okay," she said softly. "I'd love to help you in any way I can."

And Izzy smiled, because it felt like more than just a yes.

CHAPTER 18

She wanted to say something — something teasing, something flirty and suggestive — but then her phone buzzed in her pocket. Maggie's name lit up her screen with a call coming through.

"Should we tell her we're on a date?" Kiera said, grinning mischievously.

"Only if you're ready for the meddling," Izzy said.

"Pete and Danica are already bad enough. What's one more?" Kiera quipped.

Izzy grinned, swiping to answer. "Well, hello there." She held the phone up to Kiera in case she wanted to chime in, then continued. "Maggie, you have excellent timing. We have to tell you something scandalous."

But instead of the playful retort she expected, there was nothing. Just a shaky inhale, a wobbling, gasping breath.

Izzy's stomach turned cold. "Mags?"

Then Maggie sobbed. A sound so raw, so devastating, that it made Izzy's knees feel weak.

Kiera's smile vanished in an instant. "Maggie?" she asked softly, stepping closer.

Izzy's heart was already racing. "Maggie, what's wrong? What happened?"

Another breath, another choked, unsteady exhale.

"My mom," Maggie finally whispered, her words sounding strangled. "My mom... a heart attack."

Izzy's throat tightened, and she didn't know how, but she *knew*. The words weren't there yet, but they didn't have to be. "What do you mean? Is she in the hospital?"

"She came over for dinner, and then I walked back in from the kitchen, and she was gone. Just like that. The paramedics just left like an hour ago, and I... I don't know what to do."

"Oh, Maggie," Izzy breathed.

Maggie let out another broken sound.

Kiera's hand lay gently on her shoulder, grounding her. Izzy squeezed her eyes shut, inhaled through her nose, then forced the words out. "Is Gwen there? Do you want me to come?"

Maggie didn't answer — just cried, and Izzy could *hear* the devastation in it, the bottomless grief, the way her whole world had just turned upside down. It reminded her of when Maggie had called after her pregnancy termination. How Izzy had helped just by being there to do whatever Maggie and Gwen needed, taking care of the kids, helping her two friends through one of the worst traumas of their lives.

Kiera had her phone out, texting someone. She turned her phone toward Izzy and showed her Gwen's response. She was in Lisbon and trying to get a flight, but even hopping a flight immediately, she couldn't make it back until tomorrow afternoon. Kiera met Izzy's gaze and nodded, encouraging.

"Okay, Mags, I'll be there soon," Izzy said, as steady as she could.

"Okay," Maggie said, her voice small.

Izzy swallowed past the lump in her throat, forcing herself into action. She immediately opened the airline app, her hands shaking so badly she could barely type.

"God, poor Maggie. Are you seriously going to fly out there tonight?" Kiera asked, her voice gentle.

"I have to." Izzy was already moving, already turning back toward the parking lot.

Kiera was right beside her, matching her frantic pace. "Okay, I get it, especially with Gwen overseas. I'll drive you home, help you pack—"

"I'm... I think I'm just going to go straight to the airport." Izzy was already looking at flight options while she walked, looking for the soonest possible departure. She blinked back tears as her hands shook.

Kiera stopped them both in their tracks, reaching out, her hands gripping Izzy's shoulders. "Izzy. *Breathe.*"

Izzy sucked in a sharp breath, trying to keep it together, but her whole body was vibrating with worry, with grief that wasn't even *hers* but felt like it might swallow her whole. She looked up at Kiera, who reached to wrap her in a tight hug. Izzy let herself be held tightly, taking slow, deep breaths against Kiera's soft T-shirt.

"Hey, I'm here to help however I can," Kiera said in a hushed, gentle tone.

When Izzy was ready, she leaned back and looked up to Kiera, who was watching her with a steady gaze. "Can you drive?"

Kiera nodded, no hint of uncertainty. "Okay. I'll drive you to the airport, and then I'll drive your car to my parent's place."

Izzy wrapped her arms around Kiera and gave her another tight hug. "Thank you."

It was late by the time Izzy pulled up in front of Maggie's house. The porch light was on, casting long shadows across the lawn, but the house was oppressively still and dark — like it was holding its breath.

Izzy sat for a moment in the silence of her car, hands gripping the steering wheel until her knuckles ached. She had barely slept on the flight. Couldn't eat. Every part of her body was heavy with exhaustion, but her mind wouldn't stop racing, grasping at the edges of every memory she had of Maggie's mom — her easy laugh, the way she always made Izzy feel welcome, like she was family.

The weight of it hit her all over again. *Maggie's mom is gone.*

Izzy swallowed hard and climbed out of the car. Her feet carried her to the front door on instinct, and she punched in the security code — still the same as it had been the last time she was here, when Maggie needed her after the pregnancy loss. That moment had felt like the end of the world. This felt worse.

She didn't bother knocking. The lock clicked open, and she stepped inside.

The house was dark except for a single lamp glowing dimly in the living room, casting long shadows against the walls. It smelled faintly of lavender and something burnt — maybe an untouched meal left too long in the oven.

Maggie sat curled up on the couch, wrapped in a blanket. Her eyes were swollen and red, her face blotchy with the evidence of hours of crying. And clutched tightly in her hands was a photo frame. Izzy didn't need to see the picture to know it was of her mom.

Maggie crumpled like paper folding in on itself as soon as she looked up at Izzy. Her breath hitched and then came the sound Izzy had been dreading — the kind of sob that shattered everything in its wake.

Izzy didn't think. She just moved.

She crossed the room in seconds, dropping to her knees in front of Maggie and pulling her in close. Maggie collapsed into her arms, shaking so hard it seemed like she might break apart. The photo frame clattered to the floor, as she clung to Izzy with every ounce of strength she had left.

"Fuck," Maggie choked out, her voice raw and barely audible. "She's gone. She's really gone."

"I'm so sorry," Izzy whispered, running her hand gently over Maggie's hair, pressing her cheek against the top of her head. "I'm here. You're not alone. I'm not going anywhere."

Maggie's sobs came harder, wrenching through her like something primal — like grief was clawing its way out of her. Every breath was ragged, every cry a reminder of what had been lost.

Izzy held her tighter, whispering soft, useless comforts. "You're not alone. I promise. I'm right here."

There were no words that could make this better. No comfort deep enough to patch the hole left behind by losing someone who had been integral in Maggie's world. This wasn't the kind of pain that could be fixed — it could only be endured.

So Izzy stayed there, on the floor of the dim living room, holding her friend as she broke apart. And when the sobs slowed, tapering into soft, hiccupping breaths, Izzy didn't let go.

CHAPTER 19

Kiera

Kiera sat stiffly at the kitchen table the next morning, staring at her phone beside a cooling cup of herbal tea that her mom had placed in front of her with gentle insistence. She'd texted Maggie an hour ago, just a quiet *I'm here if you need me,* and hadn't expected a reply. The scent of sage lingered in the air — a residue of the cleansing and calming ritual her parents had performed earlier that morning in the house after Kiera had told them about Maggie's mom passing. Her dad had finished pacing through the rooms, murmuring affirmations under his breath, ringing a small brass bell meant to bring peace and clarity.

Instead of clarity, Kiera felt a tension throughout her body, like a rope tightening inside her chest, pulling tighter with every breath.

Rationally, she knew that Maggie's mom dying shouldn't affect her so much, but it brought so many intense thoughts to the surface. She worried about her own parent's dying, her friend's grief, Izzy's panic. The way Izzy's hands shook as she booked her flight to get to Maggie.

She sent Izzy a good morning text, then asked how Maggie was feeling.

Izzy: She's existing. Barely eating. Barely sleeping. Just… frozen. It's awful, actually.

Kiera: Fuck, that does sound awful.

Izzy: And the kids, they're like extra weird because Maggie's weird. Arlo tried to push Jude down the stairs like some little psycho this morning.

"Mommy, can we have cookies for breakfast?" Eliza asked suddenly, her hopeful eyes cutting through Kiera's spiraling thoughts. "They are oatmeal chocolate chip, and oatmeal is a breakfast food."

"Yeah, cookies!" Quinn chimed in, bouncing on her toes.

Kiera forced a smile and reached out to ruffle Quinn's hair. "That is a surprisingly good argument, Eliza. Go for it."

The girls cheered and ran toward the cookie jar, their excitement cutting through the heavy silence that had settled over the house. It should've been comforting — these small, ordinary moments — but her thoughts kept drifting back to Maggie. To the raw, broken sound of her voice on the phone. The exhaustion laced into every word when Izzy called late last night.

Maggie's mom was gone. Just like that. She'd died of a heart attack, gone within seconds. Every life ended too soon was a dark reminder of how fragile every day was.

A wave of grief for both Maggie and her mom washed over Kiera, an unexpected ache blossoming in her entire body.

Her parents were moving around the house in a gentle, hovering way — close but giving her space. Her mom puttered near the sink, pretending to busy herself with dishes that didn't need washing. Her dad was adjusting a plant by the window for the third time.

Kiera couldn't take it anymore.

She crossed the kitchen and wrapped her arms around her

CHAPTER 19

mom in a tight hug. Her mom stilled for a moment, surprised, before returning the embrace with soft, steady hands on Kiera's back.

"I love you, Mom," Kiera whispered, her voice catching.

Her mom pulled back just enough to look at her, brushing a tear off Kiera's cheek with her thumb. "Aw, love you too, honey. More than I probably say out loud."

Kiera turned to her dad and stepped into his arms. He wrapped her up in a firm, familiar hug and kissed the top of her head.

"I just... needed to say it," she murmured. "I don't want to take any of this for granted."

Her dad gave her a squeeze. "You don't. You never have. We've got you, kiddo. Always."

Their presence helped her breathe easier, but it didn't make the heaviness go away.

"Do you want us to watch the girls so you can go out and be with Maggie?" Her mom asked, voice soft as she rubbed Kiera's back. "And Izzy?"

Tears welled in Kiera's eyes and she sniffled, nodding. "I think flights might be pretty expensive, and I think her mom's service is in just a few days."

"Money is a stupid thing to get in the way of being there for the ones you love. We can help with whatever cost and watch the girls for however long you need," her dad responded.

Kiera wiped at her eyes. "Thank you, both. So much. Have I told you lately—"

"That I love you," her mom burst into song, interrupting her.

Kiera shook her head. "Oh, no."

"You fill my heart with gladness," her dad added, not even trying to be in the right key. Or a key at all, it seemed.

"You're being ridiculous." Kiera smiled through her tears. "I was going to say that I really do appreciate you."

"Could you say we ease your troubles?" her dad said, ruffling her hair in exactly the same way she'd ruffled Quinn's hair a few moments before. "That's what we do."

"How did I ever turn out normal with parents like you?" Kiera teased.

"Oh, John," her mom said, pressing a hand to her chest like she was emotional over something adorable. "She thinks *she's* the normal one."

Kiera rolled her eyes.

Her dad put a hand on her shoulder, steadying and supportive. "Okay, now go to Austin and don't worry about us."

KIERA

> I can be there around 2pm, if you need me. And if you think Maggie would be okay with that.

IZZY

> I would never say no. But you don't have to. I'd never want to ask you to be away from your girls.

KIERA

> I'm coming. I'll send you my flight details.

IZZY

> Okay. Yeah. Yeah, I'd really like that. See you soon, then.

THE FLIGHT to Austin was a blur. When Kiera finally arrived, Maggie's house was heavy with the kind of silence that lingered after loss. She let herself in with the code Izzy had given her, the weight of grief pressing against her chest before she even stepped inside.

CHAPTER 19

Maggie was curled up on the couch, her blonde hair pulled into a messy bun. She was wrapped in one of her mom's old cardigans, her body small and hunched over, like she was trying to disappear. Izzy sat beside her, a hand on her arm. The kids sat on the floor, watching a movie and playing with a magnetic tile set. "Hey champs," Kiera said gently to the kids, who she'd only ever met on Facetime. They barely even looked up from the elaborate garage they were building as Kiera crossed the room and sat next to Maggie, pulling her into a gentle hug.

"Hey, Mags," Kiera whispered, brushing Maggie's hair from her face. What else was there to say? That she was sorry? That she was here to help? No words could come close to being the right ones, so instead she did the only thing she knew was right. She held space for whatever Maggie needed.

Maggie didn't speak, didn't react. She just folded into Kiera's embrace and shook with silent, gut-wrenching sobs. Kiera gently rubbed Maggie's back, offering comfort.

She met Izzy's eyes, noticing the heavy circles there. She was right to have come. She reached out and squeezed Izzy's arm in silent greeting.

Kiera and Izzy sat like that for hours, flanking Maggie on the couch, shifting only when she needed something — someone's hand to squeeze, a shoulder to lean on, a tissue passed wordlessly. One of them would get up occasionally to fix snacks or warm leftovers from the fridge, to refill juice cups or remind the kids to take a few bites of something. They kept encouraging Maggie to eat too, nudging a bowl of soup into her hands or unwrapping a granola bar and setting it beside her without saying anything. No one filled the silence with advice or platitudes. They just stayed close, offering what they could.

They watched both *Frozen* movies, then *Moana*, the TV quietly looping through familiar songs and bright animation while the afternoon slipped quietly into evening.

Eventually, the front door clicked open and Kiera glanced up to see Gwen walk in. Her shoulders were tight with worry, dark eyes shadowed by exhaustion. She looked worn, like she had been carrying her own version of heartbreak the whole way here. The kids ran to her, shouting and excited to see their mom. Maggie flinched at the noise, then turned toward Gwen but didn't move. Her face was unreadable — no tears of relief, no rush into Gwen's arms. Just... blank.

Izzy glanced toward Kiera, brow furrowed, but didn't say anything.

Kiera stiffened slightly, then moved from Maggie's side. She and Izzy both stood to give Gwen a hug, then cleared out of the way and ushered the kids toward the kitchen to give Gwen and Maggie some space.

Kiera tried not to eavesdrop as she passed out fruit snacks to twins Arlo and Jude and their little sister Rosie.

She needn't worry about overhearing something. The silence coming from the living room was thick and uncomfortable. When she glanced toward the couch, she saw Gwen and Maggie sitting together on the couch. Maggie, however, pulled her cardigan tight like a shield, turning slightly away from Gwen.

Kiera's heart twisted painfully in her chest. She leaned into Izzy, wanting to feel the comfort and warmth of her. Instead of her usual scent of cherry and ginger, Izzy smelled simply of fresh laundry. Izzy's gentle hug was a balm to her soul, an easy thing to hold onto in the darkness of the moment. "I just feel powerless to help her," Kiera whispered.

Izzy chest hummed against Kiera's ear as she spoke. "I know."

"She's just *so* sad," Kiera murmured.

Izzy sighed, her voice softening. "I know."

. . .

CHAPTER 19

Later, after the house quieted and the kids were finally asleep, Kiera sat on the back patio with Izzy, sharing the silence between them. The night air was thick with the scent of jasmine. The Texas heat had relented, a slow breeze rustling the trees in the backyard, carrying the distant buzz of cicadas.

Kiera sighed, stretching her legs out in front of her, the wooden deck warm beneath her bare feet. She rolled a cold bottle of beer between her palms before taking a sip, the grapefruit and spice a welcome change from the herbal tea she'd been making Maggie all afternoon.

"I don't get it," she whispered, staring out into the night, her voice barely more than a breath. "Why is Maggie being so cold to Gwen?"

Izzy was curled up in the patio chair beside her, one knee pulled to her chest, the other foot tucked beneath her. She exhaled slowly before taking a drink of her own beer, tilting her head back slightly as she swallowed. The glow from the patio light caught the angles of her face, the shadow of her lashes against her cheekbones.

"When my dad died," Izzy said, her voice quieter than usual, "I couldn't handle being close to the people who should have made me feel better."

Kiera turned to look at her, studying the way Izzy's fingers tightened just slightly around the bottle in her hands. "Like, your mom?"

Izzy gave a small, tight smile, though there was no humor in it. "Yeah. Well, I don't know why I ever expected that. My mom wasn't the most... affectionate, I guess. I do believe my therapist has used the word, 'withholding of love.' After Dad died, that tie completely unraveled. We aren't close or anything now."

"That's so hard. I'm so sorry you had to endure that." Kiera said quietly, waiting for Izzy to feel comfortable enough to continue.

"But grief has this way of sneaking up on you when you least expect it. Like, now, being around another grieving person makes me feel my own grief all over again." Izzy let out a soft, breathy laugh. "Like some asshole lurking in the dark, waiting for the right moment to punch you in the gut."

Kiera smiled despite herself at the frank description, shaking her head.

A silent moment followed Izzy's words, a shared understanding hanging in the air between them. Kiera sipped her beer again, feeling the fizz on her tongue, the cold glass a contrast to the evening's heat.

"I just wish I could help more," Kiera admitted, rubbing a thumb over the condensation on the bottle. "I thought that when Gwen got here, Maggie would feel a little better, but it's like she can't even look at her for more than a few seconds."

Izzy shifted, resting her head against the back of her chair, her gaze flickering over to Kiera. "I wonder if the person you love the most is the hardest person to be around when you're falling apart." Her voice was softer now, more thoughtful. "Because they know you. They see all of it. And if they reach for you and you let them in, it's like admitting to yourself just how bad it really is. It's like... it hurts more to be comforted because it forces you to feel everything."

She understood now in a way she never would have before — before the divorce, before she was forced to rebuild from the ground up. Sometimes it was easier to keep moving, to avoid looking too closely at the wreckage. Letting someone witness the full extent of your grief meant acknowledging it yourself, and maybe Maggie wasn't ready for that.

Kiera nodded slowly, letting the thought settle. "I don't know. I think there's something really beautiful in letting the people you love most see you and love you through the mess."

The cicadas buzzed through the brief silence that stretched out.

CHAPTER 19

Izzy let out a small hum of consideration. "Maybe I've just never had that kind of love."

Kiera sighed. "Yeah, I certainly haven't had it in a partner."

Still, Kiera hated feeling helpless when it came to helping Maggie through it.

She looked at Izzy, watching her fingers trace idle patterns along the condensation of her bottle, catching the distant look in her eyes. "How long ago did your dad pass?"

"My senior year of high school." Izzy hesitated for a moment before nodding. "Yeah. I shut down. Pushed my brother and my mom away... though, to be fair, neither put up much of a fight. I don't regret not talking to either of them, don't get me wrong." A small, bitter smile flickered across her lips before disappearing. "But I got really good at pretending I was fine."

Kiera watched her for a long moment, feeling the weight of that admission settle in the air between them. Izzy had been dealing with that all those years ago and Kiera had never even known. She wondered if Izzy even realized how much she was revealing, how much she was letting Kiera see.

On impulse, Kiera took Izzy's hand, her fingers entwining with Izzy's. "You don't have to pretend with me," Kiera murmured.

Izzy pressed her mouth into a thin line as though she was thinking deeply. She looked down at their joined hands, her thumb brushing lightly against Kiera's before she squeezed back.

"What I'm trying to say is, you're doing enough for Maggie by just being here," Izzy whispered. "And for me."

"Listen, before Danica and Pete get here... should we talk about..." Kiera started, gesturing with her bottle to Izzy and back to herself. "Us?"

"Can I be honest? I'm so emotionally exhausted from

being here that I don't think I can take Pete and Danica's pestering questions on top of everything," Izzy admitted.

"No, I completely agree. I was going to say that maybe we should just keep it quiet for now, since we need to all focus on Maggie. But we're still... good, right?" She asked, feeling only slightly awkward.

Izzy smiled, pulling Kiera's hand to give her knuckles a kiss. "We're still good."

Kiera swallowed past the sudden lump in her throat, nodding. "Good."

Kiera balanced her phone between her shoulder and ear as she poured pancake batter onto the griddle, the sizzle of the batter filling the quiet kitchen. "I know you and Pete are stressed about not being able to get here today," she told Danica, flipping a pancake with practiced ease. "But Maggie's aunt will be here soon, and a few of her cousins just arrived, so the house is already packed. It's no problem to get here tomorrow for the service."

Danica sighed on the other end of the line. "That makes sense. I just..." She groaned. "I hate not being there."

Kiera glanced over at the dining table, where Maggie's five-year-old twins, Arlo and Jude, were coloring. Their little sister, three-year-old Rosie, was perched on her knees beside them, gripping a crayon like it was a sword. A few feet away, Gwen sat at the far end of the table, a mug of untouched coffee in front of her, her hand running absently through her short salt and pepper hair. She hadn't been talking much since she arrived. She was there, present in the house, but the space between her and Maggie felt so thick it was almost suffocating.

"I know. But Izzy and are keeping the wheels on for now," Kiera reassured Danica. She paused, glancing at Gwen again.

CHAPTER 19

"Just trying to make sure everything stays as steady as it can."

"I trust you," Danica said. "And how are *you* doing?"

Kiera hesitated, pressing the spatula against one of the pancakes. The warmth of her connection with Izzy from the previous night lingered; she recalled Izzy's shy smile that morning in the guest bathroom as they brushed their teeth. Izzy had crashed on the couch after insisting that Kiera take the guest bedroom. Kiera finally said, "Just trying not to think of how many chickens the girls are going to con my parents into buying while I'm gone."

"Oh, you think they're hatching a plan?" Danica said with an amused tone.

"Of course they are — Wait a second, I just got that." Kiera laughed.

"Took you a moment. I thought it was pretty egg-cellent."

"Did my parents give you this script?" Kiera teased.

Danica let out an even louder laugh. "You're right, I should text your mom to remind her how funny I am."

"She'd love it," Kiera assured her.

"Chicken puns aside, how are you doing there?" Danica pressed.

"I'm doing fine," Kiera finally said.

"If you say so." Danica made a small sound that told Kiera she wasn't convinced, but thankfully, she didn't push. "Just let me know if anything changes. And tell Maggie we love her, okay?"

"Of course." Kiera slid the last of the pancakes onto a plate, then balanced it on her arm as she turned back toward the table. "Gotta go, I'm on breakfast duty."

She hung up just as Arlo perked up. "Is it ready now?"

"Patience, my tiny minions." Kiera set the plate of golden pancakes in the center of the table, ruffling his hair and suddenly feeling homesick to see Eliza and Quinn. She'd called them early this morning, and they'd sounded sweet and sleepy. She hoped she'd get to call them again that afternoon. "But yes. It's ready now."

Jude gasped dramatically. "Butter! We need butter!"

Kiera told them to take a deep breath, setting down a bowl of softened butter and a jar of syrup. The kids dug in immediately, all sticky fingers and happy chatter. She let herself take a beat, absorbing the normalcy of the moment, the illusion that, for a little while, everything was okay.

As she turned to grab her cup of coffee from the counter, she caught sight of Gwen finally stirring from her seat, rubbing at her temple before standing. It was the first time Kiera had seen her look anything other than frozen since she arrived.

"Gwen, do you want something to eat?" Kiera asked, keeping her voice light.

Gwen blinked, as if only just realizing she was being spoken to. "Oh. Uh, sure. Thanks." She hesitated, then sighed, rubbing the back of her neck. "Sorry. I'm still — jet lag, I guess."

"This is a lot. You're allowed to feel exhausted about it." Kiera tilted her head. "You flew in from Lisbon, right?"

Gwen nodded, pressing her lips together before finally sitting back down. "Yeah. I was at a conference for work when Maggie called. I caught the first flight I could, but..." She exhaled slowly, shaking her head.

Kiera handed her a plate, watching Gwen poke at the pancakes absently. "Was it an architecture thing?"

"Yeah. I was supposed to present on sustainable urban development. Spent months preparing, but..." She trailed off, jaw tightening as she set her fork down. "None of it feels important now."

Kiera hesitated before sitting across from her. "That seriously sucks. I'm so sorry. Do you think you'll be able to reuse your presentation at another conference?"

CHAPTER 19

Gwen looked at her for a long moment, then nodded. "I hope so."

Before Kiera could say anything else, Izzy appeared beside her, close enough that Kiera could feel the brush of her arm. Izzy reached for a spoon, stirring her own coffee absently.

Kiera glanced at her, catching the faint dark circles under Izzy's eyes, the tension in her shoulders as she slid into a seat beside her. The past two days had taken a toll on all of them.

Izzy exhaled, then, without a word, reached under the table and gave Kiera's hand a quick, firm squeeze.

A secret moment just for them. Kiera stifled a smile that would have revealed exactly how much just a simple hand squeeze could make her feel giddy.

The spell was broken when Jude shouted, "Aunt Izzy, I need more syrup!"

Izzy pulled back, clearing her throat. "On it, kiddo," she called back, reaching for the syrup bottle and handing it over.

Kiera swallowed, her hands still tingling where Izzy had touched her.

CHAPTER 20

Izzy

The morning of the funeral, the house was quiet with the kids taking naps in their rooms, leaving only the muffled sounds of Maggie's aunts murmuring in the living room and the occasional clatter from the kitchen. Izzy leaned against the counter, nursing the last of her coffee, when the front door suddenly swung open with zero warning.

"The Comfort Brigade has arrived!" Pete's voice boomed through the house, immediately breaking the fragile silence.

Izzy nearly choked.

Kiera, sitting at the table flipping through the funeral program details, did not even flinch.

Izzy barely had time to react before Pete came barreling into the house, suitcase in tow. Danica followed behind with a much more reasonable expression of concern.

Maggie looked up from her spot on the couch, where she had been staring blankly at the ceiling. Her face shifted slightly, relief flickering through the exhaustion. "You guys are here."

Pete dropped her bag immediately and crossed the room in four strides, dragging Maggie into a bone-crushing hug.

"Of course we're here." Pete's voice was softer now, her usual bravado muted by the reality of why they were all gathered. "You think we'd let you go through this without us?"

Maggie let out a shaky breath against Pete's shoulder, clutching her back like she was grounding herself. "You don't know how much I need this right now."

Danica, less of a human battering ram than Pete, settled next to Maggie and offered a gentle smile. "We brought emergency snacks, and I have a fully drafted medical excuse to get you out of talking to any relatives you don't want to deal with."

Pete grinned, finally pulling back. "And by emergency snacks, she means we raided a gas station on the way here, and I may or may not have bought a questionable amount of gummy worms."

Maggie actually huffed out a weak laugh, shaking her head. "Appreciate it."

Pete moved to hug Gwen on the opposite side of the room next, and Izzy watched as Gwen tensed before relaxing into the hug. Izzy glanced toward Maggie to see if she was looking at Gwen, but she was consumed in giving Danica a bone-crushing hug. There was distance, thick and heavy, every time Gwen and Maggie were in the same room.

Pete, oblivious to the underlying tension, greeted Izzy and Kiera, then flopped onto the couch beside Maggie like she had claimed it as her personal throne. "What do you need, baby cakes? Coffee? Please tell me someone has coffee. Danica made me get to the airport like two hours early."

Gwen finally piped up. "I could make a fresh pot if anyone else wants some?"

For the first time in days, Maggie actually looked right at Gwen. "Yeah, that sounds good."

CHAPTER 20

Izzy had never seen a person move so fast. Gwen's desperation to help Maggie was palpable. Kiera raised a brow, locking eyes with Izzy, as if to question if they'd both noticed it. Perhaps the stalemate was over.

IZZY HAD ASSUMED that the most stressful part of the afternoon of the funeral would be keeping Maggie from spiraling into a complete emotional shutdown. She was wrong.

The most stressful part was the dress.

"Ohmyfuckinggod," Maggie whispered as she sat down on the edge of her bed, staring at the black dress in her hands in utter horror. It was ruined, covered in dozens of spots in shades of gray and yellow.

"It's really bad, isn't it?" Gwen asked, her face stricken with guilt as she hovered nearby, her nervous energy palpable in the way she was wringing her hands. "I was trying to get the wrinkles out and used the spray bottle, but I must have grabbed the wrong one."

Maggie didn't move or respond. She just kept staring at the dress like it had personally betrayed her. Or worse, like Gwen had personally betrayed her.

Izzy had only come in to ask Gwen for a pair of black socks when she'd seen the spotted dress in Maggie's hands. She now attempted to leave, determined not to witness a murder. Unfortunately, she had nowhere to escape, because the second she reached the hallway, Kiera and Danica nearly collided into her.

"What happened?" Kiera asked, her hand on Izzy's arm.

Izzy pinched the bridge of her nose. "Gwen accidentally bleached the funeral dress."

Kiera and Danica both froze.

Then, at the exact same time: "Oh, shit."

Izzy chanced a glance behind her. Gwen looked miserable.

"Maggie, I'm so sorry," she said, taking a tentative step forward. "I should've double-checked—"

Maggie finally moved, running a hand through her blonde hair before pressing the heels of her palms against her eyes. Her breathing had gone a little too shallow, a little too fast, and Izzy recognized the signs of an anxiety attack.

"It's fine," Maggie said, her voice oddly and terrifyingly detached. "I'll just — I'll wear something else."

Kiera and Danica exchanged a silent, panicked conversation via eyebrow movements. Before Izzy could stop them, Kiera said in a voice that was half-strangled with panic and half-desperate with optimism, "Or, we can fix it!"

Maggie dropped her hands, looking at Kiera with flat skepticism. "Fix bleach? Is there some magic un-bleaching potion I don't know about?"

Kiera, undaunted, announced, "I have a Sharpie."

A long, tense silence ensued.

Izzy blinked. "I'm sorry... what?"

Kiera ignored her, already digging through her purse. "Look, we just color it in, and no one will notice. It's mostly at the bottom of the dress anyway. Who is staring at your hemline during a funeral?"

Maggie stared. Then looked at Danica. Then back at Kiera. "You're actually suggesting that I color the dress that I am wearing to my mother's funeral with Sharpie."

Danica sighed, rubbing her temples. "I can't believe I'm saying this, but... Kiera might be right."

Maggie, to everyone's surprise, didn't immediately shut it down. She looked at the dress again, brows drawn tight, jaw tense. Then, slowly, painfully, she exhaled. "...If it looks terrible, I am not liable for any ensuing homicidal rage," she warned.

"It would be deserved," Kiera said solemnly, pulling a marker out of her bag with a large smile.

Izzy watched warily as Kiera and Danica dropped to the

floor near where Maggie sat on the bed, Sharpie in hand, and got to work. Danica held the dress taut while Kiera scribbled.

Gwen, still hovering nearby, shifted uncomfortably. "Baby, I really feel awful about this."

Maggie shook her head, rubbing at her face. "It's fine," she muttered, voice tight. "It's not a big deal."

Maggie, whether she realized it or not, had been keeping a space between them.

Worse yet, Gwen didn't seem to be pushing to close it.

Izzy watched Gwen's face carefully. Her expression was frustrated but muted, like she wanted to argue but didn't know how.

A few minutes later, Kiera and Danica sat back, surveying their work like two proud artists unveiling a masterpiece.

"Okay," Kiera said, wiping her hands dramatically. "It's done."

Maggie leaned forward cautiously, inspecting the freshly Sharpied section of her dress.

After a long pause, she narrowed her eyes. "I cannot believe I'm about to say this, but… it actually looks fine."

Kiera grinned. "Told you. We're professionals."

Izzy couldn't help noticing how adorable Kiera was with her self-satisfied smile.

Danica stood, dusting her skirt off. "Crisis averted. Now, go get dressed."

Maggie exhaled slowly, then stood, rolling her shoulders like she was physically shaking off the stress. "Yeah," she murmured. "Okay."

As she disappeared into the bathroom to change, Izzy exchanged a glance with Gwen. Gwen looked… adrift, hollow. Izzy didn't know what to do with that. Instead of acknowledging it, she turned to Kiera and Danica, arms crossed.

"I can't believe you just Sharpied a funeral dress," Izzy said, completely deadpan. "How do you sleep at night?"

"Danica snores," Pete said, and Izzy turned to find Pete leaning against the doorframe.

"I do not," Danica said.

"You do," Kiera said with a sigh.

Gwen sighed and pushed past Pete, mumbling something about Arlo's suit, and Pete gave the group a wide-eyed look of surprise.

"What is going on with Gwen and Maggie? They've hardly even looked at one another today," Danica said, her voice a whisper.

Kiera shrugged. "I don't know. It's been like that since I've been here, so I'm not sure if it's something bigger or just Maggie's way of grieving."

"By pushing away her wife? Nah. Something's way off," Izzy said. "Even after Maggie's pregnancy loss, it wasn't like this."

"Well, now's not a good time," Danica said, glancing over her shoulder toward the hallway. "Maybe in a few weeks we could check in with Mags about it, but not now."

Izzy and Kiera both nodded.

"Alright, who is ready for a funeral?" Pete asked in a forcefully cheerful tone. "Any bets on how many salads that aren't really salads will be at the church after?"

THE SUN HUNG low in the sky, filtering soft light through the tree line beyond the church parking lot. The reception hall inside was still packed, filled with murmured condolences and the clinking of catering trays, but outside, tucked away on the worn stone steps at the back of the church, the five of them sat in much-needed silence.

Pete stretched her legs out, tipping her head back against the brick wall. "So... we all made it out alive."

"Debatable," Maggie muttered, making Izzy choke on her drink.

"Oh, yeah. Sorry. Wrong choice of words," Pete said with a grimace.

Danica, ever the doctor, gave Maggie a once-over. "You should eat something."

Pete shuddered. "Who the hell decided funeral food had to be so aggressively 1950s? Who wants to mourn and eat *jellied salads* at the same time?"

"I mean, it's a miracle we haven't all burst from the casserole table alone," Izzy said, eyeing the nearly translucent potato dish Pete had abandoned earlier.

Kiera, who had been quiet for most of the conversation, finally spoke. "Who even invented the funeral potato? Like, at what point in history did someone decide, 'You know what this grief buffet needs? A metric ton of hash browns and cream of mushroom soup.'"

Maggie let out a heavy sigh, and Izzy followed her line of sight to where Gwen was playing with the kids on the small church playground.

Danica nodded solemnly. "And why is there always a rogue cereal topping? Like, 'We have to mourn, but let's not forget to add a solid layer of Corn Flakes for crunch.'"

Pete snorted, shaking her head. "I'm just saying, I better not die before you guys, because if I look down from the afterlife and see y'all serving up a tray of Funeral Surprise in my honor, I *will* haunt your asses."

"Haunt us all you want," Izzy said, nudging Pete's boot with her own. "You think we're *not* going to serve a buffet of aggressively Midwestern comfort foods at your funeral? We'll make sure there's an entire table dedicated to things suspended in Jell-O."

Pete groaned. "Disrespectful."

Maggie shook her head, lips twitching up into an almost-smile. "I would like to formally request zero Jell-O at my funeral, please."

"Noted," Kiera said, pressing a hand over her heart like

she was taking an oath. "But, in return, you have to promise that if I die first, you'll all sit here and reminisce about me while eating an exorbitant amount of cake."

"Oh, absolutely," Danica said without hesitation. "Red velvet, right?"

Kiera gave her an approving nod. "Exactly. None of that dry-ass vanilla cake. I want layers."

Pete let out a dramatic sigh, looking up at the church behind them. "I'm still relieved none of us spontaneously combusted upon entry. I was fully prepared for a queer flames situation."

"Oh, same," Izzy said, pulling her knees up and wrapping her arms around them. "I haven't stepped foot in a church in years. The whole time, I kept waiting for some old priest to sniff out the gay divorce and start throwing holy water on me."

"Please," Danica scoffed. "I was waiting for them to see all of us and start whispering about the woke gay agenda."

Maggie laughed, her voice catching slightly.

Kiera turned to Maggie, nudging her knee lightly. "Seriously, though, how are you feeling?"

Maggie exhaled slowly, staring out at the parking lot. "I don't know. It's all weird. It doesn't feel real yet."

No one had a good response. Because what could they say? It *was* weird. And awful. And none of them could fix it, or change it, or make it better.

Instead, they sat there, pressed together on the steps, their quiet presence doing more than words could. Pete pulled a granola bar from her pocket and handed it to Maggie without comment. Maggie rolled her eyes but took it anyway.

"You guys missed a spot," Maggie said calmly, pointing to her side.

Kiera pulled her Sharpie back out of her bag and pulled the cap off with her teeth, reaching to color directly on Maggie's dress while she was wearing it.

CHAPTER 20

"This is one of the stupidest things we've ever done, and that's really saying something." Maggie was the first to laugh, then Kiera, and then the rest joined in.

And for the first time all day, they weren't drowning in grief. They were just friends, sitting on a church step, cracking jokes, finding solace in each other's company.

CHAPTER 21

Kiera

Izzy and Kiera sat side by side at a picnic table tucked into the back patio of a coffee shop just off South Congress, the afternoon light keeping everything just a little on the warm side of comfortable. Izzy's iced matcha was sweating into a ring on the wood; Kiera's black coffee had already gone lukewarm.

They'd stolen a moment while Maggie still had plenty of family around the day after the funeral. Danica and Pete had left that morning, a whirlwind of a trip before Danica's next 36-hour shift started that evening.

A legal pad sat between them, half-filled with Izzy's looping handwriting and a smattering of post-its that Kiera had meticulously color-coded by theme.

Kiera liked the quiet buzz of the place — the low hum of conversation, the faint clink of dishes behind the counter. But mostly, she liked sitting here with Izzy, completely unhurried. It reminded her of the staff lounges she used to hide in between classes — except this time, someone actually wanted her opinion.

Izzy tapped her pen against her mouth, staring at the page. "So we've got guest speakers, resume workshops, and mock interviews. That's solid. But it still feels a little... flat. We need something with more impact."

Kiera glanced at the notes. "What about a science module?" she offered. "Something hands-on — a mini STEM challenge that builds over a few weeks. They'd get collaboration, time management, trial and error — it sneaks the life skills in without making it feel like school."

Izzy turned to her, eyes bright. "See? This is exactly why I asked you. You know how to make this make sense to kids. I've got the dream, but you've got the structure."

Kiera's face warmed, and she looked down at the pad. "I can definitely do structure."

"And I know these kids," Izzy went on, her voice softening. "I don't want to throw a generic playbook at them. I want to make something real — and I want your help to do it right."

Kiera looked over at her, surprised by the sincerity in Izzy's voice. "I want that too. Honestly, it feels good to be useful again."

Izzy smiled and scribbled *STEM Project Arc* onto the pad. "You are. In, like, a wildly impressive way."

Kiera let out a quiet laugh. "You're the big-picture thinker. I just know how to build the scaffolding to hold it up."

Izzy leaned her elbow on the table and bumped Kiera's shoulder. "Scaffolding is underrated. Let's build something that holds."

They bent back over the notes, arms brushing occasionally as they worked, both of them leaning in without realizing it. Kiera didn't say what she was thinking — that this, all of it, felt like more than just curriculum planning. It felt like momentum. Like belonging.

Like maybe this was the beginning of something neither of them had words for yet.

CHAPTER 21

. . .

Silence filled the house. Not just the absence of voices, but the kind of deep, settling quiet that only came after days of relentless noise — hushed conversations, dishes being washed, and children laughing. Now, with most of the guests gone and the rest asleep, the heavy weight of grief settled back over the space.

Kiera moved carefully through the dim hallway, her socks barely making a sound against the hardwood floor. The guest room door was slightly ajar, just enough for her to see the faint glow of a bedside lamp and the rise and fall of Izzy's breathing beneath the blankets.

She should go back to her own room. She knew that. But she hesitated, lingering in the doorway, her fingers wrapping around the edge of the frame.

Tomorrow, she'd be leaving, and she didn't know when she'd see Izzy next.

Taking a quiet breath, she slipped inside, shutting the door softly behind her. Izzy was lying on her side, her back to the door, one arm tucked under her pillow. The blanket had slipped down slightly, exposing the line of her shoulder, the soft curve of her back.

"You okay?" Izzy asked. Her voice was thick with exhaustion, but there was no surprise in her tone. Like she had expected this, or needed the company, too.

"Yeah, just... couldn't turn my brain off," Kiera admitted.

Izzy reached and pulled the covers aside, inviting her into the bed.

Kiera hesitated for only a moment before slipping into the bed behind her, careful not to jostle Izzy too much.

For a moment, there was only silence between them. The steady tick of the clock on the nightstand. The distant creak of the house settling. Kiera exhaled, slow and deliberate, before inching just a little closer, letting her arm drape lightly around Izzy's waist. A small ask. A quiet permission.

Izzy didn't pull away. Instead, she shifted just enough to fit against Kiera more fully, her back to Kiera's chest, their ankles entwined.

The way they fit together felt... easy. Right.

Kiera closed her eyes, feeling the steady rhythm of Izzy's breathing beneath her palm, the way their bodies naturally aligned. It wasn't like the hesitant, fleeting touches they had shared before — brushes of hands, quick embraces, lingering glances. This was something quieter, something steadier. Something she wasn't quite ready to name but wasn't willing to let go of either.

She wasn't sure how long they lay like that, just breathing, just existing together.

Then, softly, Izzy murmured, "You leave tomorrow."

Kiera nodded against the pillow. "Yeah."

Izzy was quiet for a long moment, her fingers resting lightly over Kiera's hand where it lay on her waist. When she spoke again, her voice was barely above a whisper. "I'm gonna miss you."

Kiera's heart squeezed at the admission, simple as it was. She could feel the truth of it in the way Izzy's grip tightened, just slightly, like she didn't want to let her go.

"Me too," Kiera admitted, her voice just as quiet. Maybe even quieter.

She had spent the past few days watching Izzy — watching the way she had taken care of Maggie, the way she had held everything together even when no one asked her to. She and Izzy had cleaned the house, taken the kids to the local playground to get out their energy, and spent most evenings sitting out on Maggie's back patio, drinking iced tea and beer and relaxing with one another in mostly exhausted silence. They hadn't had any time for intimacy past a stolen hand squeeze or lingering look. And now, lying there, pressed

CHAPTER 21   209

close in the stillness, Kiera realized how much she didn't want to leave Izzy's side.

Her voice was hesitant when she finally asked, "Are you heading back to San Francisco after this?"

Izzy tensed slightly, just for a second, before she let out a slow breath. "I don't know yet."

Kiera frowned, lifting her head to look at her. "You don't know?"

Izzy's thumb traced a small, absent-minded circle against the back of Kiera's hand. "I've been thinking... maybe it's time for something new."

Kiera's pulse jumped, though she tried not to let it show. "Something new?" she echoed carefully.

Izzy let out a small, quiet laugh, turning slightly so their faces were closer. "Yeah. A change of scenery. I've been thinking about Denver."

Kiera stilled in surprise, trying not to overreact. She tried — really tried — to keep her body language neutral, to not let the words sink too deep before they were real. But the thought of Izzy in Denver, of her not leaving, of this — whatever this was — not ending before it even really began, sent a warmth through her that she hadn't felt in a long time.

She should be careful. She should temper her expectations. Izzy moving to Denver didn't even necessarily mean they were going to date. But instead, she found herself smiling.

"You're thinking of moving?" she asked, her voice softer now.

Izzy turned in Kiera's arms until they were facing each other, her eyes searching Kiera's face in the dark like she was looking for an answer before she even asked the question. "Would you hate that?"

Kiera barely hesitated before shaking her head. "No," she whispered. "I wouldn't hate that at all."

Izzy's lips twitched, like she was holding back a smile of

her own. And Kiera, lying there, heart beating too fast, realized she had already lost the battle with herself.

For the first time in a long time, she *wanted* something. *Really* wanted it. That terrified her, but it didn't stop her from pulling Izzy just a little bit closer.

"Can I sleep in here tonight? Nothing... you know, just sleep," Kiera asked.

Izzy didn't answer right away. Instead, she studied Kiera, her gaze flickering over her face like she was committing every detail to memory. Then, slowly, deliberately, she reached up, brushing a loose strand of hair from Kiera's cheek. Her hand stayed, her thumb tracing over Kiera's cheekbone.

"Yeah," Izzy murmured. "Just sleep."

But she didn't move away. Didn't shift back into the pillow or turn away to settle in. Instead, she lingered, her fingers still resting against Kiera's cheek, her breath warm between them.

Kiera felt her pulse hammer in her throat, felt the slow, inevitable pull of gravity drawing them together. She knew that this was new and delicate and terrifying in ways she hadn't let herself think about yet. But none of that seemed to matter when Izzy was looking at her like this, like she was already halfway gone.

She wasn't sure who leaned in first, only that it was pure instinct. When their mouths met, the kiss wasn't rushed, wasn't desperate. It was slow, confident — they didn't need to rush anything right now, as if the outside world no longer existed and every worry of tomorrow had faded. The kiss was a promise of more to come. Izzy's lips were tender and gentle, and Kiera found herself gripping the fabric of Izzy's shirt, holding on like she was afraid of what would happen if she let go. The kiss deepened, just slightly, just enough for Kiera to feel the warmth spread from her chest downwards. Their bodies moved together, their hips moving slowly, carefully, like they were testing the waters.

When they finally pulled back, neither of them moved far. Izzy's forehead rested against Kiera's, the moment stretching between them.

A noise startled them both and they stilled, listening. Music. Gentle guitar, then Michael Stipe's crooning. Kiera turned her head, her brow crinkling. "Is that what I think it is?"

Izzy grimaced. "Yeah, it's... REM's "Everybody Hurts" coming from Maggie's room. She's lucky those kids sleep deeply."

"Should we go check on her?" Kiera asked, though neither moved.

"Let's give Gwen a chance to take that one on. We're a little busy," Izzy said. She shifted her thigh away from Kiera's legs. "Though, to be honest, I don't want to have sex with you for the first time in the guest bedroom of our grieving friend's home."

Kiera's eyes widened. "Okay, when you put it like that... I agree."

Izzy bit her lip. "I know you've never had sex with a woman, and I want your first time to be... good, you know?"

Kiera raised an eyebrow. "What, you're like on the welcoming committee or something?"

"No, not like that." Izzy blinked in surprise.

Kiera leaned forward to kiss Izzy's lower lip. "I'm joking. I don't think there's any way it's possible for us to not have incredible sex, but yeah, this is... not the place for that."

Izzy visibly relaxed.

"Are you, um, worried about the fact that I've never... you know, had sex with a woman?" Kiera hedged, watching Izzy carefully.

"Are you worried about that?" Izzy asked.

"You can't answer a question with a question," Kiera said.

Izzy rubbed at the back of her neck. "It does freak me out a little, you know? I don't want you to be disappointed."

"Izzy," Kiera breathed. "I think that's honestly impossible at this point." She leaned in again, and just as their lips brushed, REM's 'Everybody Hurts' started anew.

"I can't believe we're being cockblocked by 90's alt rock right now," Izzy grumbled.

"Do you remember that kiss in college?" Kiera asked.

Izzy scoffed. "Of course I do."

Kiera raised a brow. "Why do you say it like that?"

"Because I've thought about that kiss... a lot," Izzy confessed.

Kiera's stomach clenched with excitement and nerves. She ran a hand affectionately through Izzy's hair, playing with the short strands. "Oh, really?"

"Mostly I've thought, how did we wait so long to do it again?" Izzy said, her voice dropping lower.

Kiera squeezed her eyes shut in the darkness, needing the extra illusion of privacy. "I wish I'd been braver back then," she whispered. "I wish I'd just been honest with how attracted I was to you."

"I thought I was just some experiment," Izzy said.

Kiera traced the shell of Izzy's ear with her thumb. "I'm sorry I ever made you feel that way. That's not fair of me. I was just a coward."

"I think you're one of the strongest, bravest women I've ever met," Izzy said, so quiet it was barely audible.

Tears pricked at the edges of Kiera's eyes. "That might be the kindest thing anyone has ever said to me."

"I mean it," Izzy insisted.

"Well, thank you." Kiera leaned forward and smiled against Izzy's lips. "Everybody Hurts" hit volume 11, absolutely blasting for a moment, before abruptly turning off. Suddenly, they could hear Gwen say, "Hey baby..." as the primary bedroom door shut.

"Okay, I think it's a sign," Izzy murmured, her lips curving into a smile so small Kiera barely caught it. "*Now* just sleep."

Kiera's shoulder shook in quiet laugh, and she leaned to press one last lingering kiss to Izzy's jawline, then waited for Izzy to flip back over and be her little spoon. She held Izzy tight, grateful to have someone so open and honest with her on this strange and thrilling new adventure.

THE PLANE RIDE BACK to Denver felt like floating in limbo — neither here nor there, just suspended in the air with nothing but her thoughts to keep Kiera company. It was a reminder of how the world didn't stop for grief, how life around her spun on as if nothing had changed. The hum of the engines was a poor distraction from the pit in her stomach. Leaving Austin felt wrong, like she was abandoning Maggie during one of the worst moments of her life. But Izzy had insisted she go home, and Maggie... Maggie had whispered, voice raw and quiet, "I'll be okay. You need to be with your girls."

She didn't seem okay. Of course she didn't seem okay — how could she?

When the plane landed and she turned her phone back on, an email notification popped up. She swiped it open, ready to face yet another rejection, but the subject line surprised her. There, in capital letters: OFFER. She stared down at the email, skimming the details. Teaching position. Offer. ...Lincoln, Nebraska.

That last detail hit her like a punch to the gut. Lincoln. So close to Omaha, where Alex was. The girls could be close enough to see their dad. Her teaching license wouldn't have to change...

She swiped open her spreadsheet, trying to remember even applying to this job. She scrolled down the column of application dates, finding that she'd applied to this nearly four months ago, right around Christmas. She must have been feeling mighty desperate. Still, it seemed the desperation was going both ways if they were extending an offer without meeting her.

She walked through the airport in a daze, nearly getting on the wrong train in all of her distraction. Nebraska. Did she really want to go back? A job was a job... but she finally felt settled here. And a small part of her instantly felt disappointment at the thought of Izzy moving to Denver just as she was moving away. That would pretty much close the door on their future, wouldn't it?

Her parents were waiting at the Passenger Pickup curb, their expressions a blend of relief and concern. Her daughters, bundled in oversized jackets despite the mild spring day, were the first to spot her. Eliza broke free from her grandmother's grasp and sprinted toward Kiera with reckless abandon. "Mommy!"

Kiera crouched down just in time for both girls to crash into her arms. The sheer relief of holding them, feeling their small bodies against her chest, made her want to cry. "I missed you both so much," she whispered into their hair, clinging to them as if she could anchor herself there. "Did you have a nice time with Grandma and Grandpa?"

"Chicken Nugget Dinosaur Monster Truck Rocketship missed you," Quinn admitted.

"Dinosaur Monster Truck?" Kiera asked. "This lady is really racking up the names."

Quinn's brow furrowed the same way when Kiera was making a very important point. "She's very important, Mama."

"Should we add Her Highness to the beginning of her name, then?" Kiera asked, nuzzling her face against Quinn's cheek.

"That's a great idea!" Quinn said with excitement.

Back home, everything felt painfully normal. The incense

from her mom's latest cleansing ritual swirled faintly in the air, and her dad was already preparing an early dinner, humming an off-key tune under his breath. The familiarity should have been a comfort, but it gnawed at her instead, highlighting just how much she felt like she didn't belong anywhere at the moment.

Kiera settled at the kitchen table, her girls beside her, their chatter filling the space with life. They told her about their days, about Quinn's daring leap off the back of the couch into the pillow fort they'd built, and Eliza's latest drawing obsession — chickens, naturally. Yet, beneath it all, a heavy guilt simmered — guilt for leaving Maggie, for feeling relieved to be home, for wanting something as simple as peace.

KIERA SAT at the edge of her bed, staring at her computer screen. The house was quiet except for the distant clinking noise of the dishwasher running in the kitchen. The weight of exhaustion pulled at her bones, but sleep felt impossible. Her mind was racing, thinking about the offer, about moving back to Nebraska, about leaving her parents and her friends and... Izzy. She'd been tossing and turning for over an hour when she'd just given up and opened her laptop to watch New Girl episodes. Again.

Her phone lit up from the bedside table.

IZZY

Did you make it home okay?

KIERA

I did. Her Highness Chicken Nugget Dinosaur Monster Truck Rocketship was very happy to see me.

IZZY

Was she really?

> **KIERA**
> No, she's a chicken.

> **IZZY**
> Correction: She's chicken royalty.

> **KIERA**
> I'm not convinced they feel emotion.

> **IZZY**
> I'm pretty sure I've seen an enraged chicken before.

> **KIERA**
> A valid point. How's Maggie?

> **IZZY**
> Well, she showered today.

> **KIERA**
> That's a start! How's Gwen?

> **IZZY**
> I'm pretty sure she slept on the couch in the family room downstairs?

> **KIERA**
> I wish I could be there for both of them. And you.

> **IZZY**
> Me too. I wish you were still here.

A soft flutter sparked in Kiera's chest, a hopeful, terrifying little beat she wasn't ready for but couldn't ignore. She stared at the message longer than she should have, her fingertips hovering above the screen, trying to decide if she should respond. Instead, she set the phone down and curled into her blanket, pulling it tight around her shoulders.

The connection was still there — palpable and undeniable, hiding beneath the surface of everything left unsaid.

As she stared up at the ceiling, the memories of Austin pressed in — the loss, the heartbreak, the tenderness of holding Izzy in her arms. Despite the sorrow, it wasn't Maggie's pain that lingered in her mind. It was Izzy's voice from last night, soft and hesitant: *"I'll miss you."*

She should tell Izzy about her job offer. Well, maybe first she should figure out what she was going to do about the job offer. She knew she shouldn't let the idea of what might happen with Izzy hold her back from providing for her family, but she couldn't help but shake the feeling that going back to Nebraska was just that — a step backwards.

She picked her phone back up and typed a reply before she could overthink it.

KIERA

I wish you were here, too.

THE POLE STUDIO smelled faintly of coconut and old wood, the mood light with the sound of pop music pulsing through the speakers. The polished floors gleamed under the glow of the overhead lights, and the scattered mirrors lining the walls reflected flashes of bodies in motion — women of all shapes and sizes spinning, climbing, moving with a kind of confidence Kiera still wasn't sure she could possess.

She stood near the back of the room, clutching the metal pole in front of her like a life raft, its cool surface grounding her in the moment. Her palms were already slick with sweat, though she'd been coming to class for a couple of weeks now.

She exhaled slowly, rolling out her shoulders and flexing her fingers, trying to shake the tension from her body. But her nerves weren't just about the class, not really. She had spent too long feeling like she was waiting for something. Now, she had Izzy's affection and a job offer and it felt like all the right pieces were falling into the wrong places.

The instructor's voice cut through her melancholy. "Remember, this is for you. There's no wrong way to move your body here."

Kiera nodded and swallowed, adjusting her grip. She let herself lean into the spin, pushing off the floor, the pole guiding her into a graceful, slow twirl. The first moment of flight always took her by surprise — how her body moved without her overthinking every step and gravity let her go, just for a second. The rush of momentum brought a brief flicker of freedom, and for a moment, she wasn't a single, unemployed mom, or testing the waters of a new relationship, or a woman stuck between who she'd been and who she wanted to be.

Here, she was just Kiera.

She liked that.

She liked the version of herself that existed in this room — this Kiera didn't hesitate, didn't shrink herself down to fit into spaces she had outgrown. She wasn't constantly trying to balance being a good mother, a good daughter, a good ex-wife, a good everything. Here, she wasn't responsible for anyone but herself.

She finished the spin, landing lightly on her toes, heart hammering from a combination of nerves and exertion. For the first time since she had started coming here, she didn't feel awkward or out of place. She felt... present. Strong. Capable. Brave.

By the end of class, her muscles burned and her heart pounded — not just from the effort, but from something quieter settling underneath it all. As her breath slowed and her body stretched into stillness, a different kind of release took hold. Not adrenaline, but understanding.

I don't want to keep living out of fear.

She stood in front of the mirror, running a towel over the sweat glistening along her collarbone. She'd spent years making choices that made sense on paper — safe, sturdy, selfless. Always what was best for everyone else. But somewhere along the way, she'd stopped asking what she wanted. Now, when she looked at her own reflection, all she saw was someone trying to understand the person she'd become — and what it meant that Izzy had started to feel like something she couldn't ignore.

Kiera had spent years making careful, measured choices — doing what was best for the people around her, always putting their needs first and pushing her own to the side. And what had it gotten her? A life half-lived. A marriage that had unraveled long before it officially ended. A version of herself she barely recognized.

But this? Showing up for herself? Making the choice to pursue things with Izzy. Moving her body in ways that terrified but thrilled her. It didn't feel like fear. It felt like power. Like agency. Like she was finally getting a handle on exactly who she'd always been too afraid to be.

As she packed up her things and slipped on her sneakers, a thought unfurled in the back of her mind, one that she couldn't stifle back down. What if she let herself *want* Izzy — fully, unapologetically, without bracing for the fallout? What if, for once, she didn't overthink it or talk herself out of it, and just reached for the thing that made her feel alive?

Her fingers hovered over her phone as she walked to her car.

She could wait to tell Izzy about the offer. She could overthink it like she always did. She could keep telling herself that slow and careful was the only way to do this.

Or she could be brave. She could tell Izzy about the job offer before it loomed over every conversation.

She exhaled, pulse still thrumming from class, from clarity, from possibility. Then, before she could talk herself out of it, she unlocked her phone and hit call.

Izzy picked up on the second ring. "Hey," she said.

Kiera could hear Maggie's kids laughing in the background. She smiled to herself, climbing into her car. "Hey, I was just leaving pole class and was thinking about you."

"Oh? Thinking about me during pole dancing sounds like something I'd like many, many more details about. Does this mean I get a seat in the audience for future performances?" Izzy asked.

Kiera snorted in amusement. "Keep playing your cards right."

Izzy laughed. "Other than class, how was your day?"

Kiera sank back into the driver's seat, her hands motionless on the steering wheel, not quite ready to turn the ignition. The silence of the parked car felt loud, too full of the thing she hadn't said yet. "Good, actually. Um, I wanted to tell you something."

"Sure, what's up?" Izzy's tone was light, casual — unprepared.

Kiera stared straight ahead, the streetlamp outside casting soft shadows across the dash. "I got a job offer," she said, trying to keep her voice steady.

"That's huge!" Izzy's voice brightened instantly, warm and effortless, a genuine smile tucked between the words. "How are you feeling about it?"

"In Lincoln, Nebraska," Kiera added, her thumb dragging along the ridge of the steering wheel like she could smooth out the tension building in her chest. She couldn't look at her. Couldn't breathe too deep. The moment felt fragile, like one wrong move might collapse it.

There was a pause. Then, softer: "Oh."

And just like that, the air shifted — not cold, but quieter. Heavier. Kiera didn't know what she wanted Izzy to say. Only that she already missed whatever ease they'd had a second ago. "Yeah."

"I mean, that's still awesome. I didn't even know you were considering going back."

"With all of the licensing issues, I applied like a random

shot in the dark months ago. I didn't expect to hear back, but it's a sister district to where I taught before," Kiera explained, hating that she felt like she had to explain herself about this.

"I'm happy for you. I know it's been stressing you out," Izzy said.

And goddammit, she sounded so genuine, like she was happy for Kiera.

"I don't know if I'm going to take it yet," Kiera admitted.

"If you do, I support you completely," Izzy said.

The words hit deeper than Kiera expected. Her throat tightened, but she didn't let the silence stretch too long. "Thank you. That really does mean a lot." She cleared her throat, shifting in the seat. "And you? How's Maggie doing?"

Izzy let out a shaky sigh. "It's not easy, but I think she's doing a little better every day."

"And you? Are you okay?"

Another pause. "It's still heavy here, and there's still a lot to figure out," Izzy admitted quietly. "But hearing your voice helps."

Something twisted low in Kiera's ribs. "Yours, too."

A high-pitched wail broke through the uncomfortable quiet on the line, and then Izzy cursed under her breath. "Um, Rosie just took a header. Can we talk later?"

"Of course," Kiera said. "Give Rosie a kiss for her owwie. Those always help."

Izzy agreed, and as they hung up, Kiera was left with a strange mix of emotions — guilt still coiled low in her stomach, but also something like relief. Kiera stared at her phone for a moment, the sound of Izzy's voice still echoing softly in her head. She exhaled and pressed the phone to her chest, letting the quiet fill the room around her. Everything still felt fragile, still unsettled, but Izzy hadn't immediately pulled away. Maybe if she took this job, they could still figure things out between them. it felt like a small anchor in the middle of all the unknowns.

Pete named the conversation, "date court™".

PETE

WAIT

HOLD ON

MAGGIE

What now.

PETE

I JUST REALIZED SOMETHING

I NEVER ASKED HOW THE DATE WENT 😱😱😱

MAGGIE

...???

MAGGIE

WHAT DATE.

MAGGIE

EXCUSE ME.

DANICA

Oh wow. I was NOT expecting this to be the scandal of the day but I'm invested.

KIERA

Pete. It is after midnight.

IZZY

Pete. Go to sleep.

PETE

WHAT??

i was respectful, okay??

i gave you two your space, let you do your thing, and i JUST realized we haven't debriefed

MAGGIE

WHAT. DATE.

KIERA

Petra Pancott, you are so nosy.

IZZY

We were THIS CLOSE to escaping without this coming up.

MAGGIE

YOU WENT ON A DATE AND DIDN'T TELL ME?

LIKE WITH EACH OTHER?

DANICA

Yeah, wow, I have to admit, I'm a little disappointed in you both. We have a system. You date, we debrief.

MAGGIE

EXACTLY. I THOUGHT WE WERE FRIENDS.

Pete named the conversation, "The Nosy & The Restless".

PETE

NOPE

you don't get to dodge this

I want DETAILS! did anyone do the awkward reach for the check at the same time thing? did you KISS?!

MAGGIE

HAVE YOU KISSED MORE THAN ONCE.

KIERA

You people are unbearable. Turn off your caps, Mags.

DANICA

Oh, 100% owning the unbearability. Now spill.

IZZY

No.

PETE

YES

MAGGIE

I CANNOT BELIEVE YOU TWO WENT ON A DATE AND DIDN'T TELL ME. THIS IS A PERSONAL BETRAYAL.

Maggie named the conversation, "The Betrayed Besties".

KIERA

We were slightly busy and distracted in Austin.

IZZY

Goodnight, everyone. Go to bed.

MAGGIE

WHAT COULD YOU HAVE BEEN BUSY WITH

KIERA

...

IZZY

...

KIERA

It was nice.

MAGGIE

OH MY GOD THAT'S ALL YOU'RE GIVING ME??? I AM A GRIEVING WOMAN, GIVE ME SOMETHING HERE.

PETE

UNACCEPTABLE

SHE IS A GRIEVING WOMAN

DANICA

This is an absolute failure of the system.

KIERA

Fine. Yes, we kissed.

IZZY

Technically. Not on the date, though.

MAGGIE

!!!!!

PETE

!!!!!

DANICA

!!!!!

MAGGIE

In my house?! Did you guys have a "moment" à la Pete and Danica in Aunt Jade's bunk room?

DANICA

omg

PETE

hey! i take offense

we took way longer than one moment

IZZY

I hate you all.

PETE:

okay but WHEN is the next date??

. . . . . .

KIERA:

...Goodnight.

DANICA

Not before you tell us if there was bunk bed action.

Izzy named the conversation, "Oops, All Meddlers!".

MAGGIE

COWARDS

CHAPTER 22

Izzy

THE TEXAS HEAT WAS STICKY AND RELENTLESS, EVEN IN THE early hours of the morning, as the first rays of light stretched across Maggie's quiet Austin neighborhood. Izzy sat on the back porch, legs pulled up onto the worn wooden chair, a mug of coffee cradled between her hands. The cicadas buzzed in the trees, their constant, low drone a comfort at this point in her visit. She didn't know how long she'd been there — two weeks? The days blurred together.

Inside, the house was quiet. The kids were still asleep, giving Izzy a rare sliver of stillness. Her shoulders ached from holding everything in. For days, she'd been the steady one — wiping counters, ordering takeout, intercepting awkward visits from neighbors. She didn't know why Maggie seemed to freeze every time Gwen entered the room, only that the silence between them was starting to feel like a wall. That morning, Gwen had made eggs, and Maggie had managed the smallest smile. It wasn't a fix, but it was something. Izzy couldn't glue them back together. She could keep the laundry moving, keep the fridge stocked, keep the lights on.

Work was another thing entirely. When Gwen was home or the kids were in school, Izzy had thrown herself into Second Star with a focus she hadn't felt in months. She was tired of feeling like a barnacle to Pete's brilliance. The guilt from Maggie's loss had morphed into a burning need to take control of *something*.

It was a major step out of her comfort zone to talk to community members who would be good mentors. It was only when Denver-based soccer star Sage Carson and her wife Willa signed on to mentor a few teenagers who were interested in sports after barely hearing two sentences, that Izzy felt like maybe this was something she could do. She believed in the work and she believed in Pete, and it was heartening that others seemed to believe in it, too.

When Izzy wasn't busy, the quiet caught up to her. The moments when Maggie was asleep or the kids were at school were when her thoughts spiraled. It wasn't like she could ask Kiera to stay in Denver on her account — Izzy knew that. Kiera had kids, a life to rebuild, real decisions to make. But still, the sting of it surprised her. Just as she'd finally let herself imagine something here, something real — Denver, Kiera, all of it — the ground shifted again. And what was worse was how selfish it felt to even be upset. This wasn't about her. But knowing that didn't make the ache go away. It just made her quieter about it. Like if she kept her disappointment small enough, maybe it wouldn't matter so much when Kiera left.

Of course. Of *course* she'd fallen for someone who might leave. Izzy wanted to laugh at herself, but it wouldn't come out right. She should've known better — *did* know better — and still, she'd let herself hope. Let herself picture something solid this time, something mutual. But Kiera was already slipping through her fingers, and Izzy was left wondering if she'd learned anything at all. It was the same pattern in a prettier disguise: want the person who can't stay. And then act surprised when they don't.

"I want to tell you not to take that job, but that's not my place, and I'm scared of what might happen if I push too hard, too fast."

She had typed those words more times than she could count. Every time, she deleted them before she hit send. It had felt exciting to see that Kiera told the group first... Maybe that meant she was ready for more.

It felt wrong to be thinking about Kiera while Maggie was buried in grief, but Izzy couldn't help it. Her mind kept pulling back to Denver — to the way Kiera had looked at her before that first kiss, to the quiet hesitation in her voice when she said she wanted more. Izzy could still feel the press of Kiera's hand at the small of her back, the way she'd leaned in like it meant something. She tried to push it aside. This wasn't the time. Not when Maggie could barely get out of bed, not when Gwen couldn't make it through a conversation without shutting down. But the feelings were there anyway, sharp and persistent, threading their way through every quiet moment.

The back door creaked open behind her. Izzy turned her head just enough to see Gwen stepping onto the porch, her salt-and-pepper hair slightly mussed, her eyes heavy-lidded with exhaustion. She was still in the clothes she'd worn the night before, the fabric wrinkled from sleep — if she'd even gotten any. She'd been sleeping in the family room again.

Gwen blinked at Izzy like she was surprised to see her there. "Didn't think anyone else would be up yet," she murmured, her voice still rough from sleep.

Izzy shifted in her chair, setting her coffee down on the armrest. "I'm an early bird."

Gwen nodded and rubbed at her face before crossing the porch to lean against the railing. For a long moment, neither of them spoke. The cicadas droned on, filling the silence.

Izzy watched her from the corner of her eye. Gwen was usually so meticulous, so put-together, but she seemed to be unraveling at the edges. Her sharp, architectural mind was always oriented toward solutions — finding a flaw in the design, fixing it before the cracks could spread.

Izzy watched Gwen yawn and rub at her eyes. "You should go back to bed," Izzy said after a moment.

Gwen let out a hollow laugh. "I can't sleep. Not much point in trying."

Izzy frowned. "Gwen—"

"I don't know what she needs from me," Gwen interrupted, her voice barely above a whisper. "I've never not known how to fix something with her before."

The admission was unexpected. Izzy had been prepared for Gwen's usual stiff silence, the way she held herself just far enough away from things to maintain control. But this? This was something else.

Izzy shifted forward in her chair, resting her forearms on her knees. "I don't think she knows either," she said. "

Gwen sighed. "She won't talk to me. Barely looks at me. I know she's grieving, but it feels like... like I'm not even here." Her fingers drummed on the deck railing. "Like she's already decided I'm part of what she's losing."

Izzy bit her lip. She had noticed it, too — that strange, intangible space Maggie kept between them, like something had already broken that neither of them could name.

Gwen shook her head, a rough sound escaping her throat. "And I don't know how to stop it."

Izzy sighed, leaning back in her chair. "I don't think you can."

Gwen finally looked at her then, brow furrowing. "You're shockingly bad at pep talks."

Izzy huffed a soft laugh. "I mean it. This isn't something you can fix with logic. Maggie's going through something bigger than either of you and all you can do is be there for her."

CHAPTER 22

Gwen swallowed. "Waiting for her to come back to me is making me feel insane."

As Gwen said it, the words hit harder than Izzy expected. Because wasn't she doing the same thing with Kiera? Sitting back, waiting, hoping things would sort themselves out — just like she always had. Letting other people lead, afraid to want too much in case they didn't want her back. But watching Gwen hesitate, stay silent, refuse to move even when everything was falling apart — it made something snap into focus. Izzy didn't want to float through this. She didn't want to keep waiting for Kiera to wake up one day and suddenly see her standing there. She wanted to be chosen *on purpose*. And she was done pretending that wasn't what she needed.

Gwen dropped her hands, letting them fall to her sides. She turned fully to face Izzy, something searching in her expression. She hesitated, exhaling. "It's like I'm clinging onto what we had with all our might and she's not even trying. Has she said anything to you about it?"

"She hasn't," Izzy said honestly. "But I do know Maggie still loves you, and if you still love her, then there's still something worth fighting for."

Gwen fell silent, staring up at the trees for a long moment.

"Did you know that cicadas live on all continents except Antarctica?" Izzy offered.

Gwen glanced back over her shoulder toward Izzy with a confused expression.

"They only leave the ground when it's 64 degrees," Izzy added.

"How do you know this?" Gwen asked.

"The internet."

"Should have guessed." Gwen nodded, then sighed. "I'm going to go wake up Arlo and Jude with my new weird bug facts."

Izzy sat back as Gwen slipped inside, leaving her alone again with the dawn stretching over the Austin sky.

Watching Gwen shut down again had left Izzy feeling raw. She could see how much Maggie needed her, how much Gwen loved her, and yet neither of them could say the thing that mattered most. It made her heart ache — not just for them, but for all the ways people missed each other while trying not to need too much. Izzy had been waiting quietly, trying not to press, hoping someone would choose her without being asked to. But that wasn't enough anymore.

She would stay here for as long as Maggie needed her — of course she would — but the next time she saw Kiera, she wasn't going to hold back. She was going to say what she wanted. And this time, she wouldn't apologize for wanting it.

ANOTHER HANDFUL of days passed in a haze of grief, responsibility, and exhaustion. The household began to settle into something resembling a routine — morning playtime, packing lunches, driving the boys to and from school, taking Rosie to the playground to wear her out, evening board games that ended with scattered pieces and sleepy yawns. The house never felt truly quiet, not with Maggie's other family members checking in, Gwen moving around like a ghost, and the ever-present neediness of small children demanding snacks or attention. But somehow, it still felt hollow.

Gwen had locked herself in her office most days, and Izzy tried not to notice the blankets on the family room couch.

Izzy wasn't sure what was keeping her in Austin anymore. At first, it was Maggie. The need to be the one solid thing Maggie could lean on without guilt, without explanation. In the past few days, Maggie got back into the swing of parenthood, though Izzy frequently helped when Maggie was exhausted or needed a break. Lately, she'd started wondering

CHAPTER 22   233

if it was also a way to delay making decisions about her own life. About Denver. About Kiera.

One evening, after the kids had gone to bed and Gwen was still hidden away in her office, Izzy found Maggie in the kitchen, staring out the window with a faraway look. The kitchen light cast soft shadows against the walls, the half-empty glass of wine in Maggie's hand reflecting amber in the dim glow.

The exhaustion was still there, but something had shifted. Maggie's shoulders seemed just a little less weighed down.

"Izzy," Maggie said quietly, her voice so soft it was difficult to hear.

"Yeah?" Izzy organized a few pieces of mail on the counter.

"You need to go home."

Izzy froze, setting down one of the never-ending Hello Fresh advertisements. "I'm not sure—"

"You've done more than enough," Maggie interrupted, finally turning to face her. Her eyes were bloodshot and puffy, the skin beneath them dark and swollen like bruises — the kind of exhaustion that clung to the bones, untouched by sleep. "You've been here for me in ways I didn't even know I needed. But I can't keep leaning on you like this. You need to get back to your life." Her voice was steady.

"I'm fine staying here as long as you need," Izzy said.

Maggie shook her head, her smile small, bittersweet. "I'll never be ready for you to leave," she admitted, raw honesty in her voice. "I wish I could shrink you and keep you in my pocket. But I need to figure some things out." Her voice wavered slightly, but she held Izzy's gaze with quiet resolve. "And you've got a job to get back to."

"My job is flexible, and Pete's my boss, so she knows I've been taking care of more important things and working from here when I can."

Maggie leveled her with a look Izzy was pretty sure came

in some kind of *How To Be A Parent* handbook, equal parts concerned, disappointed, and exasperated.

Izzy swallowed hard. The thought of leaving felt like abandoning Maggie in the middle of a storm, but deep down, she knew her friend was right. Still, it was hard to let go.

Maggie reached out and took Izzy's hand in hers, squeezing gently. "Don't you need to go figure things out with Kiera?"

Izzy exhaled a laugh, shaking her head. Her voice was light, teasing. "We're taking things slow."

Maggie arched a brow. "Taking things slow or avoiding things altogether?"

Izzy narrowed her eyes. "You're way too smug for someone who's kicking me out."

Maggie grinned, just for a moment, before her expression softened. "I like the idea of you two together. I like that you're not afraid of heartbreak anymore."

"I've never been afraid of heartbreak," Izzy admitted. "What scares me is being fully seen and still left behind, and I can't help but wonder if that's about to happen yet again." She hadn't ever admitted that out loud, barely even to herself.

"Only one way to find out," Maggie said, reaching to squeeze Izzy's shoulder as she turned away.

Izzy hesitated, studying Maggie's face. She was avoiding direct eye contact now, suddenly preoccupied with an invisible speck on the countertop. "And you and Gwen? Will you be okay?"

Maggie's easy expression faltered for the first time. "Oh, yeah, sure," she said, but the words were rushed, forced. She lifted a shoulder in an almost careless shrug, but it was obvious, painfully obvious, that she was putting on a front.

Izzy frowned. "Mags."

"I mean it," Maggie said quickly, reaching for the drying rack to start putting away cups. "We're fine."

Izzy bit her lip. "I'm going to put my Meddling Maggie

hat on real quick here. You leave the room or don't respond when she tries to talk to you. She sleeps in the family room. I've barely seen you look at her. Do you want to talk about it?"

Maggie swallowed visibly, staring down into the drinking glass she was holding. For a second, Izzy thought she might say something — might finally crack and let it spill. But instead, Maggie let out a breath, set the glass in the cupboard with careful precision, and shook her head.

"Okay," Izzy said, backing off. "Well, I'm here when you're ready for that." She hesitated, then added, "You're not alone, okay?"

Maggie paused, her back still half-turned toward Izzy. "I know. I love you for that."

She felt tears begin at the corners of her eyes, but she willed them away. "I love you, too."

Maggie finally turned back to her, her eyes glassy. "Izzy," she said, softer now, more careful. "I know it feels like leaving is the wrong thing. Like you're letting go too soon. But you're not. You're allowed to want something for yourself, too."

Izzy swallowed hard. She thought of Denver, of Kiera, of what she wanted but had been too afraid to really acknowledge. And she thought of Gwen — of the slow, silent way things had unraveled between her and Maggie, of what happened when two people loved each other but never quite reached for each other in time.

"I know," Izzy said quietly.

They stood in silence for a long beat, the only sound the clinking of glasses as she put them away, the gravity of goodbye settling around them.

Maggie was right.

It was time to go home.

CHAPTER 23

Kiera

Kiera sat at the dining table, laptop open, scrolling through job listings she wasn't even sure she needed anymore. The offer in Nebraska sat quietly in her inbox — safe, expected, easy to fall back on. But something in her couldn't stop looking. When a new email notification blinked across the top of her screen, her breath caught.

Subject: Interview Invitation

A middle school near the girls' elementary school. She stared at the screen, heart thudding. This wasn't just another listing — it was a chance to stay. To build something real here. To stop feeling like she was camped out in someone else's life, waiting for her own to restart.

"Mom?"

Eliza's voice startled her. Kiera turned to find both girls standing in the doorway, dirt smudged across their faces and flower crowns crooked on their heads. Quinn's tiny hands were caked in mud, clutching a small plastic chicken figurine like it was treasure.

"Grandma and Grandpa said we could name the new ducks!" Eliza announced proudly.

The words took a second to land. *"Ducks?"*

Eliza nodded furiously, adjusting her flower crown. "I'm going to name mine Francine."

Quinn beamed. "Mine's called Captain Quackington."

Kiera couldn't help the laugh that bubbled out. "Perfect duck names."

Before she could say more, the front door creaked open and her mom stepped into the room with her dad in tow. "Surprise!" her mom said cheerfully. "We figured a few new additions to the coop would keep the girls busy."

"Ducks?" Kiera repeated, still processing the new information. "You're really just leaning into the fowl play over here."

Her dad winked, grinning. "That was good."

"Thanks, I learned the dad jokes from the best of them," Kiera said, shooing the girls back outside. "But let's talk ducks."

"Let's not," her dad added, shooing the girls back outside as her mom slid into a seat beside her.

Her mom dug a letter out of her gardening apron. "I accidentally opened this. It's an offer from a school in Nebraska. Wanna talk, kiddo?"

Kiera didn't reach for the letter. She just stared at it like it might say something new if she waited long enough.

Her dad leaned a hip against the counter, arms crossed. "We figured it was time to ask what you're really thinking."

Kiera let out a breath. "I don't know. It's a good offer."

Her mom sat down across from her, hands folded neatly in her lap, eyes steady. "No one's saying it isn't."

Kiera closed the laptop slowly, like that might help quiet the noise in her head. "It's safe. It's a real job, in a district I did my student-teaching in. I could have the girls back in their old schools. I'd know the grocery stores, the weather. My way around."

"But?" her dad asked.

She swallowed. "But I keep wondering if going back would just be... rewinding. Not moving forward. And I don't know what forward even looks like yet."

The silence stretched, not uncomfortable, just full.

Her mom nodded. "You've been working so hard to hold everything together — the girls, your routines, this job search. We're happy to help where we can, but you're stubborn like your Aunt Jade. You don't have to prove anything to us. We know you can make either choice work. That's not the question."

Kiera glanced toward the back door, where Quinn and Eliza were still running in circles in the yard, yelling about ducks. Her heart ached a little — for them, for the life she was trying to shape, for the version of herself she had really started to like.

Her dad's voice was quieter now. "Just don't go back to something that didn't serve you just because it's easier to explain than staying here."

That made her look up.

He shrugged. "We've been watching you soften. Not fall apart — soften. And that's not a bad thing."

Kiera blinked hard, pressing her fingertips to the edge of the table.

"Tonya says you're nearly at the end of your metamorphosis," her mom said with the nonchalance of a remark about good weather.

Kiera's brow furrowed in confusion. "Tonya..."

"You know, Tonya. My spiritual guide," her mom said, and Kiera took a deep breath.

"How'd Tonya know about the goo phase?" Kiera said, tilting her head.

"The what?" Her dad asked, opening a few drawers before finding whatever he was looking for. He slid a slim manila envelope across the table. "Jade wanted us to give you this, too."

Kiera frowned, hesitating before pulling the flap open. Inside was a lease agreement — already signed — for a furnished townhouse near the girl's school. A key was paper-clipped to the top. Her stomach flipped. "She — what is this?"

Her mom gave a small shrug. "She wants to spend more time here in Denver but figured you could crash there with the girls until you land on your feet. It's already paid through the end of the year."

Kiera stared at the document, throat tightening. "I can't accept this."

Her dad snorted. "Then don't tell her that. You think she asks for permission? Have you ever tried telling Jade no? It's impossible."

"She said if you so much as *try* to thank her, she'll pretend she doesn't know what you're talking about," her mom added, standing to ready a cup of tea as if this wasn't absurd.

Kiera ran a hand through her hair, overwhelmed. "It's too much. I don't even know if I'm going to get a job. It's just way too much."

"Jade has a different definition of 'too much' than the rest of us," her dad said. "She loves you. She's always had a soft spot for the girls. And she's not going to let you make a decision based on where you can crash rent-free."

Kiera looked back down at the lease. Her name was already written in neat, looping script at the top. The key felt small and heavy in her palm.

Her mom reached out, resting a hand on hers. "You don't have to use it. But it's there if you need it. You're allowed to choose something for yourself."

Kiera didn't say anything, but she didn't hand the key back either.

THE LATE AFTERNOON sunlight filtered through the sheer curtains of the two-story townhouse, casting shadows across the hardwood floors. It was small — cozy, as her mom had phrased it. She'd even lit her favorite candle, the scent of citrus and greenery filled the room, making it feel like it could one day be hers.

Her parents had offered to keep the girls for the night to let her stay over at the townhouse and get her bearings — to make an "informed" decision as they'd worded it. She had spent the first few hours of the day putting clean linens on the bed, cleaning, and shifting the couch in the living room into a configuration she liked better.

Kiera stood in the middle of it all, feeling the surrealness of starting over settle around her shoulders. It wasn't the sprawling family home she'd once shared with Alex. There was no suburban backyard or impressive foyer. It also wasn't her childhood home, so tied to her parents and who she'd been that she'd never had the space to figure out a different version of herself there. But this townhouse felt like freedom — a breath of fresh air after months of suffocating uncertainty.

A knock at the door snapped her from her thoughts.

Kiera froze at the knock, her heart stuttering. She wasn't expecting anyone — the only possibility would be her parents or Aunt Jade, and neither seemed likely. She crossed the room slowly, brushing crumbs off her sweatshirt, still barefoot, still unsure if she even would be staying here. When she opened the door and saw Izzy standing there, everything inside her tilted.

For a second, she couldn't speak. Her brain needed time to catch up to what her eyes already knew. Izzy — hair wind-tousled, cheeks pink, looking both sure of herself and completely out of breath — stood with one hand in her pocket and the other loosely holding something that looked like takeout. Like it was just any other afternoon.

Kiera's stomach flipped. Not from nerves exactly — more like recognition. Like something she'd been holding back finally surged forward, uninvited and undeniable. She hadn't realized how much she'd missed Izzy's face until it was right in front of her. Now that it was, she had no idea what to do with all the feelings rushing in at once.

"Hi," Izzy said, her smile shy.

"Hi," Kiera said, though she was unable to hide her confusion.

"I stopped by your house, but your parents gave me this address," Izzy said. "I grabbed some food on my way over."

Kiera raised a brow. "What kind of food?"

"Now I know where Eliza gets her intensity from," Izzy joked. "It's Thai. I got you drunken noodles."

Kiera stepped back. "Well, lucky for you, drunken noodles is the password."

Izzy grinned, looking around as she crossed the threshold into the entry, pausing in the kitchen. "So, um, what is this place? Did your parents' kombucha operation finally get off the ground and you're hiding in this safe house from a rival booch gang?"

Kiera couldn't help herself. She moved, wrapping her arms around Izzy in a hug bordering on strangulation. She heard the rustle of Izzy setting the takeout down on the kitchen counter behind her, and then Izzy's hands were on her back, in her hair, reassuring. Here. Izzy was here.

"I missed you," Kiera whispered.

"I missed you, too," Izzy said with a small laugh. "Should we, um, talk or maybe we could just silently eat this food, or…"

Kiera leaned back, looking into Izzy's face.

CHAPTER 23

Izzy's eyes were dark, her gaze drifting to Kiera's mouth. Kiera's breath caught, her heart thudding against her ribs. The quiet stretched out, charged with possibility. She reached out slowly, her fingers brushing against Izzy's hand. Izzy didn't pull away — if anything, she leaned in, just enough to close the space.

Kiera swallowed, scanning Izzy's face for any flicker of hesitation. When she found none, she leaned forward and kissed her. It was careful, tentative — a question more than an answer. Izzy let out a soft, uneven breath against her lips, and Kiera felt her nerves melt into something warmer, steadier.

The room faded around them, like everything outside this moment had gone quiet. Izzy looked up at her, eyes wide and unreadable. Neither of them moved. Time felt suspended, held by the thread of what they weren't saying yet.

Kiera stepped in. "I... I don't know how to say this so I'm just going to try," she whispered, voice low, shaking just enough to betray how much this mattered. "I just — God, Izzy, I want you so fucking bad."

Izzy's lips parted like she might respond, but nothing came out. Kiera didn't wait. She lifted a hand to Izzy's jaw, her fingers trembling as she leaned in and kissed her again — deeper this time, with every ounce of emotion she hadn't said out loud.

Izzy's hands found her waist, pulling her close until their bodies met. The warmth of Izzy settled into Kiera's skin, into her chest, everywhere. Kiera pressed in, her breath catching as Izzy's thigh slipped between hers, slow and deliberate. Her whole body sparked at the contact — a jolt of heat rolling through her, sharp and sweet.

The counter dug into her back, but she barely noticed. Izzy's mouth was on hers again, surer now, and Kiera kissed her back like she couldn't help it. Her fingers slid into Izzy's hair, holding tight, grounding herself in the dizzying rush of it all.

She moved against her, chasing that friction, that closeness, her breath growing more uneven with every second. Izzy exhaled roughly, her grip tightening at Kiera's waist, guiding her closer, deeper into the kiss. Everything else — the silence of the house, the unanswered questions, the job offer sitting in her inbox — disappeared.

Hands roamed — over ribs, up backs, gripping hips. Kiera's breath stuttered as Izzy's teeth grazed her lower lip. She responded without thinking, chasing that edge, deepening the kiss until her knees nearly gave out. Every touch felt amplified, drawn tight with want.

She moved against Izzy's thigh again, a low sound catching in her throat. Izzy's hand slipped beneath her sweatshirt, fingers brushing hot against her skin, and Kiera gasped into her mouth.

And then a beat later she pulled back, chest rising and falling, lips still parted. "Wait," she said, breathless but suddenly remembering the very real world around them. Izzy's eyes went wide with worry. "We should... put the noodles in the fridge. Before we get distracted, and it goes bad."

Izzy blinked, still dazed, and then broke into a laugh, resting her forehead against Kiera's shoulder. "Right. Priorities." She stepped back to open the fridge and unceremoniously tossed the bag inside.

"How dare you treat my noodles like that," Kiera joked.

Izzy grinned, smirking. "How can I make it up to you?"

"I mean, I have a few ideas," Kiera said, reaching for Izzy again. She leaned back against the kitchen counter, tugging Izzy closer as she dropped her voice. "Though all of them end with us in bed, if I'm being honest."

"I'm a fan of honesty." Izzy's hand slid up, fingers threading through Kiera's hair, voice husky in the quiet. "Are you sure?"

Kiera nodded, voice soft but certain. "Yeah. I'm sure. I'm ready."

CHAPTER 23

As if those words were all she needed, Izzy's lips crashed against Kiera's, unraveling anything left of the careful restraint they'd been holding onto all this time. Kiera barely had a moment to gasp before Izzy's hands gripped her waist, strong and sure, lifting her effortlessly onto the kitchen counter. She clutched Izzy's shoulders as a startled gasp slipped from her lips.

"Holy shit," Kiera whispered in awe, staring down at Izzy.

Izzy stood between Kiera's legs, hands sliding slowly up her thighs. "Surprised?" she murmured against her throat, voice teasing, but her eyes had gone dark, hooded with intent.

Kiera swallowed hard, heart hammering as she tilted her chin up, daring, wanting. "A little," she admitted, breathless. "But I like it."

Izzy's hands drifted up her sides, slow and warm, fingertips skimming skin before finding the hem of Kiera's sweatshirt. She paused, her gaze holding steady — one last check-in. Kiera gave a barely-there nod.

Izzy tugged the sweatshirt up and over Kiera's head in one fluid motion, her glasses disappearing with it. Kiera shivered — not from the air, but from the look Izzy gave her. Like she was seeing all of her and didn't want to look away.

Izzy's palms traced her sides, thumbs brushing beneath her ribs, and Kiera's pulse skipped. Her lips found Kiera's collarbone, the edge of her plain, thin bra, trailing down with soft, careful grazes of teeth.

"You're so fucking gorgeous," Izzy murmured, voice rough at the edges.

The words punched right through her. When was the last time someone had looked at her like this — said it like they meant it? Izzy's mouth was on her again, lips brushing down, tongue smoothing over each place her teeth had teased.

Kiera melted into it, her whole body alive to every movement, every breath. Her fingers slid into Izzy's hair, holding on.

Izzy's hands slipped lower, finding the button of Kiera's shorts. She paused, her breath warm against Kiera's stomach. "Still good?"

"Yes," Kiera breathed, arching into her. "Yes."

Izzy's smirk was slow and knowing as she eased the shorts and underwear down, fingertips dragging softly along her thighs. She dropped a kiss to the inside of one knee, then another, higher, slower. Kiera trembled, her breath uneven, the electric energy in her body building.

"Izzy," she exhaled, her voice rough. Her whole body drawn tight with anticipation, every nerve lit and reaching. She leaned back against the cabinet, head tipped, eyes half-lidded as Izzy kissed her way up. Hands firm at her thighs, parting her gently, reverently.

Izzy glanced up, eyes steady. "You're going to be so fucking beautiful when you come for me," she murmured. And before Kiera could answer, before she could even catch her breath, Izzy's mouth was on her.

The moan that ripped from Kiera's throat was almost embarrassingly loud, instinctive. Her back arched as sensation overtook her. Her hands reached blindly — Izzy's shoulders, the counter edge, anything to hold on to. Izzy didn't rush. She moved with slow, devastating control, taking her apart piece by piece. Every breath, every sound Kiera made, seemed to draw Izzy deeper.

Kiera had never been touched like this — not with such attention, such hunger. With Izzy's mouth on her, she came undone. Izzy's hands mapped her skin, grounding her, worshiping her, making her feel like she was the only thing that mattered.

When Izzy pressed two fingers inside her, Kiera let go. She cried out, hips jerking, body trembling under the rising wave.

CHAPTER 23

The pleasure was sharp, full, dizzying. It swallowed her whole.

She came with Izzy's name on her lips, her fingers tangled in blonde hair, pulling her close as the rhythm crested and broke. Izzy didn't stop — just eased her through it, her mouth pressing gentle kisses along Kiera's thighs as she shuddered and sagged against the cabinets.

Kiera's breath came in shallow pulls, her chest rising and falling in sync with the thrum still moving through her limbs. When Izzy finally lifted her head, her lips were kiss-swollen, her expression soft and impossibly smug.

Kiera let out a breathless laugh, dazed and entirely undone. She reached down, threading her fingers through Izzy's hair, pulling her up into a kiss that was slow and deep — full of an emotion Kiera didn't want to name just yet. She could taste herself on Izzy's mouth, something she realized she'd never done before. It was intoxicating — the way Izzy kissed, the way she moved, the way her hands skimmed along Kiera's skin, warm and knowing. Every touch sent a jolt through her, a reminder that this was real, that this was happening.

"We should go upstairs," Kiera murmured against Izzy's lips, her voice shaky, her fingers gripping at Izzy's hips like she needed to keep herself steady.

Izzy let out a breathy laugh, resting her forehead against Kiera's for a beat. They didn't move right away. The suggestion hung in the air, unhurried.

Eventually, they stumbled toward the stairs, hands exploring, mouths finding each other again and again in kisses that burned slow and hot. Kiera had never been kissed with this kind of intensity — not just wanting but knowing. Her body pulsed with need, her skin flushed with it. She wasn't shy about being naked against Izzy's clothed body, a first for her.

They only made it a few steps before Izzy groaned against

her mouth, pulling back just enough to say, "If we don't stop kissing, we're not making it to the bedroom."

Kiera grinned and pressed her hands to Izzy's chest, gently pushing her down onto a step, straddling her hips without hesitation. "Then we won't make it."

She kissed Izzy's jaw, then down her neck, taking her time as her fingers tugged at the hem of Izzy's shirt. Her mouth brushed lower, and Izzy's breath came rough and fast, her skin warming under Kiera's touch.

"I think this is the perfect place," Kiera whispered, her voice low, lips grazing the hollow of Izzy's throat, "to take this off you."

There was no doubt in her movements. No second-guessing. She explored Izzy's body with a hunger she didn't try to hide. Not worried about doing it right. Just letting herself want, and take, and feel.

"I always knew you'd be trouble," Izzy teased.

Kiera slid her hands beneath Izzy's shirt, pushing it up. "You like trouble," she teased, her voice husky as she peeled the fabric up and over Izzy's head, tossing it somewhere behind them.

"I like *you*," Izzy said, her gaze steady.

Kiera smiled. The sight of Izzy beneath her, out of breath and flushed, sent a wave of want through her so strong it shocked her. She leaned down to brush her lips over Izzy's collarbone. "You are like, unfairly attractive," she whispered against Izzy's skin.

She could feel Izzy's silent laugh as she kissed down Izzy's sternum, her lips brushing the warm skin there, trailing lower, lower, feeling every shift of Izzy's body beneath her as she navigated down a step or two, reveling in every small sound she made. It was overwhelming, the taste of her, the softness of her skin, the way she arched under Kiera's touch.

She had never wanted someone like this before, never felt such a deep pull to touch, to taste, to learn someone so intimately. She kissed just below Izzy's navel, exhaling slowly, savoring the way Izzy arched beneath her. Then, with aching slowness, she tugged Izzy's shorts and underwear down, fingertips tracing every inch of newly exposed skin.

When she finally dipped her tongue between Izzy's thighs, she felt Izzy exhale a shuddering breath, felt Izzy's fingers tighten in her hair. Kiera took her time, reveling in the way Izzy melted beneath her touch, the way Izzy tasted like warmth and earth and salt. She couldn't get enough. She was desperate to experience it all. The uneven rise and fall of Izzy's chest, the soft gasps spilling from her lips. Kiera pressed harder, her tongue teasing, exploring, drawing Izzy closer and closer to the edge with every calculated movement.

Izzy let out a broken moan, her hips lifting against Kiera's mouth, one hand gripping the railing while the other stayed tangled in Kiera's hair. "Don't stop," her voice cracked, desperate.

Kiera glanced up, catching the wrecked expression on Izzy's face — her parted lips, the blush blooming across her skin, how her eyes were squeezed shut with pleasure. It made Kiera's stomach tighten with a rush of satisfaction that had nothing to do with ego and everything to do with the fact that she was the one making Izzy fall apart like this.

She didn't slow down, didn't stop, not until Izzy was gasping her name over and over like a prayer. Her body tensed, trembling, then shattering in Kiera's hands.

Izzy exhaled sharply, collapsing back against the stairs. Kiera pressed a lingering kiss against her inner thigh before shifting up, kissing a slow path back up Izzy's body, taking her time to explore every inch of her. When their mouths met again, Izzy kissed her like she needed Kiera for air, like she needed her closer still.

"Jesus," Izzy finally managed when they broke apart, her voice shaky. She let out a dazed laugh, fingers trailing over

Kiera's heated cheek. "You—" she exhaled, shaking her head. "You're unreal."

Kiera smiled. "You're not too bad yourself."

Izzy let out a soft, contented hum before pulling Kiera up onto the step beside her. Izzy brushed a hand through Kiera's hair, her thumb skimming over Kiera's jawline.

"We really didn't make it upstairs," she murmured, amusement threading through the exhaustion in her voice

Kiera laughed, nudging their noses together, then reached down to take Izzy's hand. "Not yet. But I've got big plans for christening the bedroom, so hurry up."

"You're relentless," Izzy sighed.

CHAPTER 24

Izzy

Izzy wasn't sure how they made it up the stairs, tangled as they were in sloppy, desperate, exhilarated kisses and wandering hands. Every step they took was interrupted — Kiera pressing Izzy back against the wall, Izzy pulling Kiera closer until their bodies were flush, their mouths meeting again and again like they were making up for lost time. Each kiss deepened, more insistent, more consuming, until neither of them could think beyond the heat of the other's body.

By the time they finally stumbled into the bedroom, they were both laughing and tripping over boxes — breathless, full of anticipation. Kiera reached for Izzy, but this time, Izzy was the one who guided her backward until the backs of her knees hit the edge of the bed. Kiera fell backwards, bouncing slightly against the mattress, looking up at Izzy with dark, wanting eyes, her lips parted, her breath uneven.

Izzy climbed over her, knees bracketing Kiera's hips, and kissed her again — slow and deep, her weight settling fully as their bodies rocked together in a steady, deliberate rhythm. This time, there was a different kind of urgency — one threaded with a deeper intimacy, a need to touch, to explore, to memorize every inch of each other. Kiera's body was utter perfection, lush and curved and soft. Kiera's breasts demanded far, far more exploration, and her nipples peaked against Izzy's fingers, drawing a gentle gasp from Kiera's mouth.

Kiera's fingers skimmed over the sensitive skin at Izzy's hips, making her shiver. Izzy's own hands continued their languid exploration down Kiera's body, fingertips tracing the soft curve of her waist, the heat between her thighs. Kiera gasped at the touch, her body arching, her fingers digging into Izzy's skin with desperation.

They found a rhythm, hands moving with growing purpose — searching, adjusting, responding. Izzy dragged her fingers through the slick heat between Kiera's thighs, slow and deliberate, just enough pressure to make Kiera's breath stutter and her hips roll into the touch. Kiera's hand slipped between Izzy's legs in return, hesitant at first, then more confident when Izzy moaned low against her shoulder, her body tipping forward with the intensity of it.

Kiera like this — open, responsive, chasing her own pleasure — undid Izzy completely. Not just the heat of her skin or the way she gasped when Izzy's mouth skimmed over her chest, but the way she gave in to it. No walls, no second-guessing, just raw want. Izzy wanted to memorize every shift of her hips, every tremble in her thighs, every breath that caught when Izzy's fingers moved just right.

They didn't speak, didn't need to. Their bodies communicated in short exhales and tightening grips. Izzy had spent so long keeping herself reined in, but this — this felt like permission to let go.

The pressure built, slowly at first, then all at once — a rush beneath her skin, a demand she didn't want to deny. "Come for me," she whispered, voice rough as she kissed along the side of Kiera's neck, teeth scraping gently before her lips soothed the sting. Their hands kept moving, synced without effort now, chasing release together.

Kiera's thighs tightened around her, stomach pulled taut as her hips jerked once, twice — the kind of full-body tension Izzy had already learned to read. She leaned in and grazed her teeth along Kiera's jaw, feeling the way Kiera's breath hitched, how her fingers dug into Izzy's back like she was trying to hold on through the rush of it. "Good girl," she gasped. The next words came in stutters as she pitched closer toward the edge: "Let go. Just like that."

A moan escaped Kiera's lips as she trembled beneath Izzy's touch. The sound, the feeling of Kiera falling apart in her arms, was enough to send Izzy over the edge right after, her own release crashing into her like a tidal wave. Everything else dropped away: just their ragged breathing, the grip of fingers against skin, and the wild, unsteady thud of their hearts.

Izzy lay still, her skin cooling, heart starting to slow as Kiera's breath tickled the edge of her shoulder. Everything felt a little disoriented — her limbs heavy, her thoughts sluggish — but not in a bad way. More like she'd been poured out and hadn't quite settled back into herself. Kiera's lips brushed her shoulder again, and Izzy didn't flinch or pull away. She just breathed.

Kiera's fingers traced lazy shapes across her back, and Izzy focused on that — on the quiet, repetitive movement, the solid weight of her next to her. It wasn't dramatic. It wasn't overwhelming. It was calm. Steady. And maybe that's what caught her off guard most — the steadiness. Not having to guess what came next, not having to armor up or keep her distance.

The room was quiet except for the sound of their breathing evening out. And somewhere underneath the leftover adrenaline and the rising awareness of how emotionally exposed she felt, Izzy could tell: she didn't want to leave this.

Whatever *this* was. It didn't come with guarantees. But it made her want to stay long enough to see what might happen.

Morning light filtered through the gauzy curtains of Kiera's bedroom, casting pale shadows across the sheets. Izzy lay on her side, Kiera's body warm against her. It was comfortably quiet, and the silence felt like a bubble around them, fragile but full of something unspoken.

Izzy watched Kiera's face, relaxed in sleep, her breath slow and steady. A soft pang of tenderness hit her square in the chest.

She didn't know how to explain what had happened the night before — not out loud, not yet. But she felt it in the way they'd fit together without needing to talk it through, how hesitation had shifted into certainty. At first, their hands had been unsure, searching; but slowly, they'd started to figure each other out. The way Kiera gasped when Izzy curled her fingers just right. The way Izzy's breath caught when Kiera mouthed along her collarbone. They adjusted. They learned. By the end, it felt less like guessing and more like remembering — as if their bodies already knew the language, even if their mouths hadn't caught up yet.

Kiera stirred, eyelashes fluttering against her cheeks before her eyes opened, still hazy with sleep. She blinked at Izzy with a slow, sleepy smile. "Hey," Kiera murmured, her voice rough with sleep.

Izzy's heart did an embarrassingly traitorous flip. "Hey."

For a moment, they just lay there, caught up in something that felt dangerously close to *more*.

Then Kiera's stomach growled loudly, breaking the spell.

Izzy couldn't help the snort that escaped her. "Romantic."

Kiera laughed, cheeks flushing a delicate pink. "I used up my romance quota last night."

"Oh, was that romance? The part where you fucked me on the stairs?" Izzy teased.

Kiera's eyes flashed and she leaned in to kiss to Izzy's jaw. "I didn't hear you complaining."

"Oh, I wasn't complaining at all," Izzy clarified.

Kiera nuzzled into Izzy's neck. "It's funny. I've thought about this for so long, and now…"

Izzy sighed contentedly. "Did it live up to the hype?

"I think I'd put exceeds expectations on your review," Kiera said, her face still nuzzled in Izzy's neck.

Izzy blinked in surprise. "Really?" She pulled back to look down at Kiera, her thumb brushing along Kiera's jawline. "Does that mean I get a raise?"

Kiera's mouth quirked up in a smile. "Sorry, best I can offer is more sex."

Izzy laughed. "All this time, I thought I was the only one. We could have been having kitchen counter sex for *decades*."

Kiera playfully nipped at Izzy's collarbone, and then her thigh found its way between Izzy's knees. "Literal decades."

THEY EVENTUALLY UNTANGLED themselves from the sheets and padded to the kitchen. Kiera made coffee while Izzy sat on the counter, swinging her legs, trying not to think about how comfortable this all felt.

The mundane act of making breakfast felt intimate in a way that surprised Izzy. It wasn't big gestures that undid her — it was the small moments of closeness that made her feel loved.

"I would just like to announce that I formally retract my cheese statement," Kiera said, holding a spatula in her hand, her brunette waves adorably mussed, her glasses slipping down her nose. "I think I was mistaken. I would *not* be choosing cheese over any of what happened on this counter." She pointed with her spatula.

Izzy laughed. "We aim to please."

Kiera looked at her a little shyly, then bit her lip. "So, what happens now?"

"What do you mean?" Izzy asked, buttering a piece of toast.

"Like..." Kiera angled the spatula toward Izzy, then back toward herself. "What... do we do now?"

"I have a few ideas," Izzy said with an exaggerated wink.

"I do want to talk more about my offer in Nebraska. And this townhouse. And—"

"Do we really need to decide anything right now? We've been waiting forever for this, right? Can't we just bask in it a little longer?" Izzy interrupted, hopping off the counter to wrap an arm around Kiera's waist, desperate to keep ahold of the fragile moment, the ease of the morning. As soon as the words left her mouth, she knew it was the wrong thing to say. She could see Kiera's body tense as the question landed like an insult.

Kiera's body felt stiff as she tried to force a nonchalant nod. "Oh, um, yeah. You're right," she said, clearing her throat and pushing her glasses back up her nose with the back of her hand. "We have time for all of that."

Izzy could feel the shift in the room. Kiera pushed the scrambled eggs around the pan in silence.

"What's on your agenda for today?" Kiera asked with a tone that Izzy could hear was slightly strained.

Izzy cleared her throat. "I have that big meeting with Pete tomorrow for the project you helped me with, so I'll be out of commission for most of today, but then I was thinking maybe we could do dinner tonight?"

"I'll be with the girls," Kiera said, and Izzy hated how Kiera's tone suggested that Izzy wasn't invited. "It's their first night in the new place... Maybe tomorrow night?"

Izzy didn't want to admit that she felt disappointed. She understood exactly where Kiera was coming from, and she

CHAPTER 24

didn't want her own selfish desires to get in the way. "Sure, of course. Tomorrow sounds great."

PETE LEANED back in her chair at Second Star's main office — Pete's dining room table — crossing her arms and giving Izzy a knowing look. The remnants of their celebratory lunch, a veritable feast of half-eaten sandwiches and an empty plate of pastries, were scattered across the table. Gladys was lying nearby, enjoying a few slices of turkey that Pete had slipped to her.

The partnership Izzy had been chasing — a major mentorship organization that had been highly recommended by Sage Carson — had been her biggest challenge yet. It wasn't just about expanding their outreach. It was about proving that Second Star had the infrastructure, the vision, and the leadership to handle something stateside.

When she'd first pitched the idea to Pete, her voice had trembled with doubt, but Pete's enthusiasm had been unwavering. Still, finalizing the partnership had taken a lot of determination. She spearheaded the project, fine-tuned details late into the night, and fought to ensure that Second Star's mission didn't get lost. Then, finally, after weeks of back-and-forth, the agreement was official.

The victory wasn't just hers — it was the kind of breakthrough that would help communities across the country. And Kiera had helped with an essential planning part of it.

"So," Pete started, breaking the comfortable silence. "You gonna let yourself celebrate this win? Because this new partnership isn't something you just brush off like it's no big deal."

Izzy let out a laugh, leaning forward to rest her arms on the table. "It's... huge. I know. I just—" She hesitated, rolling a pen between her fingers. "It still feels like I'm waiting for you to realize you made a mistake by letting me lead on this."

"*Ex-fucking-cuse me*, Isabel Tierney?!" Pete balked, her brows high.

Izzy gave a weak smile, the weight of imposter syndrome still clinging stubbornly to her shoulders. "It just doesn't feel real. Like... this is your baby, Pete. You built Second Star from the ground up. You just gave me a job because we're friends."

Pete snorted. "Because we're friends? You're kidding me, right? You convinced an organization with national reach to partner with us. You presented the idea, you led those meetings, you handled the details. You're not just helping — you're steering the damn ship."

Izzy shifted in her seat, the praise making her uncomfortable, though a tiny part of her clung to it like a life raft. "Everything is happening so fast. I keep thinking I'm going to screw it up."

Pete leaned forward, her voice gentler now. "I get it, but you're not going to screw it up. You are not the same hesitant person who began this job unsure of their direction. You've had incredible ideas to grow what we're doing, that I wouldn't have even thought of."

A sense of accomplishment sank in slowly. She had led the project. Not Pete, not anyone else. Her.

Pete's expression was sincere. "Iz, come on. You earned this. The job wasn't a pity offer, and I've never doubted my decision to bring you on."

Izzy took a beat, absorbing the words. She picked at the edge of her notebook, then glanced up. "Do you ever feel like you've finally figured your shit out, but instead of feeling settled, you just... start looking for the exit? Like some part of you is already scanning for the next move, even if nothing's wrong?"

Pete's smile looked suddenly sad. "Are you kidding? I started Second Star because I was bad at staying still. But that's not a sign of failure. It's a sign that you're still growing.

You're allowed to grow. You're allowed to want more, to do more."

Izzy nodded slowly, her gaze dropping back down to the table.

Pete's brows lifted with curiosity. "What's going on?"

She thought of Kiera — her laugh, her eyes, the awkwardness of their goodbye yesterday morning. Izzy swallowed hard. "I think I fucked things up with Kiera."

Pete didn't press, just offered a small smile. "I doubt that. Kiera seems head over heels for you. I bet you could start wearing cargo shorts and she'd not only tell you they looked good but also defend their usefulness."

Izzy rolled her eyes. "Well, unfortunately, I panicked yesterday when she tried to talk about the future."

"Yeesh." Pete grimaced, which didn't make Izzy feel better at all. "Why?"

Izzy rubbed at her temple. "I think I'm figuring out I don't know how to be still in love. I only know how to reach for it."

"Well, here's what I know. Danica and I got our second chance. We remembered just how much we liked each other. And then because we didn't actually communicate with each other about what was going on, we didn't talk for months. Months where we were miserable."

"Oh, I remember." Izzy grimaced.

"And you meddled, giving her my location in the airport, if I remember correctly," Pete added. "And didn't you fake sick, too?"

Izzy felt a grin tug at the corner of her mouth. "Which I have no regrets about. You two just needed to get out of your own way."

Pete looked at her for a long moment, eyebrows raised. "And I would like to extend the courtesy back to you in this moment. If you're scared of stillness, that's only because you've never had someone fully reciprocate love back to you, and so you're sabotaging it before it even gets to the good part. Pull your head out of your ass and go fix it. I will not tolerate months of wallowing when I know that a simple conversation can change this. You want to be with her. Don't be such a baby."

Izzy sat with the words. Pete was right. She'd messed up this morning by not letting Kiera be honest with her. Kiera hadn't pushed her away. She hadn't disappeared. Izzy had misread the pause, assumed silence meant retreat. But it didn't. Not this time. If she wanted something to come of this — *really* come of it — she had to stop waiting and say what she felt.

Because this wasn't just about hooking up. She liked being around Kiera. She liked the quiet steadiness of her. The way her presence made things feel less chaotic. And if there was a chance for more — for something steady, something that could actually last — Izzy didn't want to waste it by letting Kiera move away without knowing exactly how she felt. And if Kiera needed to move, she was going to fucking figure that out, too, even if it meant spending much more time than she'd like in Nebraska, visiting her and the girls.

"That was like, some *really* tough love," Izzy said after a long while.

Pete smiled, giving her a gentle punch on the shoulder. "I'm just basking in the idea that it's finally my turn to be the voice of reason."

HEART POUNDING with a powerful combination of hope and nerves, she drove to the townhouse. She rehearsed what she might say — *I do want this. I want you. The whole package. Let's make it official.* She took a deep breath before knocking, the memory of that epic night they'd spent together still fresh and tangled in her chest.

Kiera opened the door with a confused smile. "Hi," she said.

CHAPTER 24

"Hey." Izzy took a deep breath. "I just needed to tell you —" She was interrupted as two little heads popped out from behind Kiera — Eliza and Quinn, both wearing oversized pajamas, grins wide and messy with paint, or perhaps frosting.

Eliza giggled, grabbing Izzy's hand without hesitation. "Izzy! We're playing princess-pirates! I can make you a crown."

Before Izzy could react, she was being tugged inside, watching Kiera shake her head with a bemused smile. Kiera walked back into the kitchen, looking absolutely stunning in a soft cream sweater and jeans. Her hair was tied back in a loose bun, and Izzy's stomach fluttered at her casual beauty. Kiera's gaze met hers, shy yet welcoming.

Quinn interrupted before they could exchange a word, holding a crown made of construction paper and glitter. "You're the pirate queen now!" Quinn declared, placing the crown precariously on Izzy's head. "We're about to go on a treasure hunt!"

Izzy couldn't help but laugh. "Guess I better earn my title, huh?"

The next hour dissolved into delightful chaos. They crafted treasure maps, built pillow forts, and turned the living room into an imaginary pirate ship. Kiera played along, her laughter infectious, and Izzy couldn't take her eyes off her — especially when Kiera looked so at ease, so happy with her girls. Kiera even seemed at ease around her, like she was glad Izzy was here with her.

At one point, while Kiera and Eliza debated whether the couch cushions were a good hiding place for their treasure, Quinn crawled into Izzy's lap with her favorite stuffed bunny. "Do you love my mommy?" Quinn asked in a whisper, looking at her with wide, curious eyes.

Izzy froze, the question landing like a small, sharp stone tossed into still water. Her eyes flicked toward Kiera — who was laughing as Eliza climbed over the arm of the couch, her cheeks pink from the effort — and something in Izzy's chest shifted. She thought of the way Kiera always made space for other people, how her hands were always busy caring for someone else, but she still managed to look at Izzy like she mattered. How she was still figuring herself out but trying. Really trying.

"Yeah," Izzy said quietly, her voice low and honest. "Yeah, I do."

She didn't notice Kiera looking over until it was too late — her head tilted, lips parted like she'd caught the tail end of something unexpected.

Izzy met her eyes, heart tripping in her chest. But Kiera didn't say anything. Not yet.

"She's really great, isn't she?" Izzy whispered conspiratorially.

"She's the best." Izzy's arms wrapped around Quinn without thinking, and the feeling that settled in her chest was sharp and bright, like being handed something fragile and precious.

Later, after Kiera took the girls upstairs for baths and pajamas and Izzy picked up toys and began to clean the kitchen, Kiera came down to join her.

Kiera wiped down the counter, her voice quiet. "They really like you."

Izzy placed a plate in the dishwasher, glancing up with a bashful smile. "Yeah? I like them, too. They're... amazing."

Kiera turned to face her, holding a towel in her hands. "You're so good with them."

Izzy hesitated before answering, her throat tight with emotion. "I didn't expect to feel so, um... It was really easy to hang out with them."

Kiera took a step forward, closing the distance between them.

For a heartbeat, Izzy thought Kiera might kiss her, but

instead, Kiera reached out, brushing a loose strand of hair behind Izzy's ear. The tenderness of the gesture made Izzy's breath catch.

Eliza's voice, calling from the hall, interrupted them before either could speak. "Mama, Quinn stole my blanket!"

"Duty calls." Kiera's soft laugh made Izzy's insides swirl with affection and tenderness.

Izzy watched her disappear down the hallway, heart pounding, realizing that she wasn't just falling for Kiera. She was falling for everything that came with her — the girls, the chaos, the laughter. All of it.

When Kiera returned downstairs, they curled up on the couch together, watching a mindless sitcom. Halfway through the episode, Kiera rested her head on Izzy's shoulder.

"I'm sorry for what I said yesterday morning," Izzy said finally, taking an unsteady breath. "I panicked, and I should have listened to your concerns so we could talk through it instead of acting like they weren't important."

"And I think I could be more realistic about what it truly means for you to consider being with me. It's not just me you're signing up for. I'm a package deal, you know?" Kiera said. "We can take our time, if you want to figure some things out."

Izzy just reached out, squeezing Kiera's hand gently. "I'm ready for the next step when you are. I love you, Kiera."

Kiera's eyes stayed locked on hers for a moment. Izzy held the silence like a breath, waiting for it to shift into something — a word, a nod, even just the soft *yes, I love you, too* she was hoping for. But Kiera didn't say anything. Just looked at her, eyes wide and unreadable. And that look — that *not knowing* — dug in deeper than any spoken rejection might have.

She didn't flinch. Didn't pull her hand back. She just nodded like she understood, even if she didn't yet.

Because this was always the risk, wasn't it? Wanting

someone who was still figuring out if they could want you back.

Her stomach twisted, but she kept her smile gentle, careful. She'd meant what she said — she *was* ready. But now, she had to accept that maybe Kiera wasn't. Maybe she never would be. And Izzy would have to decide what to do with that truth — how much she was willing to wait, and how long she could sit in uncertainty without losing herself in it.

CHAPTER 25

Kiera

Kiera stepped out of the middle school and into the mid-May afternoon warmth, the door swinging shut behind her with a quiet click. Her heart was still thudding from the interview — not because it had gone badly, but because it hadn't. The principal had been kind, engaged. The questions had felt like real conversations. For the first time in what felt like forever, Kiera had walked into a school and imagined herself there — standing in front of a classroom, her girls just a few blocks away, the rhythm of a life she could actually see unfolding.

And that scared the hell out of her.

She crossed the parking lot slowly, keys in hand but not unlocking the car just yet. It would be so easy to want this too much. To picture school supplies stacked in the front hallway. To imagine her girls growing up with the same neighborhood routes, the same familiar routines. Even without Izzy in the picture, it felt possible. It felt steady. Real.

But then came the flickers of doubt, just behind the hope. What if she got the offer and Izzy didn't want this after all?

What if Izzy said she was ready for the chaos — for the girls, the co-parenting schedules, the stress — but then realized it was too much?

And what if *she* wasn't ready? What if this whole thing with Izzy was just a moment, a break in the current before everything returned to normal? Kiera had been the one to put on the brakes before. Could she trust herself to say yes now, even if every piece of her still felt mid-recovery?

Izzy had said she loved her. And Kiera had heard it — *really* heard it. But she'd stayed silent, not out of doubt, exactly, but out of fear. Because what if she said it back and then took a job somewhere else? What if she made the wrong choice again, for herself and everyone else?

The truth was, she didn't want to go back to Nebraska. Not really. But staying meant choosing uncertainty — professionally, emotionally, in every way. She would be asking Izzy to mean what she said. To show up. To share a life that wasn't always convenient or easy.

She would have to show up, too.

She opened the car door and sat for a long moment before starting the ignition, the buzz of the cicadas filling the silence around her. Maybe she wasn't ready to say everything out loud yet. But she was here. She was still trying.

For now, being honest with herself — even quietly — would have to count for something.

The girls' squeals of delight from the backseat made Kiera smile as she parked the car in front of her parents' house, the full moon casting silver light across the yard. The girls were nearly vibrating with excitement in the back seat, clutching their overnight bags with gleaming anticipation. They'd been begging to stay with Grandma and Grandpa again, even though it had only been two days since they'd seen one another. As soon as the car stopped, they scrambled out, racing toward the coop with excited shrieks. Hard to compete with the flock.

Kiera watched them before stepping out, stretching her sore muscles from the long day. Not just physical, but a profound exhaustion settled in; the weight of unsaid things, unfinished matters, heavy on her soul.

Her parents were in the yard, standing barefoot in the damp grass, arms stretched skyward, their crystals glinting in the moonlight.

Kiera exhaled sharply. "Mom, Dad... what are you doing?"

"We're blessing the chickens and ducks!" her mom said brightly, shaking a small brass bell with sharp, purposeful movements. "The moonlight helps them lay healthier eggs. Tonya says it's all about energy alignment."

Kiera groaned, shaking her head. "Of course it is."

Eliza and Quinn were already at the coop, showering Chiquitita, Her Highness, and all of their feathered friends with adoration. The girls were so lucky to have this connection to their eccentric grandparents, and Kiera felt a small wave of relief and comfort knowing she had such a phenomenal support system.

She kissed them both goodnight, promising to call in the morning. Then, as she walked back to the car, a knot formed in her chest, thinking about how Maggie didn't have the same kind of support. Well, she could be that for her friend, then, the same as Izzy had. Her hands gripped the wheel, but she didn't start the engine.

Instead, she pulled out her phone. She hesitated for only a second before calling Maggie. It'd been almost a month now since Maggie's mom had died, and she still sometimes wondered if calling randomly was intrusive or helpful.

Maggie picked up quickly. "Well hello, Kiera," Maggie's voice no longer held the raw strain she'd been used to over the past few weeks.

"Well hello, gorgeous. Just checking in. How are you?"

"Better, actually," Maggie said. "I'm doing okay today. My therapist said we can go down to just one session a week now."

"Look at you, winning therapy," A quiet smile tugged at Kiera's lips.

Maggie snorted. "Yeah, well, apparently she wouldn't agree to give me a trophy for my achievement."

"I didn't realize your therapist was such a monster," Kiera joked.

"Speaking of monsters, is it bad that I'm already fantasizing about a solo vacation? I just want to lie on a beach somewhere in absolute silence." Maggie sighed wistfully.

"Not bad at all. You deserve all the beaches and quiet and relaxation," Kiera encouraged.

Maggie took a deep breath. "I might do that. You guys should come down soon for a visit. I could use the distraction. And the wine."

"Definitely. We'll plan something."

Unspoken things filled the heavy pause. Then Maggie sighed. "How're you and Izzy?"

Kiera drummed her fingers on her steering wheel, still staring at the front of her parent's garage. "Oh, um. Did she call you?"

"No, I'm just making sure I don't find everything out via group chat," Maggie said.

Kiera chewed her bottom lip. "We're just still taking things slow. I'm not actually sure if she knows what she's getting into. She… um… She said she loves me."

Maggie released an exaggerated noise, half-groan, half-sigh. "Oh my god, are you serious?"

"What?"

"Kiera, you're being a complete idiot."

Kiera choked. "Uh, thanks."

"I'm serious." Maggie's voice softened slightly, but the

exasperation was still there. "She loves you. And you love her. It's obvious to literally everyone except you two."

The words landed hard, not because they were surprising, but because Kiera had run out of ways to pretend they weren't true.

She did love Izzy.

She had been trying to be responsible, to not let herself want too much, to be realistic in what it meant to be with someone like her. But hadn't that been her problem all along? Hadn't she spent too much of her life holding back, second-guessing, waiting for the right time?

And all this time, Izzy had been standing there — not walking away, saying the hard thing.

She thought about the night before, curled on the couch — the comfort of Izzy's arms around her, the unspoken promise in every touch, the way Izzy had been trying to tell her without pushing, without demanding anything in return. She had given Kiera space, had let her set the pace, but she had been there, waiting, willing to take the risk if Kiera just said the words.

And Kiera had frozen, the words caught somewhere between her chest and throat. Not because she didn't feel them, but because she did — too much, too clearly. Because saying them meant choosing this life fully, with all its chaos and complications. It meant trusting that Izzy wouldn't change her mind when things got hard. That she wouldn't regret choosing someone with kids, with baggage, with a whole orbit spinning around her.

Kiera had spent years putting everyone else first. She'd made peace with being the stable one, the practical one, the one who didn't ask for more. But now that more was right in front of her — in Izzy's touch, her words, her presence — it terrified her to reach for it. What if she wasn't enough to hold it? What if she broke it just by wanting it too much?

"I think we're gonna need a bigger boat," Maggie stated, and just as Kiera began to ask her what the hell that meant, a beep followed by the distinct sound of someone else on the line.

"Hello?" Danica's voice came through. "Oooh, what's going on at 7:43 p.m. on a Friday night?"

Maggie didn't miss a beat. "Kiera is being an emotionally-stunted dumbass, and she needs a pep talk."

"Ah," Danica said, and Kiera could *hear* the smirk in her voice. "Classic."

Kiera let out what she hoped translated as a long-suffering sigh. "Oh my god, are you both serious?"

Danica laughed. "Sweetheart, have any of us ever *not* been serious about meddling in each other's love lives? This is prime payback."

"This is *not* my love life," Kiera protested. "This is… a situation."

"Oh? A situation?" Danica repeated. "Tell me, does this situation involve your deep-seated fear of vulnerability? Because that's the only thing I'm hearing right now."

Kiera rubbed her temples. "I am *not* afraid of vulnerability."

Danica snorted. "Kiera, I've seen house plants be more open about their needs than you."

Maggie hummed in agreement. "That's true. I mean, even my cactus wilts dramatically when it needs water. Meanwhile, you just shrugged and said, 'It's fine' when you found out Alex was cheating on you."

"*I did not*—" Kiera stopped, exhaling slowly to calm herself. "Can we not?"

Maggie's voice softened, losing some of its teasing edge. "Kiera. Just tell her."

Kiera swallowed hard, staring at her reflection in the rearview mirror. "What if she doesn't know what she's signing up for? Or what if she just likes the idea, and she's going to panic once it's not some chase anymore? Or what if I do take this job in Nebraska—"

"Ugh," Danica interrupted. "You cannot be serious right now. You're not taking that job in Nebraska. You grimaced when you were telling us about it on Facetime."

"I did not—"

Danica continued on, unphased by Kiera's protests. "And about the other nonsense, are you even *present* in your own relationship?"

"Did Izzy say 'I love you'?" Maggie asked.

"Yes," Kiera confessed.

Danica and Maggie let out matching squeals, and Kiera could hear what sounded an awful lot like Pete doing a slow clap in the background.

"Am I on speaker?" Kiera asked.

"Focus," Danica said. "But yes."

"Izzy *loves* you, Kiera," Pete said, suddenly a participating member of the conversation. "Don't fuck this up."

Kiera opened her mouth, but no words came out.

Maggie sighed. "Kiera, what is the absolute worst-case scenario?"

Kiera closed her eyes. "That I tell her how I feel, and it doesn't work out."

"And the best-case scenario?" Danica prompted.

Kiera's stomach flipped. "...That it does."

But as the memory settled in her chest, one realization hit harder than all the rest: Izzy hadn't walked away. She hadn't demanded anything. She had been patient.

Kiera didn't want to live her life standing on the edge of something that mattered, afraid to leap. She wanted to choose this — all of it. The chaos, the risk of being hurt again. She wanted Izzy. Not someday. Not maybe.

Now.

"Oh my god, I love her, too," Kiera said aloud.

As that realization sank in for Kiera, the other three people on the line yelled as if they were winning a Championship match.

Danica said, "You've got this Kiera. We're all rooting for you guys."

Maggie chimed in, "Hey, Kiera?"

"What?"

"If you don't tell her that you love her within the first five seconds of seeing her, I'm legally allowed to punch you in the arm the next time I see you."

Kiera shook her head. "That is *not* how legality works."

"Agree to disagree" Maggie said cheerfully.

Kiera rolled her eyes, but her cheeks were aching from how big her smile was. "Fine," Kiera muttered. "I'll call you all later."

Kiera could perfectly envision Maggie's face as her friend said, "Not if we call you first."

Shaking her head, Kiera hung up the phone, shifting the car into reverse, tires crunching over gravel as she pulled out of the driveway. The image of her parents' moon ritual disappeared in the rearview mirror.

Her hands trembled as she drove, streetlights passing in a blur. She drove past the turn to the townhouse. She wasn't going home. She wasn't going to spend another night wondering *what if*.

As she hit a red light, she realized she didn't know where she was going. She cursed under her breath and hit redial.

Maggie answered instantly. "Did you forget to ask where she's staying?"

Kiera let out a low sigh. "Yes, *shut up*."

Maggie laughed, but it was gentle, warm. "She's at the same hotel as before, room 604."

"Thanks, Mags."

"Now, go get the girl, dumbass."

By the time she pulled up to the hotel, her heart was pounding so hard she could feel it in her ears. She threw the car into park and stumbled out, barely noticing the valet attendant waiting for her keys.

CHAPTER 25

She rushed into the lobby, not registering the polished wood floors, the soft of jazz playing, the people checking in.

And then, all too quickly, she found herself standing in front of room 604, her breath unsteady.

Kiera knocked, sharp and quick, the sound too loud in the quiet hallway. She waited, but no footsteps came. No voice. Nothing. Her stomach clenched. She knocked again, harder this time, glancing toward the window like she might catch movement behind the curtain.

Still nothing.

Fumbling for her phone, she tapped Izzy's name and held it to her ear. One ring. Two. Three. Each one wound her tighter. When it clicked to voicemail, her breath caught. Panic surged, wrapping around her chest and tightening like a vice.

The elevator chimed behind her.

Kiera turned, heart slamming against her chest.

Izzy stood there, mid-step, her phone still in her hand, as if she had been about to call Kiera back. Her hair was damp, and she was wearing an oversized sweatshirt. Her eyes locked onto Kiera's, wide with surprise, and for a moment, neither of them moved.

"Kiera?" Izzy's voice was hesitant. "I was just calling you back, I was at the gym—"

Kiera's exhaled heavily. She had planned — at least, she had tried to plan — what to say. But now, standing there, looking at Izzy, she didn't need any of it.

"I love you."

Izzy gasped, lips parting, but Kiera kept going before she could say a word.

"I love you," Kiera said again, stepping closer. "I should have said it sooner. I should have *known* sooner, but I was scared. I kept trying to hold back, to be careful; but Izzy, I don't want to be careful anymore. I don't want to waste another second pretending that I don't want this — *you* — more than I've wanted anything in my life."

Izzy stood frozen for a moment, blinking in surprise. "I love you, too." Then, she moved. She crossed the space between them in a single breath, hands reaching to hold Kiera's face, and kissed her.

Kiera gasped, the intensity of the kiss stealing every ounce of air from her lungs. It was desperate, consuming, like they had both been starving for this moment.

Izzy kissed her like she was claiming her, like she had been waiting for this exact second to crash into Kiera and never let go. Now that nothing was left unsaid, neither of them knew how to slow down.

By the time they finally pulled apart, breathless and clinging to each other, Izzy whispered, "You love me?"

"I love you." Kiera was confident, excited, giddy. She kissed Izzy again, murmuring against her lips. "I love you."

Izzy smiled against her lips. "I love you, too. And, um, I'm sorry, I'm really sweaty. Can I shower before we do anything else?"

Kiera laughed, pressing her forehead against Izzy's. "Yeah. But you're not showering alone."

Izzy's hands tightened on her waist. "Good. Because I'm not letting you go."

Kiera kissed her again as they stumbled into the hotel room together, a tangle of hands and mouths and love. Life might not get simpler, but she wasn't scared of that anymore. Not with Izzy beside her.

EPILOGUE

ONE YEAR LATER

Kiera

The late spring sun bathed Mission Beach in warm golden light, the scent of salt and coconut sunscreen in the air. Waves rolled lazily toward the shore, foaming white before melting back into the vast blue. Kiera lay on a beach towel, reading, digging her toes into the soft sand, listening to the distant sound of laughter and the rhythmic crash of the ocean.

Beside her, Quinn was hard at work on her sandcastle, tongue poking out in concentration as she carefully packed another turret into place. Quinn looked to her mom for encouragement as her sandcastle continued to lean precariously.

Further out in the water, Izzy bobbed in the shallows, Eliza on a bright yellow foam surfboard beside her. Kiera watched as Izzy adjusted Eliza's stance, gesturing animatedly as she explained something, her body language brimming with confidence. Eliza, in contrast, was barely containing her nerves, her little arms flailing to keep her balance even before a wave approached. Kiera smiled to herself, looking around at all her favorite girls.

Izzy gave Eliza a final nod before stepping back, letting the small wave push her forward. For a second, Eliza stood, wobbling triumphantly — before immediately toppling over into the water.

Kiera winced, but when Eliza surfaced, she was already laughing, flicking water at Izzy.

"She's really bad at surfing," Quinn remarked beside her, deadpan.

Kiera stifled a laugh. "She's trying, and that's what matters."

"Yeah, she's trying really hard," Quinn added, turning back to her castle. "Like how Izzy tries really hard at everything, like when she puts broccoli in the mac and cheese."

Kiera let out a quiet laugh.

The past year had been a whirlwind, a mixture of quiet moments and milestones, of laughter, exploring their relationship and spending more and more time together. Izzy had fully immersed herself in Second Star, taking a leadership role alongside Pete, helping to launch new mentorship programs that had already started changing kids' lives.

Kiera had found her footing too — after a year of paying her dues teaching life science classes, she'd be starting chemistry classes in the fall, and would add a physics course in the spring.

Watching the girls and Izzy get to know one another, to get comfortable with each other, had been the best part of the last year. The girls adored Izzy, begged for her to stay longer every time she had to leave.

Kiera had thought she would struggle with letting someone in, but with Izzy, after they'd confessed what they wanted, it had been easy.

So easy, in fact, that the girls had started a relentless campaign months ago, constantly asking if Izzy could move into the small townhouse.

As if summoned by her thoughts, Izzy and Eliza came trudging up from the shore, Eliza dripping wet and grinning.

"That was terrible," she declared as she dropped onto the sand beside Quinn.

"No, it was great. The Izzy and Lizzie dream team," Izzy said as she sat beside Kiera.

"No, it was bad," Quinn stated. "You want to help me with the castle?"

Eliza nodded, clearly eager to escape the waves for a while, and the two of them fell into quiet collaboration, sculpting small towers into place.

Kiera took the moment of distraction and turned to Izzy, who was toweling off beside her. Izzy shot her a knowing smile, raising an eyebrow. "You're staring."

Kiera huffed a small laugh, heart racing. *Don't overthink it. Just say it.*

"Iz," she started, voice soft. "Move in with us."

Izzy's hands froze, her towel slipping from her fingers onto the sand.

"I mean it," she said, reaching out and brushing a damp strand of hair away from Izzy's cheek. "I want you to live with us. The girls love you and want you around, and so do I."

Izzy's lips quirking upward, mischief flashing in her eyes. "Kiera Phillips," she said slowly, teasingly. "I *cannot* live in sin."

Kiera rolled her eyes, laughing. "Oh my god."

Before she could respond, Izzy turned toward the girls. "Hey, Lizzie? Quinn?"

The two of them perked up instantly, sharing a glance before nodding with barely contained excitement.

Kiera looked confused. "What—"

Eliza and Quinn sprinted a few feet up the beach to their beach bag. They dug inside the bag, then ran to Izzy, depositing a small box into her hands. Quinn bounced with excitement while Eliza held her hands in a pleading gesture.

Oh, Kiera realized.

The world around them seemed to contract as Izzy knelt before her, her bright blue eyes filled with a deep and sure emotion.

"Kiera," Izzy started, her voice shaky, and fingers tight around the small box. "I was going to do this later tonight, but since you kind of walked right into it..." She took a breath, shaking her head with a small grin. "You... and the girls... and this life we want to build together — it's everything, and I don't want to wait."

The ocean blurred into background noise, drowned out by the rush of blood pounding in Kiera's ears.

"I love you," Izzy said, her gaze softening. "I have loved every moment I have spent with the three of you over this past year. And I don't just want to move in with you. I want to marry you."

Kiera let out a shaky laugh, barely holding it together. "You planned this with Eliza and Quinn?"

Izzy glanced sideways where the two pairs of wide eyes were watching them. "They've been very good at keeping this a surprise."

"How long have you known?" Kiera said, turning toward her daughters.

Eliza and Quinn erupted into giggles.

"Wait, wait, we have a thing!" Eliza said, waving her arms frantically. Quinn began tearing apart the sandcastle. Kiera watched in amusement as the girls dug wildly, sand flying everywhere, before they unearthed a small seashell-covered box and held it up in triumph, grinning ear to ear.

"We made this!" Quinn declared proudly, holding it in both hands.

EPILOGUE

Kiera opened the lid, her heart stuttering as she saw what was inside — a piece of paper, decorated in Eliza's loopy handwriting and Quinn's very enthusiastic use of stickers.

Say yes, Mommy!!!

Kiera laughed through the blur of her tears, clutching the note to her chest as Izzy reached for her hand. "No pressure," Izzy teased, though Kiera could hear the emotion in her voice. "But they worked really hard on this."

Eliza crossed her arms. "Yeah, *and* we practiced!"

It felt impossible to breathe with how much she loved the three of them. "Oh, well, in that case..." She turned back to Izzy, eyes shining. "Yes."

Izzy let out a breath before surging forward, pulling Kiera into a deep kiss, the kind that promised forever.

The girls whooped in triumph, launching themselves at Kiera and Izzy in a blur of limbs and laughter. They all collapsed into the sand in a tangled heap, breathless and grinning, the air ringing with giggles and shrieks. The tide crept closer, curling around their feet, the ocean a steady rhythm behind them. Sunlight spilled across their faces and for a brief, tender moment, Kiera found herself in awe that this beautiful, chaotic, and perfect life was real.

THANK YOU!

Thank you for reading Shift the Tide. I did not expect Izzy and Kiera to fall in love, much less need their own story, so this has been such a pleasure to write. I hope you loved Izzy and Kiera's love story as much as I do!

ACKNOWLEDGMENTS

Reader, I promised you it wouldn't be three years. Thank you so much for all of your encouragement about Pete and Danica's story and the many, many, many DMs I got asking if Izzy and Kiera were next! I bet you already know what's coming up.

Lemon, thank you for every time you called out my lazy bullshit to make this a book we can both be proud of. You're the best editor, even when you tell me something is "eh, fine" and I know I have to fix it anyways.

Tina, you beta-reader angel, thank you for cornering me at a wine bar and telling me I needed you. You were RIGHT. You are often right, it turns out.

And Steph, thank you for being such a big deal for me during this book and for the endless encouragement and for telling me not to kill Gwen.

ABOUT THE AUTHOR

Bryce Oakley is a Goldie-award winning author of sapphic romantic comedies and self-proclaimed pepperoni pizza connoisseur. She lives in Colorado with her wife, daughter, and a small herd of rescue animals.